Lisa Kleypas

"Through deft plotting and simple yet stylish prose, Kleypas distinguishes herself as a master of her craft."
Publishers Weekly (*Starred Review*)

Julia Quinn

"Julia Quinn is truly our contemporary Jane Austen."
Jill Barnett

Kinley MacGregor

"I love Kinley MacGregor's books! They brim with laughter and love."
Cathy Maxwell

When eminently sensible Lydia Craven decides to marry for security rather than love, she doesn't calculate on the determination of devil-may-care doctor Jake Linley to rewrite the romantic formula, in LISA KLEYPAS's charming romp . . .

Against the Odds

Dashing Ned Blydon is in a most unenviable predicament— he's engaged to one Thornton sister, while being secretly in love with the other— in JULIA QUINN's sensuous . . .

A Tale of Two Sisters

When Simon of Ravenswood secretly answered Lady Kenna's letters in the name of a powerful earl, he was only being polite. Little did he know the lady would fall in love with the author and come between him, his best friend and a solemn vow made long ago, in KINLEY MACGREGOR's enchanting . . .

Midsummer's Knight

Don't Miss These Other Avon Books from

Lisa Kleypas

AGAIN THE MAGIC
(Coming February 2004)

Kinley MacGregor

TAMING THE SCOTSMAN

Julia Quinn

TO SIR PHILLIP, WITH LOVE

LISA
KLEYPAS
JULIA
QUINN
KINLEY
MACGREGOR

Where's My Hero?

AVON BOOKS
An Imprint of HarperCollins*Publishers*

AVON BOOKS
An Imprint of HarperCollins*Publishers*
10 East 53rd Street
New York, New York 10022-5299

ISBN: 0-06-050524-9
www.avonromance.com

First Avon Books paperback printing: September 2003

Printed in the U.S.A.

10 9 8 7 6 5 4 3 2 1

Contents

Lisa Kleypas

Against the Odds

Prologue

If any man knew how to hold his liquor, it was Jake Linley. God knew he'd had a lot of practice at it—and it was a good thing, too, otherwise he'd be staggering drunk at the moment. Unfortunately, no matter how much he drank this evening, it was not going to numb the bitter awareness of what he could never have.

Jake was tired, and hot, his caustic resentment seeming to rise with each moment he spent in the luxurious, crowded cavern of a ballroom. Separating himself from a group of friends, he wandered to a gallery that bordered the room, glancing at the sky that loomed dark and cool beyond a row of glittering windows. At the end of the gallery, Robert, Lord Wray, was surrounded by a smiling throng of friends and well-wishers, all of them congratulating him on the betrothal that had been announced an hour ago.

Jake had always liked Wray, a pleasant enough fellow whose combination of intelligence and unoffensive wit made him welcome in any company. However, at this particular moment, a feeling of contempt coiled inside Jake's stomach as he glanced at the man. He envied Wray, who didn't begin to realize the extent of his good fortune in having won the hand of Miss Lydia Craven. It was already being said that the match was more to Miss Craven's advantage than to Wray's, that her social position would be greatly advanced when her fortune was joined to a well-respected title. Jake knew better. Lydia was the true prize, regardless of her family's common origins.

She wasn't a conventional beauty—she had her father's black hair and his wide mouth, and a chin that was a bit too decisive for a woman. Her figure was slim and small-breasted, falling short of the voluptuous standards that were considered so desirable. But there was something irresistible about her—perhaps it was the charming absentmindedness that made a man want to take care of her, or the intriguing touch of playfulness that lurked beneath her pensive facade. And of course there were her eyes . . .

exotic green eyes that seemed out of place in such a sweet, scholarly face.

Sighing grimly, Jake left the overheated gallery, stepping out into the cool spring night. The air was humid and fecund, weighted with the fragrance of damask roses that burgeoned from the terraced gardens below. The wide, stone-flagged path stretched along a series of narrow box-edged beds filled with geraniums and a heavy misting of white feverfew. Jake wandered aimlessly along the path, almost to the end, where it curled gently into a set of stone steps descending to the lower gardens.

He stopped suddenly as he saw a woman seated on a bench. Her profile was averted as she hunched over something she held in her lap. Being a veteran of London soirees and balls, Jake's first assumption was that the woman was probably waiting to meet a lover for a few stolen moments. However, he experienced an instant shock of recognition as he saw the dark silk of her hair and the decisive lines of her profile.

Lydia, he thought, staring at her hungrily. What in God's name was she doing out here alone, so soon after her betrothal had been announced?

Although he had made no sound, Lydia's head lifted, and she beheld him with a distinct lack of enthusiasm. "Dr. Linley."

Drawing closer, Jake saw that the object in her lap was a little wad of notes, which she had been scribbling with a broken pencil stub. Mathematical equations, he guessed. Lydia Craven's obsession with such masculine pursuits as math and science had been gossiped about for years. Although well-meaning friends had advised the Cravens to discourage such unorthodox interests, they had done the opposite, taking pride in their daughter's adroit intelligence.

Shoving the objects hastily into her reticule, Lydia sent him a frowning glance.

"Shouldn't you be inside with your fiancé?" Jake asked in a gently mocking tone.

"I wanted a few minutes of privacy." She sat up straighter, the shadows playing softly on the sleek lines of her body and the molded white silk of her bodice. The indentation between her winged black brows and the moody set of her mouth were so antithetical to the image of a starry-eyed bride-to-be that Jake couldn't restrain a sudden grin.

"Wray doesn't know that you're out here, does he?"

"No one does, and I'll thank you to keep it that way. If you will kindly leave—"

"Not before I offer my congratulations." He

approached her lazily, his heartbeat accelerating to a swift, strong rhythm. As always, her nearness aroused him, quickening his blood and sending frantic messages to his nerves. "Well done, Miss Craven—you've caught an earl, and a rich one at that. I suppose there is no greater achievement than that for a young woman in your position."

Lydia rolled her eyes. "Only you could make congratulations sound offensive, Linley."

"I assure you, my good wishes are sincere." Jake glanced at the space on the bench beside her. "May I?" he asked and sat before she could refuse him.

They studied each other intently, their gazes locked in challenge. "You've been drinking," Lydia said, catching the scent of brandy on his breath.

"Yes." His voice had thickened slightly. "I've been toasting you and your fiancé. Repeatedly."

"I appreciate your enthusiasm for my betrothal," Lydia said sweetly, pausing with expert timing before adding, "or is it enthusiasm for my father's brandy?"

He laughed gruffly. "Your betrothal to Wray, of course. It warms my cynical heart to witness the ardent devotion you display for each other."

His mockery brought a flush of annoyance to

her face. Lydia and the earl were hardly the most demonstrative of couples. There were no intimate glances, no seemingly accidental brushes of their fingers, nothing to indicate even a modicum of physical awareness between them. "Lord Wray and I both like and respect each other," Lydia said defensively. "That is an excellent foundation for a marriage."

"What about passion?"

She shrugged and tried to sound sophisticated. "As they say, that is only fleeting."

Jake's mouth twisted impatiently. "How would you know? You've never felt a moment of real passion in your life."

"Why do you say that?"

"Because if you had, you wouldn't be entering into a marriage that contains all the warmth of last night's table scraps."

"Your characterization of my relationship with Lord Wray is completely wrong. He and I desire each other a great deal, if you must know."

"You don't know what you're talking about."

"Oh, yes I do! But I refuse to divulge details of my private life merely to prove you wrong."

As Jake stared at Lydia, his body was flooded with longing. It seemed impossible that she would be wasted on a man as civilized and bloodless as Wray. He let his gaze fall to her mouth, the soft, expressive lips that had tempted and tormented him for years. And he reached out to close her upper arms in his hands, her flesh warm and supple beneath the layer of silk. He couldn't help himself—he had to touch her. His fingers moved in a slow upward glide, savoring the feel of her. "You've let him kiss you, I suppose. What else?"

Lydia inhaled sharply, the framework of her shoulders light and tense in his hands. "As if I would answer such a question," she said unsteadily.

"It probably hasn't gone much farther than kisses. There's a certain look about a woman who's been awakened to passion. And you don't have it."

In the four years of their acquaintance, Jake had rarely touched her. Only on occasions of obligatory courtesy, such as helping her across a rough patch of ground, or when they had exchanged partners during a country dance. Even during those perfunctory moments, his response to her had been impossible to ignore.

Staring into her shadowed green eyes, Jake told himself that she belonged to another man. And he cursed himself for wanting her, even as his body hardened with desire and all rational thought began to dissolve in a swirl of heat. He faced a lifetime of nights without her, of kisses they would never share, of words that could never be spoken. In the scheme of things, the next few moments would not matter to anyone but him. He deserved to have at least this much of her—he had paid for it with years of longing.

His voice was low and unsteady as he spoke. "Perhaps I should do you a favor, Lydia. If you're going to marry a cold fish like Wray, you should at least know what desire feels like."

"What?" she asked faintly, her gaze bewildered.

Jake knew it was a mistake, but he didn't give a damn. He bent his head and touched her lips with his, softly skimming, his large body trembling with the effort to be gentle. Her mouth was tender and sweet, her skin gossamer-smooth as he spread his fingertips along the edge of her jaw. Catching a light, elusive taste of her, he searched for more, the pressure of his mouth intensifying. Lydia's hands fluttered against his chest . . . he sensed her indecision, her surprise at the reverence of his embrace. Grasping her wrists carefully, Jake pulled them around his neck. His tongue searched the hot silken depths of her mouth, the slight penetration bringing him infinite pleasure. He wanted to fill her in every possible way, to sink inside her until he found the relief he had craved for so long.

Lydia's helpless response destroyed the remainder of his self-possession. She leaned hard against his chest, one of her slim hands sliding beneath his coat to find the body heat that was trapped between the layers of his garments. Her touch excited Jake beyond bearing, beyond sanity, and he realized incredulously that it wouldn't take much more than this for him to explode in climax. His body was clenched and hard all over, his veins throbbing with unspent desire. The effort of making himself let go of Lydia drew a groan from behind his tightly clenched teeth. He tore his mouth away from hers, breathing harshly as he fought for self-control. Sardonically he reflected that with all his experience, he had never been so unraveled by a mere kiss . . . one from a virgin, at that.

Struggling to her feet, Lydia tugged at her gown and straightened her skirts, while the night air made her shiver. After a long time, she spoke with her face averted. "That was quite instructive, Linley," she managed to say breathlessly. "But from now on, I shan't require any more lessons from you." And she left him with impetuous strides, as if she could barely keep from breaking into a run.

Chapter 1

There were two ways to pick a husband—with your head or your heart. Being a sensible young woman, Lydia Craven had naturally done the former. Which was not to say that she didn't care for her future husband. As a matter of fact, she was very fond of Robert, Lord Wray, who was kind and affable, with a quiet charm that never grated on the nerves. He was handsome in an approachable way, his refined features providing the perfect framework for a pair of intelligent blue eyes and a smile that was employed somewhat judiciously.

There was no doubt in Lydia's mind that Wray would never object to her work. In fact, he shared her interest in mathematics and science. And he mingled easily with her family—her unconventional, close-knit family, which had been blessed with enormous wealth but possessed a singularly undistinguished pedigree. It was a high mark in Wray's favor, that he could so easily overlook Lydia's ignoble ancestry . . . but then, as she had reflected wryly, a prospective dowry of a hundred thousand pounds would be a savory condiment to even the most plebeian of dishes. Since Lydia's come-out at the age of eighteen two years earlier, she had been ardently pursued by a legion of fortune hunters. However, as a peer who had come into his own sizeable inheritance, Wray had no need of Lydia's money—another mark on his side.

Everyone approved of the match, even Lydia's overprotective father. The only mild objection had come from her mother, Sara, who had seemed vaguely perturbed by her determination to marry Wray. "The earl seems to be a fine, honorable man," Sara had said while she and Lydia had wandered through the gardens of the Craven estate in Herefordshire. "And if he is the one that you've set your heart on, I would say that you've made a good choice. . . ."

"But?" Lydia had prompted.

Sara had stared thoughtfully at the rich planting of golden kingcups and yellow irises that lined the neat, brick-paved walkway. It had been a warm spring day, the pale blue sky embossed with fleecy clouds.

"Lord Wray's virtues are indisputable," Sara had said. "However, he is not the kind of man that I imagined you would marry."

"But Lord Wray and I are so much alike," Lydia had protested. "For one thing, he is the only man of my acquaintance who has actually bothered to read my article on multidimensional geometry."

"And well he should be admired for that," Sara had said, her blue eyes sparkling with sudden wry amusement. Although Sara was an intelligent woman in her own right, she had freely admitted that her daughter's advanced mathematical reasoning was far beyond her own understanding. "However, I had hoped that you would someday find a man who might balance your nature with a little more warmth and irreverence than Lord Wray seems to possess. You are such a serious girl, my dearest Lydia."

"I'm not *that* serious," she had protested.

Sara had smiled. "When you were a little girl, I tried in vain to coax you to paint pictures of trees and flowers, and instead you insisted on making lines to demonstrate the difference between obtuse angles and orthogonal ones. When we played with blocks and I began to build houses and towns with them, you showed me how to construct a dihedral pyramid—"

"All right, all right," Lydia had grumbled with a reluctant grin. "But that only serves to demonstrate why Lord Wray is perfect for me. He loves machines and physics and mathematics. In fact, we're considering writing a paper together about the possibility of vehicles being powered by atmospheric propulsion. No horses necessary!"

"Fascinating," Sara had remarked vaguely, leading Lydia away from the paved path and wandering to a wildflower meadow that stretched beyond a grove of fruit trees.

As Sara had lifted her skirts ankle-high and waded among the thick carpeting of violets and white narcissi, the sun shining on her chestnut hair, she had looked far too young to be a matron of forty-five. She had paused to scoop up a clump of violets and inhale their heavy perfume. Her speculative blue eyes had regarded Lydia over the brilliant knot of flowers. "In between all these conversations of machines and mathematics, has Lord Wray ever kissed you?"

Lydia had laughed at the question. "You're not supposed to ask your daughter things like that."

"Well, has he?"

As a matter of fact, Wray had kissed Lydia on many occasions, and Lydia had found it enjoyable. Of course, she had led an extremely sheltered life, and she'd had no basis for comparison, except . . .

Suddenly the image of Jake Linley had appeared in her mind, his dark golden head bending over hers . . . the sweet, dark fire of his kiss, the pleasure of his hands on her body . . . and Lydia had shoved the thought away immediately, as she had a thousand times before. That night had been an anomaly that she would do well to forget. Linley had only been toying with her—the kiss had been nothing more than a prank fueled by one glass of brandy too many. She had not seen Linley at all in the three months since then, and when they next met, she would pretend to have forgotten all about the episode.

"Yes," she'd admitted to her mother, "the earl has kissed me, and it was very pleasant."

"I'm glad to hear it." Sara had let the violets spill from her fingers in a vibrant shower of fluttering petals. She'd rubbed her perfumed fingertips behind her ears and darted a slightly mischievous glance at Lydia. "I would not wish for your marriage to be mostly cerebral in nature. There are many joys to be found in a husband's arms, if he is the right man."

Lydia had hardly known how to reply. Suddenly she'd felt heat gathering at the crests of her cheeks and the tips of her ears. Although Sara was discreet about such matters, it had always been obvious that Lydia's parents were a passionate couple. There were times that her father would make an oblique remark at the breakfast table that would cause Sara to splutter in her tea . . . times when their bedroom door was inexplicably locked during the middle of the day . . . and then there were the private glances her father would sometimes send her mother, somehow wicked and tender at the same time. Lydia had to admit that Wray had never looked at her that way. However, few people ever experienced the kind of love that her parents shared.

"Mama, I know what you are wishing for," Lydia had said with a rueful sigh. "You want all of your children to find true love, as you and Papa have. But the odds of that happening to me are approximately one in four hundred thousand."

Long accustomed to her daughter's habit of translating everything into numbers, Sara had smiled. "How did you decide that?"

"I started with the number of eligible men in England, and estimated how many of them might be appropriate for me in terms of age, health, and so forth. Then I assessed the number of possible outcomes to meeting each one of them, by observing a random sampling of our married acquaintances. At least half have fallen into indifference for each other, a third have been separated by death or adultery, and the rest are content, but not what anyone would call soul mates. According to my calculations, the chance of finding true love compared to the number of total possible outcomes for the process of husband hunting is one to four hundred thousand. And with odds like that, I will be far better off marrying someone like Lord Wray, rather than wait for a lightning strike that may never happen."

"Good Lord," Sara had exclaimed, clearly appalled. "Lydia, I cannot think how a child of mine has come to be so cynical."

Lydia had grinned. "I'm not cynical, Mama. Just realistic. And I've gotten it from Papa."

"I'm afraid so," Sara had said, briefly raising her gaze heavenward, as if in supplication to some inattentive deity. "Dearest, has Lord Wray ever told you that he loves you?"

"No, but that may come in time."

"Hmmm," her mother had said, staring at her dubiously.

"And if not," Lydia had said cheerfully, "I'll

have all the time I want for my mathematical studies." Seeing how distressed Sara appeared to be by her irreverence, Lydia had gone and hugged her impulsively. "Mama, don't worry," she'd said into her mother's flower-scented hair. "Everything will be all right. I'll be very, very happy with Lord Wray. I promise."

Sara soaked in a large porcelain bathtub, hoping that the steaming water would help ease the tension in her shoulders and back. The tiled bathing-room was lit by a single lamp, the gentle flame shining softly through the etched-glass globe. Sighing, she rested her head against the mahogany rim of the tub and considered what to do about Lydia. Her other children, Nicholas, Ash, Harry and Daisy, were always getting into scrapes and charming their way out of trouble. Lydia, on the other hand, was responsible, intellectual and self-controlled, possessing a head for numbers that rivaled her father's.

Since her come-out two years earlier, Lydia had kept her suitors at bay with a distant friendliness that had led many disappointed young men to claim that she was made of ice. That was far from the truth. Lydia was a warm and affectionate girl, with a reserve of deep passion that was waiting to be tapped by the right man. Unfortunately, Lord Wray was not that man. Even after a six-month courtship, he and Lydia showed no signs of having fallen in love. To Sara, their amicable relationship seemed more like that of a brother and sister than of two lovers. But if Lydia was content with the arrangement—and she certainly seemed to be—was it right to offer any objections? As a young woman, Sara had been allowed the freedom to find her own husband, and her choice had been unconventional by anyone's standards. Lydia certainly deserved the same opportunity.

Thinking back to the days of her courtship with Derek Craven, Sara slid a bit lower into the water, while her toes idly pushed soapsuds from one side of the tub to the other. Back then Derek had been the owner of the most notorious gaming club in England, making a fortune by exploiting the greed of his aristocratic patrons. By the time Sara had met him, Derek had already been a legendary figure, a penniless bastard who had eventually become the wealthiest man in London. No one, least of all Derek himself, would have claimed he was a feasible match for a young woman as unworldly as Sara had been. And yet they had been drawn together irresistibly, too desperate for each other to make any other choice.

That was what bothered her about Lydia and Lord Wray, Sara realized. One had the sense that their relationship would always remain at a safely tepid level. Of course, Sara was well aware that in upper circles, love matches were considered to be tastelessly provincial. However, she had come from the country, raised under the tender guidance of two parents who had loved each other deeply. As a young woman she had wanted to find that for herself, and as a mother, she certainly wanted no less for her children.

Sara was so intent on her thoughts that she did not hear the sound of someone entering the bathing-room. Suddenly she was startled by the sight of a waistcoat sailing to the wooden chair in the corner . . . followed immediately by a dark silk necktie. As she began to sit up, a pair of muscular forearms slid around her from behind, and she felt her husband's gentle mouth at her ear. Slowly he pulled her back against the warm porcelain wall of the tub.

"I missed you, angel," he whispered.

Smiling, Sara relaxed back against him and toyed with the edges of his rolled-up shirtsleeves. Derek had been away in London for the past three days, negotiating a deal between his telegraph company and the South Western railway to lay new telegraph lines along the tracks. Although she had kept herself busy in his absence, the days—and nights—had seemed very long indeed.

"You're late," she said, her voice tipped with a flirtatious note. "I expected you to return by suppertime. You missed a very fine sturgeon."

"I'll have to dine on you, then." His large hands plunged beneath the water.

Giggling, Sara turned to face him, and her mouth was instantly captured in a searing kiss that unsettled her breath and spurred her heartbeat to a new, urgent cadence. Her fingers gripped the hard planes of his shoulders until the fabric of his shirt was splotched with water. When their lips parted, a little skipping sigh came from her throat, and she lifted her lashes to stare into Derek's lavish green eyes. She had lived with him for more than twenty years, and yet that vibrant, audacious gaze still never failed to make her senses leap with pleasurable excitement.

Derek cradled the side of her face, his thumb smoothing the dappling of water flecks across her shining cheek. He was a big, black-haired man, with a scar on his forehead that lent an agreeable ruggedness to his handsome face. Outwardly the passing years had wrought little change in him, except to weave a few strands of silver into the hair at his temples. And as always, he possessed a devilish charm that often lulled people into forgetting the predatory nature that lurked beneath his elegant facade.

Derek's alert gaze moved over her face. "What is the matter?" he asked, sensitive to every nuance of her expression.

"Nothing, really. It's just that . . ." Sara paused and snuggled her cheek into the warm cup of his palm. "I talked to Lydia while you were gone. She freely admitted that she is not in love with Lord Wray—and she is determined to marry him anyway."

"Why?"

"Lydia has decided that she will probably never find a soul mate, and therefore she should choose a husband based on practical considerations. She claims that the odds of anyone attaining true love are negligible."

"She's probably right about that," Derek commented.

Drawing back from him, Sara frowned. "Do you mean to say that you don't expect our children to be as happy in their marriages as we are?"

"I wish for nothing less, for every single one of them. But no, I don't necessarily expect that they will each find true love."

"You don't?"

"A man or woman can spend a lifetime searching for a soul mate and never find one. In my opinion, Lydia is wise to choose prime goods like Wray, rather than wait until the best picks are all gone. I'll be damned if my grandson will be sired by some third-rate fortune hunter."

"Oh, good Lord," Sara exclaimed with a strangled laugh. "Between you and Lydia, I don't know who is more exasperating. What about hope, and romance, and magic? Some things cannot be explained by science, or measured in mathematical calculations." Reaching over the edge of the tub, she played with the dark hair revealed by the open neck of his shirt. "I waited for *my* true love, and look what it got me."

Sliding his hand behind her neck, Derek urged her face closer to his. "It got you twenty years of marriage to a ruthless scoundrel who can't keep his hands off you."

Her breath hitched with a laugh. "I've learned to live with that."

His mouth glided to the soft hollow behind her ear, while his fingertips roamed over her wet shoulders. "Tell me what you want me to do about Lydia," he said against her skin.

Sara shook her head and sighed. "There's nothing to be done. Lydia has made her decision, and one can hardly fault her choice. Now I suppose I shall have to leave everything in the hands of fate."

She felt Derek smile against her neck. "There's nothing wrong in giving fate a push in the right direction. If the opportunity presents itself."

"Hmmn." Considering various possibilities, Sara picked up a ball of soap and rolled it between her palms.

Derek stood and unfastened his shirt. He let the garment drop to the floor, revealing a lean, powerfully muscled torso and a thickly furred chest. His hot gaze slid along the water-blurred shape of her body. "Aren't you finished with your bath yet?"

"No." Sara smiled provocatively, running her soapy hands over her leg.

His hands moved to the fastenings of his trousers. "Then you'd better be prepared for some company," he said, and the note in his voice made her shiver in anticipation.

Chapter 2

In two days, Lydia would become Lady Wray. The weeklong celebration had already begun at the Craven estate, with nightly soirees, balls and lavish suppers. On Sunday, the festivities would conclude with a ceremony in the family chapel. Guests had come from all over England and the Continent to take part, until every private house, guest cottage and tavern in Herefordshire was filled. The twenty guest rooms in the Craven manor were all occupied, and visiting servants swarmed belowstairs like bees in a hive.

It seemed to Lydia that every question directed to her lately had centered around the subject of her nerves, with the general expectation that any proper young lady should be suffering from fits of bridal agitation. Unfortunately Lydia felt quite calm—a pronouncement that seemed to perturb everyone who heard it. Perceiving that her composure might somehow reflect badly on Lord Wray, Lydia tried to work up a twinge of anxiety, a shiver, a quake or a twitch, all to no avail.

The problem was, marrying Lord Wray was so sensible that Lydia saw no reason to be nervous about anything. She wasn't even worried about the wedding night, for her mother had explained such matters in a way that had robbed them of any fearful mystery. And if Wray proved to be as adept at lovemaking as he was at kissing, Lydia rather expected to enjoy the experience.

The only thing that troubled Lydia was all of this infernal entertaining. Ordinarily she was accustomed to days of tranquility, during which she could ruminate and calculate as long as she wanted. Now, after approximately one hundred and twenty hours of endless feasting, toasting, talking, laughing and dancing, Lydia had had enough. Her mind was seething with ideas that had nothing to do with romance and matrimony. She wanted to have done with the wedding and be free to work on her latest project.

"Lydia," Wray chided with amusement as he interrupted her furtive attempts to write some notes during a huge soiree on Friday. "Working on your formulae, are you?"

Guiltily Lydia slipped a scrap of paper and a pencil stub into the little fringed silk bag that dangled from her wrist. She looked up at Wray, whose lanky form towered over hers. As always, his appearance was immaculate. His smooth, dark hair gleamed with a thin veneer of pomade, his evening suit was precisely tailored, and the knot of his black silk necktie was perfectly centered.

"I'm sorry," Lydia said with a sheepish smile. "But my lord, I just had the most interesting idea about the probability analysis machine—"

"This is a soiree," he told her with a playful wag of his finger. "You're supposed to dance. Or gossip. Or linger at the refreshment table. See all the young ladies enjoying themselves? That's what you should be doing."

Lydia sighed grumpily. "I've done all that for two hours, with at least four more to go before the evening is done. I've had the same conversation with ten different people, and I'm tired of discussing the weather and the condition of my nerves."

Wray smiled. "If you're going to be a countess, you had better get used to it. As a newlywed couple, we'll be mixing in society quite a lot when the season begins."

"Lovely," Lydia said, and he chuckled.

"Come walk with me."

Taking his arm, Lydia accompanied Wray on a sedate stroll through the circuit of entertaining rooms. Wherever they went, they were greeted with approving smiles and murmured congratulations. Lydia knew that they made an attractive couple, both of them slender and dark-haired. It was obvious that Wray was a man of scholarly pursuits, with his fair complexion, his noble forehead and his beautifully manicured hands. There was nothing he loved better than long, intricate conversations concerning a wide variety of subjects. He was a sought-after guest for supper parties, where he would entertain the table with the perfect blend of wit and erudition. His academic dabblings were regarded with general approval, for a gentleman could follow his interests as long as he remained a dilettante and didn't seek to earn money from them.

They stopped to converse with a group of friends, and Lydia grinned ruefully as she saw all the signs of Wray settling in for a long discussion. Using her painted silk fan as a screen, she rose on her toes to whisper to him. "My lord . . . let's slip away together and find a private place. The conservatory, or the rose garden."

The earl smiled and shook his head, answering in an undertone that no one else could hear. "Absolutely not. Your father might find out."

"You're not really afraid of him, are you?" Lydia asked with an incredulous smile.

"He terrifies me," Wray admitted. "In fact, of all the points that Linley made when he advised me not to propose to you, that was the hardest to refute."

"What?" Lydia stared at him with open-mouthed astonishment. "Which Dr. Linley—the old one, or the son?"

"The son," Wray replied with a grimace. "Damn, I didn't mean to let that slip out. Perhaps you would be so kind as to overlook that last remark—"

"I most certainly will not!" She scowled at the discovery. "When did Linley advise you not to propose, and what were his reasons? The intolerable ass, I'd like to tell him—"

"Lydia, hush," Wray counseled softly. "Someone will hear. It was nothing, just a brief conversation we had before I approached your father to ask for your hand. I happened to mention to

Linley that I was going to propose to you, and he offered his opinion on the matter."

"A negative opinion, I gather." As Lydia struggled to control her temper, she felt a wash of color sliding over her face and throat. "What were his objections?"

"I don't remember."

Annoyance nearly suffocated her. "Yes, you do. Oh, don't be a gentleman for once, and tell me!"

Wray shook his head and replied firmly, "I shouldn't have been so careless with my words. It doesn't matter what Linley's objections are, nor anyone else's. I am resolved to have you as my wife, and that is that."

"Resolved?" Lydia repeated, making a comical face.

Wray touched her gloved elbow. "Let us join the others," he urged. "We'll have all the time in the world for private conversations after we're married."

"But my lord . . ."

He propelled her toward the gathering of friends, and they all proceeded to chat with relaxed idleness. Lydia found it impossible to keep her attention focused on the conversation. Silently she stewed and fumed, becoming increasingly irate. Even before now, she had considered Jake Linley to be the most provoking man she had ever known. How dare he try to dissuade the earl from marrying her! She wondered what he had told Wray—no doubt he had made her sound like a very bad bargain indeed.

Linley had done nothing but mock and annoy Lydia ever since they had met four years earlier, when she had twisted her ankle at a game of lawn tennis. It had been during a weekend party at a friend's estate, to which many prominent families in Herefordshire had been invited. After Lydia had injured herself during an energetic volley, her younger brother Nicholas had helped her hobble to the shade of a luxuriant maple tree.

"I believe the Linleys are here," Nicholas had told her, carefully easing her down to a cloth spread on the velvety lawn beside the remains of a picnic they had enjoyed earlier. "You sit here while I fetch the doctor." Old Dr. Linley was a kind and trustworthy man, who had helped deliver the last two of the Craven brood.

"Hurry," Lydia had told him, managing a pained grin as she saw three eager young men approaching. "I'm about to be besieged."

Nicholas had grinned, suddenly looking exactly like their father. "If any of them tries to examine your ankle, just look queasy and threaten to cast your accounts all over him."

As her brother had scampered up the hill to the main house, Lydia had indeed found herself under siege from enthusiastic suitors. She'd been helpless to do anything but sit there while the throng of men had plagued her, one of them pouring a cup of water, another pressing a moistened cloth to her forehead, another bracing his arm behind her back in case she felt faint.

"I'm perfectly all right," she had protested, smothered by their attentions. "It's just a twisted ankle—no, Mr. Gilbert, there is no need to look at it—please, all of you—"

Suddenly the three ardent young men had been shooed away by a brisk masculine voice. "Go on, all of you. I'll see to Miss Craven." Reluctantly they'd turned tail and left, and the newcomer had lowered to his haunches before Lydia.

For a moment she'd actually forgotten the throbbing pain in her leg as she'd stared into the stranger's dark-lashed gray eyes. Although he'd been well dressed, he'd been a bit rumpled, his necktie a bit too loose, his coat unevenly pressed. He'd looked to be about ten years older than herself, possessing a masculine vigor that she'd found vastly appealing. Sometimes, extremely handsome men seemed a bit vacuous, perhaps even a little effeminate, in their physical perfection. But this one had been all male, with boldly drawn features and thick, wheat-colored hair that had been cropped close to the back of his neck. He'd smiled at her, his teeth a flash of white in his tanned face.

"You're not Dr. Linley," Lydia had said.

"Yes, I am." He'd extended his hand to her, still smiling. "Dr. Jake Linley. My father sent me in his stead, as he is deep in a glass of port and didn't fancy walking down the hill."

Lydia's fingers had been enclosed in a firm clasp that had sent a pleasant ripple of sensation along her arm. Good Lord, she had heard tales of the old doctor's dashing eldest son, but she had never met him before. "You're the one with the wicked reputation," she'd said.

Releasing her hand, he'd regarded her with laughing eyes. "I hope you're not the kind to hold a man's reputation against him."

"Not at all," she'd told him. "Men of ill repute are usually much more interesting than the respectable ones."

His gaze had slid over her in a quick but thorough investigation, starting at the tumble of her wavy black hair, and ending at the protrusion of her toes from the frothy mass of her white ruffled skirts. One corner of his mouth had lifted in a coaxing half-smile. "Your brother said you'd hurt your leg. May I have a look?"

Suddenly Lydia's mouth had gone dry. She had never been so unnerved by anyone in her life. Her chin had dipped in a shallow nod, and she'd held very still as Jake Linley had grasped the hem of her skirt and eased it upward a few inches. His expression had become businesslike, his manner impersonal, but all the same she'd felt her heart begin to clatter madly in her chest. She'd glanced at his downbent head, while sunlight had spindled through the maple leaves and caused his hair to glitter with every shade from gold to dark amber. His large, gentle hands moved over her leg.

"Just a mild sprain," he'd said. "I would advise you to stay off it for the next couple of days."

"All right," she'd replied breathlessly.

Deftly he'd bound the swollen ankle with a linen napkin purloined from a nearby picnic basket. "My bag is in the house," he'd murmured. "If you will allow me to carry you inside, I'll bind your ankle properly and apply some ice . . . and give you something for the pain, if you like."

Lydia had responded with a jerky nod. "I'm sorry to be such trouble." She had gasped as he'd lifted her carefully against his chest. His body had been hard and muscular, his shoulders sturdy beneath her hands.

"Not at all," he had replied cheerfully, adjusting his arms around her. "Rescuing injured damsels is my favorite pastime."

To Lydia's everlasting chagrin, that first encounter with Jake Linley had started a wild infatuation that had lasted approximately four hours. Later in the day she'd happened to overhear a snippet of conversation between him and another male guest at the weekend party.

"Damn, Linley," the guest had remarked, "now I see why you became a doctor. You've managed to get under the skirts of every attractive woman in London, including Craven's daughter."

"Only in a professional sense," had come Linley's sardonic reply. "And I assure you, I have absolutely no interest in Miss Craven."

The comment had hurt and mortified Lydia, deflating her romantic imaginings with unpleasant abruptness. From then on, Lydia had treated Linley with coldness whenever they'd met. Through the years, their mutual antipathy had increased until they couldn't be in the same room together without launching into an argument that caused everyone else to scurry for cover. Lydia had tried to be indifferent to him, but something about him provoked her to the depths of her soul. When she was with him, she found herself saying things she didn't mean, and brooding about their fractious encounters long after they had parted company. During one of their battles, Linley had given her the infuriating nickname of "Lydia Logarithms," which family and friends still occasionally used to tease her.

And now he had tried to thwart her betrothal to Wray.

Hurt and furious, Lydia thought once again of the night her betrothal had been announced . . . the astonishing moment when Linley had kissed her, and her own mortifying response to him. If his actions had been designed to mock and confuse her, he had succeeded brilliantly.

Bringing her thoughts back to the present, Lydia decided that she could not bear another moment of the inane chatter that surrounded her. She stood on her toes and whispered to her fiancé. "My lord, my head has begun to ache, and I want to find a quiet place to sit."

The earl regarded her with a concerned gaze. "I will accompany you."

"No," she said hastily, "there is no need for that. I'll go to a private corner somewhere. I would prefer you to remain with our friends. I'll return in a little while, when I am feeling better."

"Very well." A teasing glint entered Wray's blue eyes. "I half suspect that my dear Miss Lydia Logarithms is going to sneak away to puzzle over some mathematical formula."

"My lord," she protested, scowling at his use of the hated nickname.

He chuckled. "I beg your pardon, my sweet. I shouldn't tease you like that. Are you certain that you don't want company?"

"Yes, quite certain." Lydia gave him a forgiving smile and left him with a promise to come back soon.

As she made her way out of the crowded ballroom, it was all Lydia could do to keep from running. The air was thick with the smells of flowers, perfume, sweat and wine, and the endless hum of chatter made her ears ring. She had never wanted to be alone as much as she did in this moment. If only she could reach the privacy of her bedroom . . . but there was no way to get there without going through a gauntlet of people who would insist on stopping her for mind-numbing conversation. Spying her mother, who was standing with friends near the French doors that led to the outside gardens, Lydia went to her at once.

"Mama," she said, "it's stuffy in here, and my head hurts. Would you mind terribly if I disappeared for a little while?"

Sara stared at her with concern and slid a slender, gloved arm around her waist. "You do look rather flushed. Shall I send a servant to fetch you a headache powder from the housekeeper's closet?"

"No, thank you." Lydia smiled as her mother removed a glove and pressed a cool, soft hand against the side of her face. "I'm fine, Mama. I'm just . . . oh, I don't know. Tired, I suppose."

Sara regarded her with a gently perceptive gaze, sensing Lydia's frustration. "Has something happened, darling?"

"Not really, but . . ." Lydia tugged her mother aside and glowered as she whispered back to her. "Lord Wray just told me that Jake Linley advised him not to marry me! Can you conceive of such arrogance? I'd like to bludgeon him with the nearest heavy object, the intolerable, petty, selfish cad . . ."

"What reason did Dr. Linley give for his objection to the match?"

"I don't know." Lydia let out an explosive sigh. "No doubt Linley thinks that I'm beneath Wray, and that he could do far better than me."

"Hmmm. That doesn't sound like him." Sara stroked Lydia's back soothingly. "Take a long breath, darling. Yes, that's better. Now, there is no reason for Dr. Linley's opinion to distress you, as it seems to have had no effect on Lord Wray's desire to marry you."

"Well, it *does* distress me," Lydia muttered. "In fact, it makes me want to smash something. How could Linley have done something like this?" To her disgust, she heard a note of dejection in her own voice as she added, "I've never understood why he dislikes me so."

"I don't believe that is the case at all," Sara replied, giving her a comforting squeeze. "In fact, I think I may know the reason for Dr. Linley's opposition to your betrothal. You see, I was speaking to his mother just the other day when we happened to meet at the milliner's, and she confided to me that he—"

Sara broke off as she saw a new arrival in the ballroom. "Oh, the Raifords have arrived," she exclaimed. "Their daughter Nicole had her second child just a fortnight ago, and I must ask about her. We'll talk later, darling."

"But Mama, you have to tell me . . ." Lydia began, as her mother sailed away toward her friends.

The evening was becoming more aggravating by the minute.

What in God's name had Linley's mother said about him? Filled with frustration, Lydia went to the French doors and slipped outside. Without hesitation, she headed to the one place where she knew she could be alone—the estate wine cellar.

All through her childhood, the wine cellar had been her favorite retreat. She and her younger brothers had always been fascinated by the large underground room with three chambers, each filled with hundreds of racks of amber and green bottles papered with foreign labels. It was reputed to be one of the finest collections in England, stocked with an extravagant variety of rare and expensive champagnes, brandies, ports, sherries, burgundies, clarets and cordials.

In the farthest chamber, a bench, a cupboard and small table served as a place to uncork bottles and sample their contents. Lydia remembered countless games in which she and the rest of the Craven brood had played pirates, spies, or hide-and-seek in the shadowy recesses of the cellar. On occasion, she had sat at the wine table and worked out some mathematical puzzle, relishing the silence and the fragrance of aged wood and spice and wax.

Opening a heavy wood door, she headed down a short flight of stone steps. Lamps had been left burning to accommodate the under-butler's frequent trips to the cellar to obtain wine for the guests. After the hubbub upstairs, the blessed quietness of the cellar was an unspeakable relief. Lydia sighed deeply and began to relax. With a rueful smile, she reached up to rub the taut nape of her neck. Perhaps she was finally experiencing bridal jitters, after worrying for days that she *didn't* have them.

A quiet voice disrupted the shadowy serenity of the cellar.

"Miss Craven?"

Looking up with a start, Lydia beheld the man she least wanted to see. Ever.

"Linley," she said grimly, dropping her hand to her side. "What are you doing here?"

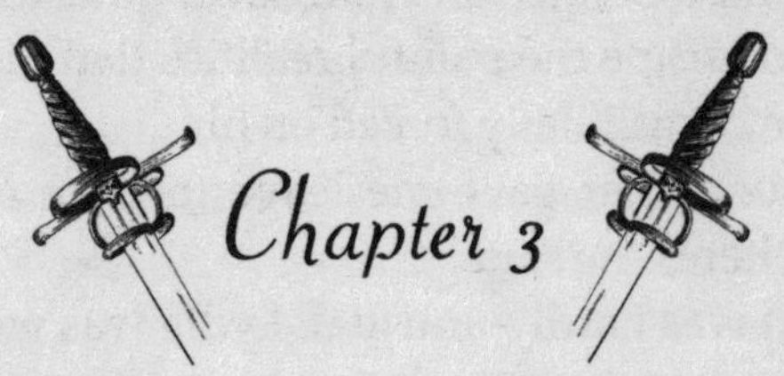

Chapter 3

In the musty, densely shadowed atmosphere, Jake Linley's tawny, sunlit coloring was even more striking than usual. Somehow it did not seem appropriate for him to be underground, even for a temporary visit to a wine cellar. Even though he was her adversary, Lydia had to acknowledge that he was one of the most attractive men she had ever met. Linley was not much older than Wray, but he was infinitely more seasoned. His worldliness was all the more apparent because of the way he tried to conceal it with irreverent lightness. Seeing the ironic flash of his smile, and the loose, easy grace of his movements, one could easily be deceived by his devil-may-care charm. But his eyes betrayed him. The light gray depths were filled with the weariness of a man who had seen and experienced far too much and had never quite found a way to escape the painful realities that his profession occasionally forced on him.

"Your father gave me leave to have a look down here," he said.

That was hardly unusual. Lydia was well accustomed to the interest that visitors took in her father's renowned wine collection. However, it was a singular stroke of bad luck that Linley should be perusing the racks at the same time that she had come here in search of privacy.

"Have you seen enough?" Lydia asked, not without an inward wince at her own rudeness. Her mother had raised all the Cravens with inviolable standards of politeness. However, Jake Linley's presence was too much for her to endure. "Because I would like to be alone."

His head tilted slightly as he fixed her with an intent stare. "Are you feeling unwell?" he asked. "If so—"

Lydia interrupted with a scornful sound. "Please don't bother to display any concern for my welfare. I know better."

Jake Linley approached her slowly, coming to stand in a pool of subdued lamplight. How unfair it was for a man to be so perfidious and yet so handsome. He wore the austere scheme of formal black-and-white, with a gray silk necktie that flattered his translucent eyes. The perfectly fitted clothes hung elegantly on his lean, powerful frame, but as always, he seemed just the slightest bit disheveled, as if he had been stretching and tugging irritably at the confining garments. The subtle signs of disarray practically begged a woman to neaten his necktie and straighten his waistcoat, the intimate gestures that a wife would make toward her husband.

"Why do you think my concern is false?" he asked.

Resentment—and some even more painful, unidentifiable emotion—caused tight knots to form in Lydia's stomach. "Because I know how you tried to convince Lord Wray that I wasn't good enough for him, and thereby prevent him from proposing to me."

His eyes narrowed. "Is that what he told you?"

"Not in those exact words. But you did advise him not to marry me, and for that I will never forgive you."

Linley sighed somewhat grimly and stared at the ancient stone-flagged floor. He seemed to be contemplating some complex problem that had no answer, much as Lydia had felt the first time she had realized that a negative number could have no square root.

"You're right," he admitted flatly. "I did advise Wray not to marry you."

"Why?"

"Does it matter now? Wray disregarded my counsel, you accepted his troth, and the matter will be concluded in about thirty-eight hours."

Lydia regarded him with sudden sharp interest. "Counting down the hours, are you?"

At that undirected shot, Linley actually backed away a step. His eyes glinted warily, as if she had struck too close to a vital secret. "I will leave you to your privacy, Miss Craven. My apologies for disrupting your solitude."

He turned and left, while Lydia glared after him. "You'll apologize for that, but not for what you said to Lord Wray?"

He paused momentarily. "That's right," he said without looking at her, and ascended the steps.

Lydia strode to the farthest chamber and plunked herself onto the creaking wooden chair. Slamming her silk purse on the table, she let out a frustrated groan and dropped her head in her hands. A soon-to-be bride should not feel this way, confounded and agitated and angry. She should be happy. Her head should be filled with dreams. In all the novels that she had read, a girl's wedding day was the most wonderful occasion of her life. If that was true, then she was once again out of step with everyone else, because she wasn't looking forward to it at all.

She'd always wanted so badly to be like everyone else. She had always tried to emulate her friends and pretend interest in dolls and indoor games, when she had infinitely preferred to climb trees and play army with her brothers. Later, when her female cousins had been absorbed in fashion, romantic intrigue and other girlish amusements, Lydia had been drawn into the fascinating world of mathematics and science. No matter how much her family loved and protected her, they could not shield her from the snide rumors and whispered asides, implying that she was unfeminine, unconventional . . . peculiar.

Now she had finally found a man who was universally regarded as a splendid catch, and he even shared her interests. When she married Lord Wray, she would finally belong. She would be part of the crowd, instead of standing apart from it. And that would be a relief.

Why, then, wasn't she happy?

Lydia rubbed her aching temples as she worried silently. She needed to talk to someone who was wise and understanding and could help clear away the inexplicable pangs of disappointment and longing that Jake Linley caused. Her father. The thought soothed her immediately. Yes, she would find her father later tonight. She had always been able to tell him anything, and his advice, though bluntly worded, was always reliable.

Feeling marginally better, she pulled a wad of paper and a pencil from her purse and arranged them on the table. Just as she began to write a long string of numbers on a scrap of paper that had already been blackened with previous scribbling, she heard the sound of footsteps.

Scowling, she looked up and beheld Linley's set face. "Why are you still here?"

"It's locked," he said curtly.

"The outside door? But that's not possible. It would have to have been barred from the outside."

"Well, it has. I put all my weight on it, and the damned thing wouldn't budge."

"There's another door in the second chamber, that leads up to the butler's pantry," Lydia informed him. "You can leave that way."

"I've already tried that. It's locked as well."

Frowning, Lydia propped her chin on her hand. "Who would have barred the outside door, and why? It must have been an accident.

No one would have reason to lock us in here together . . . unless . . ."

"Unless?"

"It could have been Eugenia King," Lydia said wrathfully. "She's wanted revenge on me ever since I managed to catch Lord Wray, when she had set her cap for him. Oh, she would love to cause a scandal by contriving to have me compromised by a libertine like you, not two days before my wedding." As another thought occurred to her, she shot him a slitted glance. "Or perhaps *you* arranged for this. It could be part of your plan to thwart my wedding to Wray."

"For God's sake," he said irritably, "I was in the cellar first, remember? I had no idea you were going to appear. And I don't care whether you marry the earl or not. I only gave my opinion when he asked for it."

Dropping the pencil to the table, Lydia turned in the chair to face him. Her indignation boiled over as she replied, "Apparently you gave it with great enthusiasm. No doubt you were all too happy for the opportunity to make derogatory remarks about me."

"I didn't make derogatory remarks about you. I only said—" Linley closed his mouth abruptly.

"What?" Lydia prompted, clenching her fist against the scarred surface of the table.

As his gaze searched hers, the silence turned so thick and intimate that Lydia could hardly breathe. For the first time, she and he had the freedom to do or say whatever they wished, and that made the situation potentially . . . explosive.

After a long pause, Linley asked softly, "Why do you give a damn what I think?"

Feeling trapped, Lydia stood and moved away from him, heading to the nearby racks that extended from floor to ceiling. She ran her finger across a row of wax-sealed corks and inspected the gray smudge of dust that accumulated on her fingertip. "I suppose I can't resist trying to solve a puzzle," she said eventually. "And I've never been able to figure out the source of the discord between you and I. It's obvious to everyone that we've never gotten along. Is it because of my family's origins? The fact that my father was born illegitimately, and his gaming club days—"

"No," Linley said swiftly. "I would never hold that against him, or your family. I have nothing but admiration for your father and what he's made of himself. And my family's origins are no better than yours. As everyone knows, the Linleys are hardly a bunch of blue bloods." He smiled darkly before continuing. "But as much as I esteem your father, there is no disputing that he's also manipulative and domineering, and he'll stop at nothing to get what he wants. And he also happens to be as rich as Croesus. In other words, Craven is the father-in-law from hell. Wray is completely cowed by him. Your father won't hesitate to make your husband dance to whatever tune he plays . . . and no marriage can tolerate that kind of interference."

"I won't let Papa bully him," Lydia said defensively.

Linley responded with a derisive snort. He half-sat on the table, one foot swinging idly. "Your husband needs the ballocks to stand up to Craven without your protection. And Wray doesn't have them. Sooner or later, he'll resent you for that, almost as much as you'll resent him."

Lydia would have given almost anything to be able to contradict him. "A man can change," she said.

"Even if he does, that won't alter the other pertinent fact."

"Which is?"

The uncertain lamplight made his rumpled hair shine like antiqued gold, and gleamed on his smooth-shaven skin. "You don't love each other."

Lydia was unable to speak, her pulse racing

wildly as he approached her. She wasn't aware of backing away from him until she felt the wine rack against her shoulders and heard the rattle of bottles.

Moving closer, Linley braced his hands on either side of her, his fingers curling around the ironwork braces fashioned to hold the bottles in place. He stood much too close, his body towering over hers. Lydia's nostrils were filled with his fragrance, the freshness of soap overlaying the warm, salty maleness of his skin. She took a deep breath, and another, but somehow her lungs wouldn't seem to work properly. How strange it was, that until now she had never realized how big he was. She was above average height, and yet he loomed over her, his shoulders blocking out the frugal lamplight.

His fingers flexed on the ironwork. "You should marry a man who would sell his soul just to spend one night with you."

"How do you know that Wray doesn't feel that way about me?" she whispered.

"Because if he did, you wouldn't be so damned innocent right now." A flush crept over the crests of his cheekbones and the bridge of his nose. "If you were mine, I never could have waited all these months without—"

He broke off and swallowed audibly, his

breath striking her lips in light, hot puffs. As he leaned closer to her, she could almost feel the animal heat of his body.

Her thoughts scattered wildly as she realized that he was going to kiss her. She felt the heat of his hands close around the back of her head, cradling, supportive. His face lowered to hers until everything blurred, and she closed her eyes. There was a velvety brush against the corner of her mouth . . . another at the vulnerable center of the lower lip. . . . His mouth settled on hers by slow degrees until he had caught her in full, moist possession. Suddenly Lydia felt drunk, just like the time last Christmas when she'd had two large cups of rum punch and had spent the rest of the evening in a pleasant, knee-weakening fog.

She swayed dizzily and was immediately caught and held against the solid length of his body. He kissed her more deeply, nudging her lips apart so that he could taste her with gentle, urgent strokes. The pleasure of it shocked her. Her mouth opened feverishly beneath his, welcoming the hot, gliding insinuation of his tongue. He gave it to her slowly, making her writhe against him. Her fingers slid into his thick hair, pulling his head harder over hers, and a soft sound came from deep in his throat.

Abruptly he took his mouth from hers, gasping harshly. "Damn. I shouldn't have done that. I'm sorry." His thumb passed tenderly over the pliable curve of her lower lip, and he stared at her with a flare of longing that astonished her. "I'm sorry," he repeated. "I'll let you go now. I . . ." His arms loosened, but he seemed unable to take them from around her. "God, Lydia," he whispered hoarsely, and his head lowered again.

His mouth took hers compulsively, savoring her helpless response. Lydia felt his hands travel downward, one pressing her hips more tightly against his, while the other slid beneath the round weight of her breast, lifting it slightly. The heat of his fingers sank through the thick silk of her bodice. He stroked the stiffening peak with the pad of his thumb, circling lazily while he kissed her over and over, unlocking a need that frightened her with its intensity.

With a low whimper, Lydia wrenched herself away from him, somehow making her way to the wine table. She sat down hard in the chair, drawing in huge gulps of air, while her damp hands pressed flat to the worn surface of the table.

Jake remained by the wine racks, resting his forehead against a shelf. Finally he stepped back and dragged a hand roughly through his hair. Lydia saw the tremor in his fingers and heard the deep shiver in his breath. "I've got to get out of here," he said gruffly. "I can't be alone with you."

Lydia waited until her heartbeat slowed before she attempted to speak. "Linley . . . Jake . . . what kind of game are you playing?"

"It's not a game." His pale eyes stared directly into hers. "I've wanted you since the first time I saw you."

"But that can't be true. I overheard you telling someone that you had no interest in me."

"When?"

"The first day we met, after you'd bound my ankle."

"You were only sixteen," he replied sardonically. "I would have sounded like a depraved old lecher if I'd admitted to being attracted to you."

"The night of my betrothal, when you kissed me . . . that was because you were attracted to me?"

"Why else would I have done so?"

Her cheeks burned at the memory. "I thought you were merely trying to embarrass me."

"You thought—" Jake began with an incredulous look, then broke off abruptly. "Hell. You're going to be married in two days. Is there any point in discussing it now?"

Lydia felt very odd, rather despairing and angry, as if she'd lost something she'd never had in the first place. As if she had somehow been cheated out of something. "You're right," she agreed slowly, "there is no point in discussing it now. Nothing would compel me to change my mind about marrying Lord Wray."

Jake was silent at that, his eyes shadowed, the set of his mouth vaguely sullen.

"Wray and I are compatible in every way," Lydia said, feeling the need to emphasize the point. "For one thing, he's the only man who has read my paper for the *Journal of Practical Science*—"

"*I* read it," he interrupted.

"You did?"

Linley smiled slightly as he saw her astonishment. "Only the first part."

"What did you think of it?"

"I fell asleep during the part about congruent and disjoint tetrahydra."

"Tetrahedra," Lydia corrected with a slight smile, knowing that to someone other than a mathematician, her paper would have been dull indeed. "Well, I hope I provided a good night's rest for you."

"You did."

She laughed, and they stared at each other for a moment of unexpected, artless delight. Slowly Lydia relaxed against the back of the chair. "If you don't like mathematics," she said, "then what *do* you enjoy?"

"Fishing for trout. Reading newspapers in coffeehouses. Walking through London at dawn." His gaze fell to her lips. "Kissing in wine cellars."

She bit back a smile at the roguish comment.

"Tell me what you like," he said.

"Billiards, and architecture, and watercoloring—even though I'm wretched at it. I also like playing cards, but only with my father, as he is the only one who can ever defeat me." *And also kissing in wine cellars,* Lydia thought wryly. Standing, she rummaged through the cabinet beside the table, unearthing a corkscrew, a wax scraper, and a pair of tasting glasses. "I know something else you'll like," she said, gesturing with an empty glass to the rack nearest him. "Look to the right of the bottom row—the bottle with the gold and green label. A d'Yquem Sauterne . . . the nicest port you've ever tasted."

Crouching to reach the bottle, Jake sent her a quizzical glance.

"We may as well," she said. "Who knows

how long we'll be trapped down here? Sooner or later the under-butler will come to fetch more wine, but in the meantime we may as well make the best of things."

Jake drew the bottle from the rack and brought it to the table. Expertly he ran the scraper around the seal of the cork, then reached for the transverse handle of the corkscrew. Lydia was mesmerized by the movements of his hands, so graceful and deft as he twisted the metal spiral into the cork and eased it from the glass throat of the bottle. Recalling the gentle skill with which those large hands had stroked her face and fondled her breast, Lydia felt a twinge of pleasure low in her stomach.

After pouring two glasses of the heavy, purplish-red liquid, Jake gave one to her, seeming to exert special care not to brush her fingers with his own. "To your wedding," he said brusquely, and they clinked the glasses. As Lydia drank, the heady flavor of rare wine rolled over her tongue and trickled sweetly down her throat.

She resumed her seat in the chair, while Jake removed his coat and half-sat on the table. "What are you working on?" he asked, glancing at the paper she had left near her purse, with its peppering of mathematical symbols.

"I'm developing a set of formulae for a probability analysis machine. Some friends from the London Mechanical Museum are designing it, and they invited me to collaborate."

"What would you do with it?"

"It could be used to calculate the outcomes of games of chance, or even for more serious purposes, such as military or economic strategy." Lydia warmed to the subject as he listened attentively. "My friends—who are much more mechanically inclined than I—have devised a system that uses brass cogs to represent numbers and symbols. Of course, it will never be built, as it would require thousands of specialized parts, and it would take up an entire building."

Jake seemed vastly entertained by the notion. "All this work for a hypothetical machine?"

"Are you going to make jest of me?" Lydia asked with raised brows.

Jake shook his head slowly, continuing to smile. "What a remarkable brain you have." The comment did not sound mocking at all. In fact, his expression was admiring.

Lydia sipped at her port, trying to ignore the sight of the way his trousers pulled tautly over his muscular thighs. He was a resplendently masculine creature, a rake with soul-weary eyes.

With no effort at all, she could stand and lean into the inviting space between his thighs and pull his head to hers. She wanted to kiss him again, to explore his delicious mouth, to feel his hands stroke her body. Instead she remained seated and gazed up at him with a gathering frown. She couldn't help speculating on how many other women must have felt this same attraction to him.

"What are you thinking?" he asked.

"I am wondering if you are as much of a rake as they say you are."

He considered the question carefully. "I'm not a paragon," he admitted.

"You have a reputation for seducing women."

Jake's face was inscrutable, but she sensed the discomfort that her comments had caused him. He remained silent for so long that Lydia thought he wasn't going to reply. However, he forced himself to meet her gaze and spoke stiffly.

"I've never seduced anyone. And I would never sleep with someone who had sought my professional services. But on occasion I do take what is offered to me."

The cool, dark interior of the cellar enclosed them in a cocoon, insulating them from the outside world, where unmarried girls did not discuss indecent subjects with wicked rakes. Lydia knew that she would never again have the chance to talk intimately with the man who had plagued and fascinated her for so many years.

"Why?" she asked softly. "Because you're lonely?"

He shook his head. "No, it's not loneliness. It's more of a need for . . . distraction."

"Distraction from what?"

Jake could have deflected the question easily. Instead, he stared at her steadily, his eyes bleak. "Without false modesty, I'm very good at what I do—but in my profession, encountering death and pain is inevitable. At times it's hell on earth, trying to help someone with a fatal wound or an incurable disease, having a husband beg me to save his wife, or a child asking me not to let his father die. Often in spite of my best efforts, I fail. I try to find the right words, to offer comfort, to give an explanation of why things happen . . . but there are no words." His face was partially averted, but she saw a faint flush of color rise in his tanned cheek. "I remember the faces of every patient who has died under my care. And on the nights that I can't stop thinking about them, I need something . . . someone . . . to help me forget. At least for a little while." He glanced at her warily. "Lately it hasn't worked so well."

Lydia had never imagined that he would

speak to her with such raw honesty. He had always seemed so eternally self-confident, so invulnerable.

"Why do you continue to be a doctor, if it causes you unhappiness?" she asked.

His throat tightened with a catch of laughter. "Because there are days when I manage to do the right things and help someone to survive in spite of all the odds. And sometimes I am called upon to deliver a baby, and as I look at the new life in my hands, I'm filled with hope." He shook his head and stared at the wall as if he were gazing across a great distance. "I've seen miracles. Once in a while, heaven smiles on the people who need it most, and they receive the greatest gift of all—a second chance at life. And then I thank God that I'm a doctor, and I know I could never be anything else."

Lydia stared at him with a stricken expression, while her heart seemed to contract with a peculiar, sweet pain.

Oh, no, she thought in a riot of confusion and panic.

In one scalding moment, all her smug complacency had been ripped away. She feared that she was in love with a man she had known for years . . . a man so familiar and yet so much a stranger.

Chapter 4

"Jake," Lydia said unsteadily, "I want to ask a favor of you."

His golden head lifted. "Yes?"

"Tell me the worst things about yourself. Be very honest—admit your worst faults, and make yourself sound as unappealing as possible."

He let out a low, rich laugh. "That's easy enough. But I'm not going to admit my faults without hearing about yours as well."

"All right," she said cautiously.

Jake took a sip of wine, his eyes narrowing slightly as he regarded her over the glass rim. "You first."

Perched on the edge of the chair, Lydia held her own glass in both hands and pressed her knees together tightly. She gave a resolute nod.

"To begin with, I am not socially adept. I don't like to make small talk, I'm terrible at flirting, and I don't like to dance."

"Not even with Wray?"

Lydia shook her head with an awkward smile.

"Perhaps you just haven't had the right partner," Jake said softly.

The rhythm of her breathing changed as their gazes meshed intimately. "Why have you never asked me to dance?"

"Because I don't trust myself to hold you in public."

Lydia colored all over and took a huge gulp of wine. She struggled to bring her mind back to her original line of thought. "More faults . . . well, I'm too impatient with people, and I hate inactivity, and I am something of a know-all . . ."

"No," he murmured with obviously manufactured surprise.

"Oh, yes," she replied, smiling ruefully in response to his teasing. "I always think I know best. I can't help it. And I hate to admit that I'm wrong. My family claims that I would argue with a lamppost."

Jake grinned. "I like strong-willed women."

"What about stubborn, unreasonable ones?" she asked with a self-deprecating grimace.

"Especially those, if they're as beautiful as you." He finished his wine and set the glass aside.

The compliment sent a ripple of pleasure through her. "Do you like to argue?" she asked breathlessly.

"No. But I like to make up afterward." His gaze stole over her body in an indiscreet sweep. "My turn now. We already know about my scandalous past. I'll also confess to a complete lack of ambition. I prefer to keep my life as uncomplicated as possible. I have few needs, aside from a nice house in town, a good horse and the occasional trip abroad."

Lydia found that difficult to absorb. How different he was from her beloved father, whose appetite to succeed and conquer was seemingly limitless. The ability to be content with what one had . . . was that a fault or a virtue?

"What if you came into a large inheritance?" she asked, throwing him a skeptical glance. "Would you really give it all away?"

"To the first charity or hospital I could find," he said without hesitation.

"Oh." Frowning, Lydia regarded the blunted

points of her knees through the layers of her skirts. "I suppose that marrying an heiress would be out of the question for you, then."

"Yes."

She continued to frown. "It would hardly be such a terrible fate, marrying into money. Having lots of servants, and nice things, and a large estate—"

"It's not what I want. Moreover, I would go hang before I became known to everyone in London as a damned fortune hunter."

"Even if it wasn't true?"

"It wouldn't matter if it was true or not. It's what everyone would say."

"Then we should add prideful to your list of faults," Lydia muttered, setting aside her glass.

"Without a doubt," he replied, his gaze daring her to protest. When she managed to hold her tongue, he smiled slightly and continued. "And unlike you, I have a great appreciation for the pleasures of inactivity. After a busy week of running about London seeing to patients, I like to laze about for hours, talking, drinking, making love . . ." He paused before adding frankly, "Particularly the last."

Lydia's brain suddenly conjured an indistinct image of his tawny body stretched over snowy white sheets. Dear Lord, what would it be like to make love with him for hours? "No doubt it is easy for you to find women who—" She stopped as her face flooded with color.

His face was inscrutable. "Usually."

"Have you ever fallen in love?"

"Once."

Lydia felt an unpleasant sting of jealousy. "Did you tell her how you felt?"

He shook his head.

Another question rose to her lips, despite the fact that Lydia didn't really want to know the answer. "Do you love her still?"

Pinning her in place with a speculative stare, he responded with a wordless nod.

Suddenly Lydia felt cold and miserable, when she had no right to be. Jake Linley was not hers. He had offered no promises or vows of love, he had only said that he wanted her. And despite her lack of experience, she was aware that love and desire could exist independently of each other.

"Is it someone I am acquainted with?" she asked dully. "Did she marry someone else?"

Jake stared at her in the burgeoning silence, his large body visibly tense. The way he leaned forward conveyed a sense of energy that would soon break free of all constraints.

Oh, the way he looked at her, his eyes light

and hot in his shadow-tricked face. . . . She would swear on her life that he felt more than mere desire for her. "Not yet," he said huskily.

Her heart began to slam against her ribs with almost frightening violence. "Who is she, Jake?" she managed to whisper.

He gave a soft groan and stood, hauling her impatiently against his body. "Who do you think she is?" he said, giving her a little shake. Then he seized her mouth with his.

The remnants of her self-possession shattered. Jake kissed her with tender fury, while his hands wandered compulsively over her body, molding her tighter, harder against him. "I adore every quarrelsome, terrifyingly logical inch of you," he said, dragging his mouth over her cheeks and chin and throat. "I love it that you're as smart as hell and not afraid to let anyone know it. I love your green eyes. I love the way you are with your family. My beautiful Lydia—"

"You idiot," she choked, tearing her lips away. She had never been so overwrought. "You *would* wait until thirty-eight hours before my wedding to tell me this!"

"Thirty-six and a half."

Suddenly the insanity of the situation struck Lydia as funny, and she began to gasp with laughter. "I love you, too," she said, overcome with a sense of the absurd. Jake kissed her more aggressively then, until her insides felt hot and molten, and her body ached with need.

She laid her hand on the side of his face, the masculine scrape of close-shaven bristle making her palm tingle. "You've never indicated that you felt anything for me other than scorn."

"I've never scorned you."

"You've been an absolute devil, and you know it."

He had the grace to look somewhat penitent. "Only because I knew that there was no chance of ever having you. It made me a little testy."

"Testy—" Lydia began indignantly, and he smothered her with his lips once more. Passion flared between them in a swift, white-hot conflagration. Panting, she opened fully to his demands, letting him explore her at will. His tongue teased hers, savoring the flavor of wine mingled with the intimate taste of her mouth. She felt the tremor that shook him, and gloried in the realization that he wanted her with a desperation that rivaled her own.

Ending the kiss abruptly, Jake held her at arms' length, as if their physical proximity posed a mortal danger.

Lydia curled her hands gently around his

wrists. "Why are you so convinced that it would be impossible for us to be together?"

"Isn't that obvious?" he countered tightly. "How can I ask you to accept a life that is so much less than what you've always had? As Lady Wray you'd want for nothing, and your children would be members of the peerage. You can't give that all away to become a doctor's wife. More often than not, I have to leave the house in the middle of the night to attend to someone, and during the day the place is always overrun with patients. It's bedlam. And on top of that, I'm not wealthy, and I have no wish to be, which would require you to make a sacrifice that you would probably come to regret."

"I would have to sacrifice something in either circumstance," Lydia pointed out. "Either I marry a peer who doesn't love me, or a professional man who does. Which would cause me more regret?"

"Before tonight, you had no objection to marrying without love," he said sardonically. "Why does it suddenly matter?"

"Because I didn't know how you felt! You never gave me a reason to hope. And if I couldn't have you, I thought I might as well take Lord Wray." She rubbed her wet eyes with the heels of her hands. "I've always cared for you—why else do you think we perpetually strike sparks off each other?"

His mouth twisted wryly. "I just thought I had a special talent for annoying you."

A breathless laugh escaped her, and she seized the lapels of his coat in her hands. "I want you," she said urgently. "I want you in every way, forever."

He was shaking his head before she even finished the sentence. "You might change your mind later. Do you really want to take that risk?"

Lydia was no coward, nor was she a fool. She understood how many obstacles lay between them, and how difficult it would be for two such strong-willed people to accommodate each other. But she was a Craven, and Cravens were notoriously relentless when it came to getting what they wanted. "I'm a gambler's daughter," she pointed out. "I'm not afraid of taking a risk."

Jake regarded her with a rueful smile. "What about making the sensible choice?"

"Some choices are so important that they have to be made by the heart."

Taking her hand, he kissed her fingertips one by one. "When did you decide that?" he asked from behind the screen of her slender fingers.

Lydia grinned recklessly as she sensed that his resistance was deteriorating. "Two minutes ago."

"Don't allow your decisions to be influenced by physical desire," he warned gently. "Trust me, when the afterglow has faded, you will see things in an entirely different light."

Although Lydia was well informed about physical passion, that particular word was unfamiliar. "What do you mean, 'afterglow'?"

"God help me, I want to show you."

"Then do," she said provocatively. "Show me what an afterglow is, and when it's gone, we'll see if my feelings extend beyond physical desire."

"That could be the worst idea I've ever heard."

"One little afterglow," she coaxed. "It shouldn't take too much effort. I already feel as if a thousand fireflies are dancing in my stomach."

"*Definitely* the worst," he said darkly.

Determined, she brought her body against his and stood on her toes to embrace him. Her soft mouth grazed his cheek and jaw, while her hand glided down the exciting length of his body, from the solid plane of his chest to the sturdy vault of his ribs. And lower. Excited and abashed, she explored the hard, heavy rise of his erection, her fingers curving over the jutting shape. He groaned faintly and caught her wrist. "My God. No, wait . . . Lydia, I'm dying for you . . . for so long I . . ." He pulled her hand away and fumbled at the back of her gown, popping silk-covered buttons from the tiny loops that tethered them.

She felt the bodice sag, the heavy celery-green silk dropping to the damp crooks of her elbows. Breathing heavily, Jake lifted her and sat her on the table, then reached for the front of her corset. He displayed an outrageous familiarity with female undergarments, unhooking the lattice of stays with an ease that even Lydia couldn't have matched. The corset, still warm from her body, was dropped heedlessly to the floor, and her body was left soft and unconfined save for the fragile muslin of her chemise. Lydia swallowed hard, experiencing a flicker of uncertainty as his large body came to stand between her thighs, his trouser-clad legs nearly disappearing in the gleaming mass of her skirts.

"For a man who claims not to be a seducer,"

she said, "you show a remarkable lack of hesitation."

His fingertips brushed the strap of her chemise over her shoulder. "I'm making an exception for you."

Her shaky laugh ended in a soft moan as she felt his hot, moist mouth graze the side of her neck. He murmured soft words of reassurance as he held her, caressed her, nudged her chemise ever lower until she was obliged to pull her arms completely free of it. Bending her backward, hooking his supportive arm beneath her, he nuzzled the tender weight of her breast. His breath teased the pale pink nipple, and his lips rubbed lightly over the very tip. Finally, after she was flushed and taut, and pleading for more, he drew the entire peak into his mouth. His tongue swirled over her in velvety passes, preparing her for the exquisite nip of his teeth.

She arched up to him in unequivocal surrender, amazed at how easy it was to trust him. It seemed impossible that she could have thought of him as her adversary, this man who made her feel so cherished and safe. Even in her innocence, she sensed the ferocity of his desire, but his every movement was exquisitely gentle and loving. His hands stole beneath her skirts, caressing the shape of her legs through the layers of silk stockings and muslin drawers. Entranced by his softly questing kisses, Lydia didn't notice that he had untied the tapes of her drawers, until she felt him tugging them down past her hips.

"Don't be afraid," he whispered, pausing to cuddle and reassure her. "I just want to give you pleasure. Let me, Lydia, let me touch you . . ."

Unable to resist him, she relaxed into the hard curve of his arm, shivering a little as he pulled the drawers from her legs. His fingers slipped behind the vulnerable back of her knee, sliding easily over the thin veil of silk stocking. He left trails of fire wherever he touched, inside her thighs, down to her ankles, gliding along the outside of her legs until he reached the naked curve of her hip. Panting for breath, she focused on that warm, large hand, suddenly wanting him to touch her in the secret place between her thighs, where she was damp and pulsing and swollen. As she felt the curve of his smile against her cheek, she realized that he was teasing her deliberately.

"Jake," she gasped. "Please. What you're doing . . . it's unbearable, I'm going mad . . ."

"Then I'll have to do it some more," came his devilish whisper, and he traced a light, tormenting circle inside her thigh.

A whimper caught in her throat, and she clutched at his shoulders, her fingers digging into the resilient muscle. He was merciless, letting his fingertips graze the edge of the dark triangle of curls between her thighs. Finally, when her need had built to an urgency that was almost painful, she felt him part the plump cleft and stroke the flesh that ached so sweetly.

"There," he murmured, his fingers circling the slick opening of her body and gliding to the delicate peak above. "Is this what you want?"

She could only respond with an incoherent sound, while delight immolated her. He kissed her deeply, while at the same time he slid one finger inside her melting flesh. Her moans were absorbed by his ardent kisses, and the intimate channel of her body clung tightly to the gentle invasion. He stroked inside her, his touch deft, gentle, rhythmic, seeming to relish the wild quivering of her body.

Driven into a sensuous frenzy, Lydia clawed helplessly at his shirt-covered back and his waistcoat, frantic to feel the hard body and warm skin beneath his clothes. Oh, God, she wanted him to be naked, for him to cover her body with his own, and ravish her for hours.

"How soft you are," he whispered raggedly,

withdrawing his finger to stroke and play with her once more. "Lydia, the things I want to do to you . . ."

"Do them *now,*" she managed to say through her clenched teeth.

He gave a husky laugh and carefully lowered her to the table. The scarred wood was hard on her back, the edge of it digging into the backs of her knees as her legs dangled helplessly.

"Don't stop, don't," she implored as she felt him rummaging beneath her skirts.

He pushed her legs wide apart, and his hot breath fell against her inner thigh. Dazedly she realized that he was sitting on the chair, with his face just above the tangle of private curls. An unthinkable notion crossed her mind . . . surely he wasn't going to . . . no, it wasn't possible . . . but his arms hooked beneath her knees, and as she groped clumsily to stop him, he grasped her wrists and trapped them at her sides.

A low cry escaped her as she felt his mouth touch her, lavishing her with wetness and scalding heat, and the slippery caress of his tongue. He suckled her leisurely, making a sound of primal enjoyment as he tasted the feminine liquor of her body. His hands released her wrists when they trembled and relaxed in his hold, and he moved to grasp her clenching buttocks in his palms. His tongue found the tiny place where sensation had accumulated in a burning knot, and he flicked it with lush strokes. She sobbed as pleasure rushed through her in waves and billows and endless ripples.

Even after the last eddies of sensation had faded, and she was quivering with exhaustion, Jake seemed reluctant to leave her, his mouth continuing to nuzzle her fragrant, salty flesh.

"Jake," she moaned, struggling to sit up, the table creaking with her movement.

He stood and cradled her head against his shoulder, and they shared a kiss that was subtly garnished with her own intimate flavor. "How is that for an afterglow?" he asked hoarsely.

"I want more of you." Lydia reached for the front of his trousers and pulled inexpertly at the placket of concealed buttons. "All of you," she clarified throatily, her fingers brushing against the thick, straining shape of him.

"God, no." He jumped back as if scalded. "I'm not going to debauch Derek Craven's daughter in his own wine cellar. For one thing, you deserve better than that. For another, he would probably castrate me by some medieval method."

"I don't know where everyone gets these ideas about Papa. He is really the kindest, most wonderful—"

"Father-in-law from hell," Jake muttered, recalling the comment he had made earlier. He heaved a sigh and picked up Lydia's discarded corset. "Well, one thing is certain—I'll handle him a damn sight better than Wray would have."

Lydia fumbled with her chemise, then sat still as Jake hooked the corset around her. "Does that mean you're going to propose to me?" she asked hopefully.

Expertly he pulled the drawers up over her ankles. "We'd better negotiate first."

Lydia hopped from the table and pulled the undergarments back into place, tying the tapes neatly. "There is one other fault of mine that I forgot to mention." The satin of her skirts rustled as she let them drop back into place.

"Oh?"

"I *hate* to compromise."

"So do I," he said, and they shared a rueful grin.

Jake went to pour another glass of wine. He drank deeply, then regarded Lydia with a steady gaze. "There is one point that I can't yield on. If we marry, I won't accept your father's money, or that damned obscene dowry. If he wants to establish an account that is yours alone, so be it. But you'll have to accept the kind of life that I can provide for you. That means no gifts of mansions and fine carriages and the like from your family."

Lydia parted her lips to argue, then closed her mouth. If that was what he required to retain his pride and self-respect, she would have to adjust to it. For heaven's sake, how much did she need to be happy? She would have her work, and a pleasant life, and most of all, a husband who loved her. That was infinitely more appealing than a luxurious but empty existence as Lady Wray.

She went to him and linked her arms around his waist, thrilling in the freedom of touching him. "What about the money that I earn from my work? Would you have an objection if I kept that?"

His brows drew together. "Is that a hypothetical question, or have you actually earned some?"

Her shoulders lifted in a modest shrug. "I've made a little here and there, inventing things. Last year I designed a relay modification for telegraph companies . . . and I have this idea about atmospheric propulsion . . ."

"How much have you made so far?" he asked suspiciously.

"Just a few thousand."

"How many thousand?"

"Not more than, say . . . twenty." The sum was nothing compared to Craven standards, but Lydia knew that the average person would probably consider it significant.

Jake closed his eyes and downed the rest of his wine.

"I'm sorry," Lydia said hastily. "It's just that Cravens can't seem to help making money. There's my father, of course, and then my mother has earned quite a lot from her novel-writing, and last year my brother Nicholas took it in his head to start a shipping company with propeller-driven vessels—"

"Nicholas is *eighteen*," he said, staring at her with patent disbelief.

"Yes, that's why Papa said he could only have two ships to start with . . ." Lydia's voice trailed away as he sat heavily in the chair and clutched his head in his hands. "Jake?"

"I give up," he said in a muffled voice. "Dammit."

"Does that mean you don't want to marry me?"

"It means that you can keep your own earnings, but what I said before still holds—not a shilling from your father."

"That sounds fair—" she began, and jumped a little as she heard the distant clank of a latch and the scrape of a door opening. The door that led to the kitchen, Lydia thought. It had to be the under-butler, finally sent to bring up more wine. She glanced down at herself and adjusted the waist of her gown, raising a hand to the pinned-up coils of her dark hair. Unfortunately, her coiffure was a bit disheveled, and her lips felt kiss-swollen, and she suspected that anyone who saw her would immediately know what she had been doing.

Jake's sardonic smile confirmed her worries.

They waited expectantly, and in less than a half-minute, the under-butler appeared. He froze with a gasp as he saw them, his small, wizened face turning pale at first, then becoming rapidly infused with color. His distress was obvious as he wondered whether to acknowledge them or hurry away.

"Good evening, Mr. Feltner," Lydia said calmly.

The servant found his voice. "Begging your

pardon, Miss Craven!" He turned and fled, his short legs churning.

Lydia glanced at Jake. "He's going to tell Papa," she said. "Don't worry, I'll go to him first, and soften him a little—"

"No, I'll handle it," Jake replied firmly.

A smile spread across Lydia's face as she saw that he was not intimidated by the prospect of confronting her irate father.

Jake stared at her, arrested. "God, what your smile does to me . . ." Reaching her in two strides, he wrapped his arms around her and kissed her soundly.

Lydia responded eagerly, then drew her head back. "Are you going to propose now?"

"I was considering it, yes."

"Before you do, I want to ask you something."

Tenderly he smoothed a stray lock of hair back from her face. "What is it?"

Her lips curved with an uncertain smile. "Will you stay faithful to me, Jake? With all your experience, I wonder if one woman will be enough for you."

Jake winced as if she had touched a raw nerve, and pain darkened his eyes. "Sweetheart," he whispered. "I've never regretted my past behavior as much as I do in this moment. I can't think of any way to make you understand how precious you are to me. I would never stray from you—I swear it on everything I hold dear. To come home to you every night, to sleep with you in my arms, is all I've ever wanted. If you could bring yourself to believe me, I would—"

"Yes, I believe you." The naked sincerity in his voice was unmistakable. Lydia smiled and caressed his lean cheek. "We'll have to trust each other, won't we?"

He covered her mouth in a long, passionate kiss and held her so tightly that she could hardly breathe. "Will you marry me, Lydia Craven?"

She laughed giddily. "*Yes.* Though everyone will say we've gone mad."

He grinned and kissed her again. "I'd rather be insane with you than sane without you."

The moment Jake emerged from the cellar with Lydia, a footman approached him with the message that Mr. Craven would like to see him in the library without delay.

"That didn't take long," Jake muttered, reflecting that the under-butler had certainly wasted no time in going to Craven.

Lydia sighed grumpily. "I suppose while you talk to Papa, I had better go find Lord Wray. Blast, how am I going to explain all of this to him?"

"Wait until after I deal with your father, and I'll help you with Wray."

"No," she said immediately, "I think it would be better if I spoke to Wray privately."

"He may not take the news well," Jake warned.

"You might be surprised," came her dry response. "Although the earl's pride might suffer some temporary damage, I have no doubt that his heart will remain inviolate." Her earnest green eyes stared up into his. "Are you certain that you don't want me to help you with Papa?"

Jake smiled as he looked into her upturned face. She was so much smaller than he that he was both amused and touched by her desire to protect him. "I'll manage," he assured her and gave her waist a squeeze before letting her go.

After going to his guest room to neaten his appearance and comb his disheveled hair, Jake went to the estate library. The heavy door had been left slightly ajar, and he knocked on it briefly.

"Linley," came a dark, quiet voice that seemed to belong to the devil himself. "I've been expecting you."

Jake entered a handsome room with walls covered in stamped and embossed burgundy leather. His future father-in-law was seated in a massive leather chair beside a heavy mahogany desk.

Though he had met Derek Craven on various occasions throughout the years, Jake was struck as always by the outsized presence of the man. Craven carried his power quietly, but he was clearly a man of consequence, a possessor of secrets, a man who was regarded with fear and respect. The amount of wealth Craven had accumulated was nearly incalculable, but it was not at all difficult to imagine him as the cockney youth he'd once been . . . dangerous, wily and completely without scruples.

Craven viewed him with menacing calculation. "Do you have something to tell me, Linley?"

Jake decided to be blunt. "Yes, sir. I'm in love with your daughter."

Clearly the revelation did not please Craven. "That is unfortunate, as she is going to marry Lord Wray."

"At the moment there seems to be some doubt on that point."

The black brows drew together in an ominous scowl. "What happened in that cellar?"

Jake met his gaze squarely. "With all respect, sir, that is between Lydia and me."

In the silence that followed, Craven seemed to be considering the options of dismemberment, strangulation, or a simple bullet to the head. Jake forced himself to wait patiently, knowing that in Craven's view, no man would ever be good enough for his daughter.

"Tell me why I should even begin to consider you as a potential husband for Lydia," Craven growled.

As he stared into Craven's hard green eyes, Jake recalled that Craven had no family other than his wife and children . . . no relatives . . . no knowledge even of the woman who had given birth to him. Naturally that made his family even more precious to Craven. He would never allow Lydia to be hurt or mistreated. And from a father's perspective, Lydia would be far better served by a marriage to an academic-minded peer than a commoner with a tainted past.

Jake sighed inwardly. It was not in his nature

to be humble. On the other hand, it appeared to be the only way he could convince Craven to give his blessing to the match. "I have my faults, sir," he admitted. "Many, in fact."

"So I've heard."

"I know that I'm not good enough for her. But I love Lydia, and I respect her, and I want to spend the rest of my life taking care of her, and trying to make her happy. The reason that I've never approached her before is that I believed Lord Wray was a better match for her."

"But now you don't?" Craven asked sardonically.

"No, I don't," Jake replied without hesitation. "Wray doesn't love her—not as I do."

Craven considered him for a long, uncomfortable moment. "We have some things to discuss," he said curtly. He gestured to a nearby chair. "Have a seat—this will take a while."

For the next three hours, Jake was interrogated in a relentless manner that would have frayed the nerves of the most scrupulous and upstanding of men—which Jake was not. It was rumored that Craven knew everything about everyone, but Jake had never fully believed it until now. The man displayed an alarmingly acute knowledge of Jake's financial circumstances, his personal history, pranks he had played at school, women he'd slept with and scandals his name had been connected to. Good God, Craven seemed to know more about him than his own father did. And as Jake had expected, he was merciless in demanding an accounting of matters so private that Jake was tempted more than once to tell him to go to hell. However, he wanted Lydia badly enough to endure this ruthless drumming of his pride with atypical humility.

Finally, just as Jake thought that Craven was going to take some perverse delight in denying him after all, Craven let out a long, taut sigh.

"I'm going to withhold my final approval until I determine for myself that this is what my daughter truly wants." His green eyes flashed balefully. "But if she convinces me that she does indeed wish to marry you, I won't stand in your way."

Jake couldn't restrain a sudden smile. "Thank you," he said simply. "You won't regret it, sir."

"I already do," Craven muttered, standing to return Jake's vigorous handshake.

Epilogue

"Mama, Lydia's kissing someone in the hallway, and it's not Lord Wray!"

Seated by the bedroom window with a cup of tea in her hand, Sara smiled at her youngest daughter, Daisy, a plump and vivacious five-year-old. Hurrying to Sara as fast as her short legs could propel her, Daisy climbed into her lap. Sara winced only a little as she saw that Daisy's hands were sticky with strawberry jam that was smearing her white lace nightgown.

Derek was shaving at the washstand, his mouth tightening as his gaze met Sara's in the looking glass. Clearly he was annoyed by the news of his daughter's torrid embrace with Dr. Linley, but Sara knew that he had grudgingly reconciled himself to the fact that his daughter would soon be Mrs. Linley, and not Lady Wray.

She and Derek had talked well into the night about the situation, and Sara had reassured him that she believed it was all for the best.

"Mrs. Linley only recently told me that she thought her son was deeply in love with Lydia," she had told him. "And he is a fine young man, Derek, even if his past has been a bit . . . adventurous."

"Adventurous?" he had repeated with a scowl. "With the swathe he's cut through London—"

"Darling," she had interrupted gently, "a man can change. He truly seems to love Lydia. And I've never seen her as happy as she was this evening—she was positively transformed."

"I wish to hell that Linley had transformed someone else's daughter," Derek had grumbled, making her laugh.

Bringing her thoughts to the present, Sara smoothed her daughter's tangled brown curls. As the child began to explain further details of Lydia's conduct with Linley, Sara tried in vain to hush her. "That's all right, Daisy. You can tell me later."

"Yes, but she was letting him put his hand on her b—"

"Don't tattle, darling," Sara interrupted hastily, seeing Derek's growing scowl. "You remember when we discussed that the other day."

"Yes," the child said sullenly. "You said I should only tell on someone when they're going to get hurt."

"Well, Lydia is not in any danger."

"He was kissing her *hard*," Daisy said after a moment's thought. "And he *was* hurting her, Mama, because she made a noise—"

"That's enough, Daisy," Sara said with a sudden gasp of laughter. "I'm certain that he wasn't hurting her unduly."

Derek sluiced his face, wiped the last trace of shaving soap from his jaw, and heaved a sigh. "My grandson was going to be an earl," he said glumly. "Now he'll probably be a sawbones like his father."

Daisy jumped from Sara's lap and went to her father, raising her arms to be picked up. "Is Lydia going to marry Mr. Sawbones, Papa?"

Derek lifted her against his chest, his gaze turning warm. "It would seem so."

Her little hand patted his freshly shaven jaw. "Don't be sad, Papa. I'll save all *my* kisses for *you*."

He chuckled suddenly, stroking her tangled brown curls. "Give me one now, then," he said, and she pressed her jam-sticky cheek to his.

The nursemaid appeared, telling Daisy that it was time to wash and dress for the day, and the child wriggled from her father's arms.

After the door had closed behind them, Sara went to her husband and smoothed her palms over the striped silk robe that covered his hard chest. "All my kisses are for you, too," she told him.

"They had better be," he said and covered her lips with his. The kiss stirred her senses pleasantly, and she linked her arms around his neck, enjoying the wicked caress of his mouth.

"Only four more to go," she said when his head lifted.

He played with the long braid that hung down her back and let his hands roam intimately over her body. "I'm afraid I don't follow you, angel."

"Our other children," she explained. "I'm going to help each of them find true love, just as I helped Lydia."

Picking her up with ease, Derek carried her to the bed. "Helped her in what way?"

"I gave her the opportunity to talk in private with Dr. Linley," Sara told him. "I was certain that if they just had a bit of uninterrupted time with each other, they would acknowledge their feelings, and then—"

"Wait," Derek interrupted, his green eyes narrowing as he dropped her to the mattress. He crawled over her and braced his elbows on either side of her head. "You're not telling me that *you* were the one who locked them in the damned cellar . . . are you?"

She smiled impishly. "You told me to give fate a push in the right direction, if I found the opportunity. And I did."

His expression was incredulous. "I didn't mean for you to trap my innocent daughter in the cellar with a womanizer like Linley!"

"Lydia wasn't trapped. She could have left any time she wanted to."

"The doors were locked!"

"Not all of them." Seeing his incomprehension, Sara smiled complacently. "Don't you remember the little passageway that goes from the back of the cellar to the conservatory? The children still use it when they play pirates. Lydia knew full well that it was there. The only reason she remained in that cellar with Linley last night was because she wanted to. And it turned out perfectly, didn't it?"

Derek groaned and dropped his head to the mattress. "My God. I'm not certain whom to pity more, Linley or myself."

Knowing exactly how to disarm him, Sara

parted the front of his silk robe and tangled her legs with his. "Pity yourself," she advised, her small hands wandering busily inside the garment. "You're about to be ravished."

She felt Derek smile suddenly against her neck. "*I* do the ravishing around here," he informed her . . . and he proceeded to prove his point.

Lisa Kleypas graduated from Wellesley College with a political science degree. As a longtime Avon Books author, her novels have appeared on both the *New York Times* and *Publishers Weekly* bestseller lists. In 2002, she was awarded the RITA Award from Romance Writers of America for best novella. She resides in Texas with her husband and two children.

Kinley MacGregor
Midsummer's Knight

Prologue

A tournament in Rouen

"Simon! Help!"

Simon of Ravenswood looked up from his table inside the blue-and-white striped tent.

Through the tent's opening, he saw Christopher of Blackmoor running toward him as fast as he could. Barely three years younger than Simon, Christopher wasn't the kind of man to ever run. He was normally slow to move, reluctant to exert himself, and had never once raised his voice. Some might call him lazy, but Simon knew otherwise.

Christopher was a dedicated man, albeit a leisurely one.

Christopher's tunic was torn, his face pale.

Simon stood up immediately, his letter forgotten as he saw the panic reflected in Christopher's green eyes.

The younger man rushed into the tent, straight to him.

"What is it, Kit?"

Christopher grabbed Simon's arm and pulled him toward the entrance. "Come quickly. Stryder needs aid. He's about to be torn asunder."

Simon didn't hesitate. Spinning out of Christopher's grip, he grabbed up his sword from the cot and belted it on as he ran for the list where Stryder had been training.

Christopher's elder brother, Stryder, the fourth earl of Blackmoor, was a man of many enemies and one of Simon's closest friends. It wasn't the first time Simon had heard of opponents attacking a man while in the confines of a tournament or practice, but woe to those who would attack Stryder in such a cowardly fashion.

No one would ever attack a friend of his with immunity. Simon would have the villains' heads.

Or so he thought.

He skidded to a halt as he came to the field where Stryder stood in the midst of what appeared to be two score of women.

Man-hungry women to be precise, who had a

taste for an earl who was still in the prime of his life and fighting prowess.

They surrounded Stryder like a sea of sharks hungry for a morsel of flesh.

Among other things.

A tall, slender blonde shrieked, "Stryder! Take my favor."

"I love you, Lord Stryder!"

"Move aside, you fat cow," another woman shouted, "I can't see him."

"Lord Stryder touched me!"

The screams of the women were deafening as they elbowed and shoved one another in an effort to reach the poor man in their center. Stryder was trying desperately to extract himself, but the more he tried to flee, the more the ladies held him fast.

Simon burst out laughing at the sight of one of the most powerful men in Christendom being captured and jostled about by mere women. It wasn't often anyone saw uncertainty from Stryder of Blackmoor.

And Simon had to admit he enjoyed seeing his friend at a loss for once. It was refreshing to know that Stryder really was human and not the soulless demon of Blackmoor legend.

"Stryder?" Simon called, raising his voice to make sure it carried over the women's. "The leech gave me the cream you requested. He said your rash should clear up soon, but in the meantime, 'tis *highly* contagious."

Silence descended on the crowd almost instantly.

"What did he say?" one of the women asked.

"Rash," another repeated.

"I've no wish for another rash," another chimed in, stepping back.

"Just how contagious is it?" Stryder asked, his blue eyes dancing with merry mischief as he joined the game.

Simon kept his face serious, his tone dire. "Extremely. The leech says you should be quarantined before you spread it about the castle and make everyone ill from it. He said it could cause you to go blind if you're not careful."

One woman shrieked and jumped away while the crowd as a whole pulled back only slightly from Stryder. Some of the more intelligent women looked skeptically at Simon.

"What sort of rash is this?" a short, dark-haired woman asked. "I've never heard of such and I see no rash on Lord Stryder."

Simon dropped his gaze to the area just below the man's belt. "That's because it resides in a most private place." He clucked his tongue at his friend. "Next time I tell you to refrain from houses of ill repute, you'll be listening to me, won't you?"

The women made various noises of distress and ran for cover.

Stryder eyed him, his face a mixture of mirth and murder. "I'm not sure if I should thank you for that, or beat you."

Simon offered him a lopsided grin. "Would you rather I left you to them?"

Stryder rubbed the back of his neck and frowned as he saw the blood on his hand where one of the women had scratched him. "Nay, I suppose not, but I wish you could have thought of a better tale."

"Very well, then, next time I shall tell them you are betrothed."

Stryder laughed openly at that. "Now there's an event that shall never happen. The earth as we know it will perish long before the earl of Blackmoor ever takes a bride."

"Never say never, my friend," Simon warned. "Far more stubborn men than you have proclaimed that and fallen to Cupid's bow."

"Mayhap, but I'm not like other men."

And neither was Simon, but then the two of them had a different calling—one that took both their lives away from the thought of matrimony.

Nay, neither he nor Stryder would ever marry. There were too many other lives that depended on both of them. Too many others who looked to them for protection.

A wife would never understand their commitments.

Stryder joined him, and they headed back toward the tents. "Just promise me one thing, Simon."

"And that is?"

"That on the day I pledge my troth to a woman, you'll run me through."

Simon laughed at that. "You'd rather be dead than married?"

Stryder's face turned deadly serious. "Aye, I would."

Simon nodded in understanding. As his mother had, so had Stryder's mother died a violent death during her son's childhood. It had been one of the things that had forged their friendship years ago, a shared tragedy that allowed them to understand each other.

Over the years, even more tragedies had bound them closer than brothers.

"Very well. But I still say a betrothal is just what you need in order to deal with your legion of rabid admirers. A wife would ease them back and allow you some time to go about your business without ladies throwing themselves at you."

The humor returned to Stryder's eyes. "Hmmm, a lady wife. Find me a wench with a level head whom I can be tempted by, Simon, and I might take you up on that."

Frankfurt, Germany
Three months later

The roar of the crowd was deafening, but then it always was whenever Stryder of Blackmoor took the field.

Knights were dressed in full tourney armor as they were introduced by the heralds to the eager crowd that had gathered for today's sport.

Simon stayed in the background, watching Stryder's back as he always did. It was what he was best at. His brother, Draven, had oft referred to him as his anchor. While others sought glory and fame, Simon sought only to protect those he loved.

He had learned long ago that glory and riches meant nothing while standing over the grave of someone who was dear. Neither brought comfort or warmth.

Neither brought true happiness.

Only friendship and brotherhood did that.

And, of course, love.

Simon didn't need troubadours to write songs about him. He held no desire to make any woman swoon.

Except for one.

She whose name he dare not say because she was the one thing he could never have.

Long ago, in a barren land, when he'd been nothing more than a starving boy yearning for home, he had made a promise that, so long as he lived, he would spend his life helping others return home to the families that loved them.

Home. It was the one thing he'd lacked growing up. Aye, Draven had loved him, but as children they'd had no real home. Ravenswood had been harsh and frightening.

Normandy had been endless and unfriendly, and even now he didn't want any thoughts at all of Outremer.

The only thing Simon had ever been able to depend upon was the three men whom he considered his family—Draven of Ravenswood, Sin MacAllister and Stryder of Blackmoor.

Draven and Sin had allowed him to survive the horrors of his childhood at Ravenswood, and Stryder had been the one who had kept him sane and whole while living in the hell that was a Saracen prison.

There was nothing he wouldn't do for them.

"Si?"

Simon looked to Stryder, who was to his right, mounting his horse.

Once settled on his horse, Stryder flashed him a taunting grin. "Are you daydreaming again, man? Pick up your sword and stand ready."

Simon scoffed at him. "Daydreaming? Ha! Merely plotting the way I intend to spend my winnings this day when I unhorse you."

Stryder laughed aloud at that. He inclined his head toward the red ribbon Simon had tied around his biceps. "Who's the fortunate lady?"

"She's no concern of yours."

He smiled knowingly. "Mayhap I'll take a bit of pity on you then and let you get in a few blows before I undignify you. With any luck, she might be willing to kiss your injuries."

If only Simon could be so lucky.

But alas, his lady was far away from him.

She would always be so. It wasn't possible for a pebble to touch a star. And she was a star. Bright, shining. Yet so far above him that he dare not even look at her because in the end, he could never lay claim to her.

He glanced down at the ribbon and his heart ached.

The heralds called them to field, and the day proved to be a long one.

How Simon grew weary of the tournament circuit. Unlike Stryder, he saw no use in it. But he stayed out of loyalty—Stryder needed someone to protect him who was beyond bribery.

And for the price on Stryder's head, those people were far too few and rare.

As the day finally drew to a close, Simon found himself with Stryder and Christopher, walking toward their tents as women tried to grab Stryder and proposition him.

"It's a sad sight, isn't it?" Christopher asked wearily. "Methinks I should have the armorer make a larger helm for tomorrow so that it can fit over Stryder's big head."

Simon laughed at that. "Indeed, but I fear a shortage in steel might occur if we tried to accommodate his ugly noggin."

Stryder scoffed. "You're both just jealous. I have my choice of bedmates, while the two of you sleep alone."

Simon passed a knowing look to Christopher. "It seems to me, Kit, that there's only enough room in his bed for him and his ego. It makes one wonder how he ever manages to squeeze a woman in."

Christopher laughed.

"A pox on both of you," Stryder said.

Simon smiled. "And one on your ego."

Stryder grunted, walking with his head down as he fumbled with a knotted lace on his cuirass.

When they rounded a tent, a shadow caught Simon's eye. He barely had time to react as a man came rushing at Stryder with a drawn dagger.

Before the assassin could reach his friend, Simon grabbed him and, after a brief struggle, threw the man to the ground. Simon disarmed him quickly and held him pinned by his neck.

Stryder curled his lip in disgust. "These attempts on my life are becoming quite monotonous."

Simon looked at him drolly. "Pray they don't become successful."

Stryder nodded as he pulled the assassin up. "Thank you, Simon. Christopher and I will see him to the guards. Would you care to join us in the hall?"

Simon went to touch the ribbon on his arm, only to realize it had been torn off during the struggle.

His stomach shrank. "Nay, I have something I need to do."

"Not another letter," Christopher moaned. "I swear, Simon, you've gotten to where you write more than I do, and I'm a minstrel."

Simon didn't say anything as they left him alone. Instead, he searched the ground until he found the tattered pieces of his ribbon.

Instantly relieved, he clutched them in his hand and pulled the letter out of his tunic, where he had laced it tightly against his chest.

It had been delivered just this morn as he'd been donning his armor for the tourney.

He broke the Scottish seal, and as he opened the letter, he found a tiny lock of brown hair.

Her hair.

He held it tightly in his hand, not wanting to let it go. Lifting it to his face, he smelled the faintest trace of her scent.

Simon smiled.

Then he eagerly read her feminine script.

My Dearest Warrior,

I hope this finds you well and unhurt. I fear the last messenger you sent will never be bribed to carry another of your letters to me. It appears I rather damaged him a bit in my enthusiasm to relieve him of his vellum burden.

I only hope his ankle heals soon.

Your words touched me deeply, and I am truly sorry that you are homesick. I was going to send you a bit of soil, but thought it might be rather ridiculous to burden you with such. Not to mention that dirt is rather the same, isn't it? And if you dropped it, you wouldn't be able to reclaim it.

So I thought perhaps my hair might bring some comfort to you. I hope you won't notice the bit of singing around the ends of it. I fear I learned a valuable lesson the day before yesterday.

While daydreaming of you and your last letter, I became distracted in the kitchen and wasn't paying attention to where I set down the candle.

But I discovered something most important. Larders catch fire rather easily. And once burned, sandstone is impossible to clean. The cook has banned me eternally from the kitchen and at first forbade me ever to partake of her services again.

After some consoling, she has at last granted me the right to eat, but only so long as I swear never again to enter her domain.

I miss you, my dearest. Know that wherever you are tonight, my thoughts and heart are with you.

Please take care of yourself and may God grant you peace and health until you find yourself home again with those who love you.

Ever yours,
K

Simon held her letter to his heart. How he wanted this woman. Needed her.

If only he were Stryder. Then he could court her. Propose to her.

But as Simon of Ravenswood, he could do nothing more than pine away for his star, knowing that the day would never come when they could be together.

He had found her only so that he could lose her.

Fate was often unmerciful.

Sighing, he took his letter and headed for his tent. At least there, for a little while, he could pretend to be someone else.

Someone who could offer his troth to his lady love.

Chapter 1

England
Eleven months later

"Congratulations, Lord Stryder. I never thought to see the day when you would take a bride."

Stryder looked up as the older nobleman's words rang in his ears. He'd just sat down no more than five minutes before to break his fast after a morning spent training in the list.

He was hot and sweaty, and not quite sure he had heard the man correctly.

"A bride?" Stryder repeated skeptically.

The old man's wizened face beamed at him, and his faded brown eyes were bright with well wishes. "And a Scots heiress, no less. A fine match you've made, my boy. Fine indeed." He clapped Stryder on the back and ambled off.

Stupefied, Stryder frowned and returned to his food. No doubt the nobleman had gone daft with his old age.

Or so he thought.

That was the first of several such encounters, and as the morning wore on while he went about his duties, Stryder could think of only one person who would spread such unfounded gossip regarding him.

Simon of Ravenswood.

He smiled to himself. Simon had promised him peace while they were in England for the yearly show of arms at Stantington. Every nobleman in England, as well as the king, was here for the event.

Along with the men had come their numerous unmarried daughters who were all eagerly seeking husbands with rich purses.

In other words, they were all seeking *him.*

Normally, he would have been hounded and mobbed by the wealth-hungry women who coveted his lands, his prowess in bed, and his body.

In that order.

Simon had promised him that if he would return home for this spectacle, Simon would keep the women and their scheming mothers far away.

Stryder still didn't know why his returning to England had been so important to Simon. After all, the man didn't owe him anything and was quite free to leave his service at any time.

Still, Simon had wanted them to come home, and so Stryder had humored him even though he hated to be in England, where the past haunted him all too vividly.

A fortnight in England, my friend. 'Tis all I ask of you. Have no fear, I shall keep the eager wenches far away.

He should have known Simon would make good his word. The man always did.

A wedding.

Stryder laughed again at the thought. Leave it to Simon to concoct such a tale. He owed his friend a flagon of ale for his inventiveness.

"Stryder?"

Stryder paused halfway across the yard as he heard the hesitant call of an unfamiliar feminine voice. His eyes focused on an average-looking woman who appeared to be around Simon's age.

There was something about her that was vaguely familiar, as if they had met once but he couldn't really recall her.

Her light brown hair was braided with a dark red ribbon. Her body leaned toward plump, and her eyes were large and brown and possessed a sweet, doelike quality.

She was pleasing enough to look at but was far from the tall, slender maids who turned his head.

She smiled a welcoming smile at him that gave him the sudden urge to bolt.

Before he could move, she crossed the distance between them and threw herself into his arms.

"Oh, Stryder!" she cried, her voice thick with a Scots brogue. "You've made me the happiest woman on earth!"

He stood woodenly as she embraced him. "I beg your pardon? Lady, who are you?"

She laughed at that and pulled back. "Who am I? Oh, Stryder, you are a funny one to be sure."

She turned back to the man and woman who had been with her. They came to rest just behind her.

Stryder knew the man, but he hadn't seen him in quite a few years.

Standing two inches taller with a body that had been made to slay any man foolish enough to get in his way, Sin MacAllister was known more by reputation than anything else. His black hair was only slightly shorter than Stryder's, and the Sin's black eyes watched Stryder and the unknown lady curiously.

"Lord Sin," Stryder said, inclining his head to the earl. "It's been a long time."

And it had been. In some ways it seemed an eternity. Stryder had just earned his spurs. During the celebration, Sin had given him sound advice that had saved his life on more than one occasion.

Let no one at your back.

Sin shook his arm. "Aye, it has. I have to tell you, I was rather surprised when my cousin told me she was to wed you. It just doesn't seem like the Stryder of Blackmoor everyone whispers about."

A feeling of dread settled over Stryder.

He wasn't sure what part of that statement shocked him most. He looked back at the plump woman.

"Beg pardon?" he asked. "Cousin?"

The woman beamed. "Remember? I told you in my letter that my cousin Caledonia"—she indicated the beautiful red-haired lady standing beside Sin—"had married Lord Sin. You said in your letter that you and Sin knew each other."

"Your letter?" he repeated in a shocked whisper.

"Aye," she said, her brow puckering with a frown. "Don't you recall it?" She moved closer to him. "Stryder? Are you all right? You look ill."

He was ill. Sick to his stomach, to be precise. "Excuse me for a moment. Please?"

Stryder didn't wait for permission. He bolted toward the hall with the speed he only used in battle, while pursuing someone he wished to kill. . . .

"How odd," Kenna said as she watched her betrothed speed away. "What do you suppose got into him?"

Sin passed an amused look at Caledonia. "Common sense, no doubt."

Caledonia lightly struck him on the stomach. "Shame on you, Sin. Kenna might think you're serious."

"I was." He sidestepped her next playful blow. "But not that Stryder should avoid Kenna per se. More that he should run from *any* woman walking about with a matrimonial noose."

Caledonia gasped in feigned indignation. "Oh, thank you so much. I never realized I was such a vile cross for you to bear."

Kenna ignored her cousin's playful bantering with her husband. She'd learned the day she met Lord Sin that he and Caledonia shared a deep, respectful love of each other. The two of them lived to tease one another.

But that wasn't where her attention was focused. "Think you Stryder changed his mind?"

Caledonia scoffed at the idea. "Nay, love. No doubt he had other duties more pressing. I'm quite certain that he will return to your side as soon as he can."

She hoped so. The alternative wasn't a pleasant thought. She'd traveled so far already just to see him, and in truth his cool reception cut her deeply.

Had she done something wrong?

Had he not meant the letters he had written to her?

Uncertain and fearful of what his reaction meant, Kenna excused herself and headed for the castle.

She entered the mammoth donjon and made her way to the stone, curving stairs that led to her chambers on an upper floor.

Surely she hadn't mistaken Lord Stryder's intent. Surely. Nervous, she made straight away for her satchel on the desk by the window. She always stored her most prized possessions inside the dark tanned skin.

Her letters.

She pulled out the one letter on top—the one she had secured with a special red ribbon that matched the one she always wore in her hair. The one she had sent to Stryder while he was in Germany. Her hands shaking from worry, she opened it and sought verification.

As she read the elegant, flowing script, the familiar joy spread through her, warming every inch of her body.

My dearest Kenna,

The sun has set now and I find myself outside the town of Frankfurt. The tournament went well today, but I am rather bored by the events, by the crowd and most especially by the knights who recount their noble deeds.

I'm bored with much of late.

I miss England a great deal, but Scotland even more. Strange, isn't it? I've only been to the Highlands once and then only briefly.

Yet when I read your words, I can feel the breath of the Scots winds on my skin, remember the sweet smell of the air. The sound of your voice speaking to me.

I cherish the story of your learning experience in the kitchen. Like you, I had no idea how easily one could burn down a larder, nor how hard it is to clean soot from sandstone. I am only grateful that no one, least of all you, was hurt and I'm sorry you have now been banished from the kitchens for eternity.

Further, I am glad that the cook has decided to let you eat again.

Like always, you remind me of the things that are gentle and good, and bring a smile to my lips when I think of you.

I was excited this morning when the messenger came with your letter. This one still held the scent of your sweet hands upon it. More and more, I find myself looking for them. Looking for my connection to you.

Your words see me through the days and especially the long nights while I remain far from home and familiar comforts. I know we have only met once, and yet I feel as though I know you in a way I have never known anyone.

I miss you, Kenna. Every moment of my day is spent wondering how you are doing and if something has made you smile in my absence.

I have the lock of hair that you sent me. I wear it inside a circlet that rests over my heart to remind me of your gentle words and kind-

ness. It is my most treasured possession, it and the letters you send.

In truth, I can't imagine living in a world where you are not a part of it. If I could, I would gladly spend the rest of my life with you, making you happy.

Meet me in England on my return, my lady, and there I would make true my heart's fondest wish. A kiss from your tender lips and a pledge from my heart to yours.

Until then, let sweet dreams be with you.

Ever your knight,
S.

Kenna closed her eyes and held the letter close to her heart. Stryder loved her. She was certain of it. Surely no man could write such tender words unless he meant them.

But perhaps she had misread them.

They had sounded like a proposal upon her first three dozen readings, but now that she had seen Stryder again, she wasn't so sure. He'd acted as if he'd had no idea who she was, and yet the two of them had been writing for well over a year now.

"Kenna?"

She turned to find Caledonia standing in the doorway.

"Are you all right?"

Kenna nodded as she folded up the letter and returned it to the satchel. Stryder's words had been written for her alone, and she had never wanted to share their precious sentiments. "I'm just trying to understand Stryder's reaction."

From the words he had written to her, she'd expected him to scoop her up in his arms and cry out in delight at her presence. Instead, he had excused himself and run for cover as if the devil himself had been after him.

Could he have been lying to her all this time?

But why would he do such?

Their letters had been innocent at first, just little notes to each other about the weather and what they were up to. He had been the one who had turned their missives into more serious matters.

Perhaps he had thought her to be another lady. Perhaps he had remembered her to be beautiful and elegant like her cousin Callie, and now, having seen her again, he was disappointed and regretful of his writings.

She shivered at the thought.

Nay, surely not. He had shared too much of

himself with her. Told her of his mother's death, of his brutal past.

He had told her things she was quite certain he had shared with no one else.

"Men can be strange beasties," Caledonia said quietly as she shut the door behind her and drew closer. "You've no idea what a hard time I had with Sin when I first met him. He was prickly and harsh, always seeking to put distance between us."

Kenna took comfort at her cousin's words. "I find that hard to believe."

"Aye, but it's true. I think you caught Stryder off guard. Give him time to think clearly and I'm sure he'll make good his promises."

Kenna nodded, even though part of her still wanted to cry at the shattering of her dreams.

Everything had started out so simply in the beginning. After her brother's death, she had gone to France to abide by her brother's dying wish—to return Stryder's heraldic emblem to the earl and to thank the man for saving her brother's life and returning him home.

Once in France, she had been enthralled by the fighting prowess of the man in the list, by the strength of his sword as he'd trained.

And when Stryder had removed his helm and she had seen his impeccably chiseled features, she had been enchanted. No man born could ever be more beautiful than he.

Stryder had been hurried as he'd left the field, barely taking time to do more than speak a quick word to her before he'd rushed off.

Her tongue had been so tied that she hadn't been able to explain to him her purpose for being there or to call him back.

Her hands had shaken so badly that she hadn't even realized she'd dropped Stryder's emblem until another knight had retrieved it from the ground and returned it to her cold hands.

"Forgive his haste, my lady," the knight had said. "Stryder is oft harried in his attempts to leave the list and make it back to his tent before he is swarmed."

She'd looked up into the face of another handsome man. His long, dark auburn hair had reminded her much of the men who graced her Highlands. His deep blue eyes had been warm and friendly.

"I only wished to return this to him," she'd said, wondering why she wasn't tongue-tied with this man. She'd always been awkward around the opposite sex. But for some reason this stranger, regardless of his handsomeness, had made her feel comfortable.

The knight had looked down at her hand and frowned at the sword-and-shield badge. "Where did you get this?"

"It belonged to my brother. He returned from Outremer with it."

His warm hand had covered hers, and she had shivered at the calluses on his rough fingers, at the sound of his deep, silken voice. "Your brother's name, my lady?"

"Edward MacRyan."

A distant light had come into his blue eyes, as if he'd been recalling the past. He'd offered her a small, gentle smile. "You're Kenna."

A sensation of heat had gone down her spine at the way he'd said her name.

"You know me?"

"Aye, my lady, your brother spoke of you often."

"You were with them in Outremer?"

His smile had faded as he'd nodded. His eyes had betrayed the same pain that her brother's had held whenever he'd remembered the years he'd spent imprisoned by the Saracens.

It was then she'd known who this man was. Edward had spoken of Stryder's right hand. The one man who had stayed in the shadows while Stryder had gained fame and renown. He was one of the men who had never allowed others to know his name, but who had comforted and protected them just the same.

"You are the Wraith."

He'd looked instantly uncomfortable at her words. "How do you know that name?"

"My brother never spoke to anyone other than me about your Brotherhood," she'd hastened to assure him. "We never kept secrets, he and I. And I've never spoken of his tales to another living soul. I promise you. He only wanted me to know of you before he died so that I could uphold his foresworn oath."

The stranger had winced at her news as if someone had struck him. It had made her feel even more tender toward him that he, too, shared her grief at the loss of so noble a man.

"Edward is dead? How?"

"Of illness. He took a pox last spring."

"I'm sorry for your loss, my lady. Edward was a good man." He'd closed his hand over the badge and started away from her. "I shall return this to Stryder and tell him the news."

"Wait."

He'd paused and looked back at her.

"I don't know your name."

All emotion had vanished from his face, and

he'd become the man of legend right before her eyes. "I am the Wraith, my lady. I have no real name. Not in this."

"Can you at least get me close enough to Lord Stryder to thank him for protecting my brother while you were imprisoned?"

He looked away at that. "Stryder doesn't like personal thank yous."

"May I at least write him then?"

The Wraith had nodded. "Aye. I shall see he receives it."

He had left her so quickly that she hadn't even had the chance to thank the mysterious knight.

But then that was why they'd called him the Wraith. Her brother had told her many stories of the Brotherhood of the Sword—the men who had banded together to escape the Saracen prison where all of them had been held.

Lord Stryder had been called the Widowmaker due to his strength of arm and willingness to kill whoever threatened those who fell under his protection.

The Wraith had been the one to gather information for them and run interference with the guards. He'd been punished countless times so that their captors would be distracted while the others tunneled their escape.

Even now, after spending a year of her life writing letters to Stryder, Kenna didn't know the name of that mysterious knight. She'd asked Stryder for it only once, and his response had been very curt and odd.

He is naught of consequence, my lady. Only a hollow, haunted ghost who is best left to the memories of the past. Let us not speak of him.

She had never questioned it further. Her thoughts had quickly been taken over by the fantasy of the fearless knight who wrote to her. Of the man who told her so much of his heart that she had been powerless against the love that overwhelmed her.

Perhaps Caledonia was right.

Stryder had shared so much with her that maybe her appearance had shocked him. Maybe he was embarrassed now by his candor and just needed a brief time to adjust to her physical presence.

Aye, that was it.

He just needed a little time to come to terms with the confidences they had shared.

Chapter 2

"Simon, you've been like a brother to me all these years. 'Tis a damn shame that I have to kill you now." Stryder's angry tone was low, lethal. Even so, it reverberated through the empty hall where Simon sat, eating a light repast to tide him over until the evening meal.

Simon choked on his bread at the unexpected words and the heartfelt sincerity of Stryder's voice.

Stryder's eyes were cold and unfeeling, devoid of the friendship that Simon was used to seeing from him.

"That's it," Stryder said, his gaze narrowed by rage. "You go ahead and choke. I'm not even going to bother saving you from it, but before you die of asphyxiation, could you at least tell me who it is I'm supposed to wed?"

Simon choked even more.

Stryder *was* going to kill him for this.

As Simon reached for his mead to help clear his throat, Stryder continued his angry rant.

"Apparently, Simon, I have been writing to my future wife. And just for clarity, let me repeat that. . . . *I* have been writing to my future wife."

His glare intensified until it would rival the devil for heat. "Don't you think that it is rather difficult for me to do such a thing since I write to no one, hmm? But then, since I don't write, who is it who answers all my personal letters? Oh, aye, I know. . . . 'Tis you, Simon. *You.*"

Simon took a deep drink of mead as his mind raced. He'd known this was coming, but he had hoped for a little more time to think up some way to extract all of them from this madness. "You told me to answer your letters as I saw fit. Not to bother you with their content."

"Answering my letters does not require a betrothal. Tell me of this woman. Is she at least wealthy?"

"She's very nice."

"Simon!"

Stryder gave him a glare so sinister that Simon could almost believe the tales that claimed Stryder had sold his soul to Lucifer.

Had Simon been any man other than himself, he might even have flinched, but Simon flinched from no man's anger, and most especially not from Stryder's.

They had known each other too long and had been through too much for Simon to fear him.

But when it came to annoying him, that was another matter entirely.

"What say you?" Stryder asked, his voice even angrier. "Is this a jest? Who is this woman who claims I have proposed to her?"

Simon met Stryder's stare levelly and wondered how he'd gotten himself into this.

Unfortunately, he knew.

It, like all ills of the earth, had come from a woman.

And not just any woman was she.

Like Eve with Adam, she had lured him into disaster against his will and his common sense. When he should have run, he'd stayed, and now he would pay a steep price for it.

His downfall had but one name.

Kenna.

Kenna with light brown hair and eyes that were golden brown and bright. She was a small slip of a woman, rather plain in looks, but she held an inner beauty that had enchanted him from the moment Simon had read her first letter.

Unfortunately, said letter hadn't been intended for him.

She'd written it to Stryder, the earl of Blackmoor, self-styled barbarian cur, known to possess the wrath of Armageddon. When Stryder entered a room, renowned warriors broke into a sweat lest they incur his notice.

Stryder who was every woman's fantasy.

Stryder who was the bane of Simon's existence. At least at this moment, because the woman Simon loved was in love with Stryder, whose heart would never be captured by a single maid.

At least not for any longer than a night or two.

Damn Stryder anyway for putting him in this position. But then if not for Stryder and his prowess, Simon would never have met Kenna.

He would do anything for his lady.

"You said if I could find you a level-headed woman, you would marry her."

Stryder sputtered at that and looked at him as if he'd grown three heads. "Are you mad?"

Aye, he was. Mad for a woman who had spilled her heart out to him as the one she thought was destined to be her husband.

"If you meet with her, you will see. She would make a good wife to you."

Stryder cursed. "Simon, what were you thinking? You proposed on my behalf? How could you do such a thing?"

Simon cringed at that. He'd been writing to Kenna for so long and signing the letters as *Ever Your Knight, S,* that he had forgotten the one small fact that in her mind the *S* stood for Stryder, not Simon.

He hadn't realized the mistake until her next letter had come to him. Instead of her writing, *My Dearest Warrior*, she had penned, *My Dearest Stryder*.

The words had struck his heart like a blow as they'd reminded him all too clearly of what he had done. Who she thought him to be.

He was such a fool.

"It just happened."

Stryder narrowed his eyes. "Nay, Simon. Foul weather just happens. Disaster just happens." He glared meaningfully. "*Death* just happens. But people do not get betrothed without design. You will get me out of this, or so help me I will have your head and your bullocks."

Simon just looked at him. "Now there's an empty threat if I ever heard one. Calm yourself, Stryder. Meet with her. She's not like other women. You will see." Simon stepped forward and lowered his voice. "Besides, she knows of us."

"Everyone knows of us, Si, we happen to be rather famous—or infamous, as the case may be."

"Nay," Simon said, giving him an arched look. "She *knows* of *us*." He spoke in an even lower tone, enunciating each word slowly. "Her brother was Edward MacRyan. Do you remember him?"

Stryder's eyes turned dull as the repressed memory of their captivity in the Holy Land came back to him. "He's the one I saved from the crocodiles."

"Aye. *She* is the sister he spoke of on so many occasions, and even after his death, she is still abiding by his oath to our cause. It was his praise of you that caused her to write to you that first time while we were in Normandy. It was her brother's fondest wish that the two of you should meet."

"Why?"

"Because the two of you are the people he loved most in this life. She wanted to thank you for saving his life and seeing him home again."

"That didn't require a betrothal."

Simon drew a deep breath as he struggled

against his untoward emotions, which demanded he beat Stryder and take Kenna regardless of the consequences.

Nay, it didn't require a betrothal.

He'd become so comfortable with Kenna that he'd let his common sense slip and his careful guard down. He had confided things to her that he had told no one. Over the course of the last year, he had laid bare his thoughts and his heart to her.

And she had returned the courtesy.

Simon sighed. "Have no fear, as soon as she comes here, I shall set things aright."

"Then you'd best be about it, since I saw her right before I came seeking you."

Simon's heart pounded at the words as happiness flooded him. "Kenna is here?"

Stryder nodded.

His food forgotten, Simon started for the door. "Where is she?"

"She was with Sin MacAllister last I saw."

Simon faltered at the name of his childhood friend. "Sin brought her here?"

"I would assume so."

Simon clenched his teeth at that. Things had just become twice as complicated. Not that it mattered.

Kenna was here.

She was the most important thing to him, and now he would be able to see her again. To touch her. Hear the sound of her voice . . .

After all these nights of struggling to remember her precious face and beautiful smile, he could see her again. Feel the warmth of her physical touch. Smell the light lavender scent of her skin.

It would be heaven.

He left Stryder in the hall and went to find the woman whose amusing insights and anecdotes had stolen his heart.

It didn't take long to ascertain her whereabouts. He found the king's steward and learned that she'd come to the castle the night before, after Simon had retired to his tent.

Lord Drexton had given her, Sin and Caledonia rooms in the castle.

Simon made for the area posthaste. He ran up the stone spiral steps, desperately seeking the woman he loved. Ignoring the maid who gasped and hurried from his path, he sprinted down the hallway to the last door.

The room that held her . . .

He knocked on the door without hesitation.

"Enter."

Simon closed his eyes and savored the lilting brogue that single word betrayed. She was here! By all the saints in heaven, she had come at his request.

As he reached for the handle, his courage faltered.

Kenna didn't know *him* at all.

All this time she'd made the assumption she was writing to Stryder. Even though he'd meant to tell her the truth about who he was, he'd never had the heart.

At first it had all seemed harmless enough. Just a few notes back and forth on nothing of any import. Until last Christmastide. In a moment of weakness, he had shared his mother's death with her.

She'd responded with such precious words of comfort that he hadn't had the courage after that to let her know his real identity.

If she ever learned the truth . . .

She will think I betrayed her.

Fear sliced through him at that thought. He would never do such a thing, and yet she would believe it. Most likely, she'd never forgive him for it.

She would hate him eternally.

Nay, he couldn't bear that.

What was he to do?

He heard her approaching the door.

His heart hammering, Simon did something he'd never done before.

He fled.

Rushing away from the room, he found a shadowy alcove where he could hide himself. He'd barely crammed himself into it before the door swung open.

Her silken voice assailed his body with pleasure. "Hello? Is anyone out here?"

From the shadows, he saw her. She was far more beautiful than he remembered. Her cheeks were flush, her eyes bright. She wore a deep scarlet kirtle that made her pale skin glisten.

He hardened instantly at the sight of her. How he yearned to go to her, take her in his arms and taste her full, moist lips. To sample the full bounty of her soft curves and pale skin.

He wanted her in a way he'd never wanted anything.

It took all his will not to leave the shadows and touch her. To yield to the burning ache in his loins that demanded he claim her for his own.

But he didn't dare.

He had no right to this woman who had

spilled her heart out to him while thinking he was someone else.

By all rights, he—who knew everything about her—should know nothing at all.

Damn him for his foolish stupidity.

She looked around the corridor, then stepped back into the room and shut the door.

Simon still didn't move.

He was torn between the desire to go to that door, kick it open and take what he wanted and the need to run for cover lest Kenna learn of his trickery.

But was it trickery when he hadn't meant it that way? He'd never really lied to her. He'd only failed to correct her misinterpretation.

Every word he'd written to her had been the truth. Every feeling real and honest.

"Simon?"

He started at the familiar voice that came from the opposite end of the hallway.

Stepping out of the shadows, he saw the MacNeely lairdess. She was even more beautiful now than when he'd left Scotland. Her long, red hair was braided down the side of her face, and she wore a deep blue kirtle that accentuated the perfection of her body.

"Callie," he greeted.

A warm smile curved her lips as she pulled

him into a sisterly hug of affection. "Whatever are you doing here, and hiding in the shadows, no less?"

Simon stepped back. "Like the others, I have come for the show of arms."

She nodded. "Is your brother, Draven, with you?"

"Nay. He didn't want to travel without Emily and the boys, and he felt it was too far for the youngest to journey."

Caledonia took his arm in hers and led him toward the room where Kenna was.

His heart pounded more with every step that took him closer to his doom.

Perspiration broke out on his forehead.

Unaware of his panic, Callie continued. "Then I shall just have to stop at Ravenswood on my way home and make sure to see them and Dermot. And speaking of my errant brother, have you seen him recently?"

Simon shook his head. "Not since I released Dermot's custody over to Draven, but Emily has written to say he is well."

"Good."

Simon swallowed as she reached for the door handle.

Run!

The command was so strong that he wasn't

sure what kept him from heeding it.

But before his common sense could return, Caledonia opened the door.

Simon's gaze met Kenna's instantly. She sat in a chair on the other side of the room, just before the open window with a small psalter in her hands. Sunlight streamed in through the window, where it lightened strands of her hair to form an angelic halo around her face.

She was beautiful.

Desire hit him fiercely. It was all he could do to breathe. His body was instantly hot and cold.

He found himself unable to move. Unable to break eye contact with the one woman who had haunted him for the last year.

The one woman he would give up his life for.

Kenna couldn't move as she saw the man beside her cousin. His dark auburn hair was a bit longer than was the English fashion, but he wore a small, stylish goatee that had been perfectly manicured.

He was taller than most men, with a lean, muscular build that bespoke power and strength. Deadly grace. His blue eyes were riveting in their striking color.

Truly, he was a most handsome man.

And it took her a full minute before she realized who he was.

The Wraith.

They'd seen each other only once, but she had never forgotten the handsomeness of his features. The way his blue eyes were able to sear her with his passionate heat.

He looked at her now like some hungry predator who had just found its next meal. The intensity of that stare made her hot and nervous. And oddly enough, it brought a strange thrill to her.

There was an aura of dangerous power surrounding him. One of possessiveness.

She couldn't fathom why, but the sensation didn't lessen.

"Kenna, have you met Simon? He is the friend of Sin's who came with him to Scotland after we married. His elder brother is the one Dermot was sent to live with."

Kenna was completely stunned by the news.

"*You're* Simon?" she said, her face breaking out into a smile. It was all she could do not to laugh at some of the stories she had heard from Callie and Sin about this knight.

It was hard to fathom that the dangerous predator before her could be the kind, good-natured man of whom they had spoken.

He was far too intense for that. Far too intense ever to follow the orders of someone else.

She had imagined Simon of Ravenswood as a small, gentle man, not as someone who towered over her cousin with such a steely and dangerous demeanor.

He inclined his head toward her. "It's good to see you again, my lady."

Caledonia looked back and forth between them. "You know each other?"

"We met in France when I went to see Lord Stryder." Kenna rose to her feet and placed her psalter in her seat.

As she neared Simon, she tilted her head to look up at him. What was it about this man that made her knees weak? Made her burn to reach out and touch him? To brush the stray lock of hair back from his forehead and to kiss the bared skin?

His gaze was guarded, cool.

"You refused to tell me your name then," she said. "Why?"

Kenna was fascinated by the way his muscles rolled under his supertunic as he shrugged his shoulders. "You were more interested in Stryder than you were in me."

She had the impression that those words seemed to wound him somehow.

"Have you heard the good news, Simon?" Callie said. "Kenna is to marry Stryder."

There was a very subtle tensing to his features. One that looked like pain. "Congratulations, my lady. I hope he makes you happy."

Callie frowned at that. "Are you all right, Simon? You seem rather reserved."

He cleared his throat and offered her a smile that didn't quite reach his eyes. "Forgive me, Callie. I didn't rest well last night."

"Do you still travel with Stryder?" Kenna asked him. "Or are you knight to another lord?"

A fierce heat came into his eyes at that. Flickering. Burning. Her question had offended him, she could sense it.

"I am always my own knight, my lady. I travel with my friends and brothers until I feel the urge to leave and go my own way."

"Brothers?" Callie repeated. "I thought Draven was the only one you had."

"Nay. I am bastard born. I fear my father was rather free with himself, and I have a large family to burden whenever the mood strikes me."

Kenna laughed at that. "You sound like Stryder. He once said the very same thing to me."

There was no mistaking the panic that flashed across his features. "I had best be going. 'Twas nice seeing you both again."

He was out the door before Kenna could even open her mouth to return the sentiment.

"Well, that was certainly odd," Callie said as she rested her hands on her hips at his hasty departure. "I don't think I've ever seen Simon so stiff and guarded. He's normally much friendlier. I can't imagine what has gotten into him."

Kenna barely heard the words. There was something strange here. Something *very* strange.

Stryder acted as if he didn't know her, and Simon quoted almost verbatim an anecdote that Stryder had once written to her. . . .

Stryder . . .

Simon . . .

A bad feeling settled over her.

Nay, surely not.

Her chest tight with apprehension, she grabbed her letters and excused herself from Callie, then went below to find one of the two men who had her perplexed.

It was Stryder she sought first. She found him alone in the stable, readying his horse for a ride.

"My lord?"

He paused and turned to face her. She had the distinct feeling that he was biting his tongue to keep from cursing.

Once again she was struck by the handsomeness of his features, by the way his black hair curled so becomingly around his face and shoulders.

Stryder of Blackmoor was a man to make any woman weak in the knees. Yet he didn't make her warm the way Simon had.

"My lady," he greeted her cooly. Dispassionately.

And it was then she knew the truth.

This wasn't the same man who had written to her. That man had spilled out his heart and soul to her. He had been open and funny. Warm and enchanting.

The man before her was too guarded and closed to her. She had been tricked, she knew it.

Now she wanted proof before she let loose her wrath on them.

So she handed Stryder her letters. "Are you the man who wrote these to me?"

He turned them over and looked at the Blackmoor seal. "They bear my mark."

"Aye, they do indeed."

He frowned as he handed them back to her. "Then they are from me."

"But you didn't write them."

He moved away.

"Please," she begged, taking his arm to stop him. "I must know."

"Why?"

"Because these are tender words," she said, holding the letters up to him. "Poetic words.

Who would dare write me such while signing your name to them? Was this some cruel game you played?"

His eyes darkened, as if her accusation greatly offended him. "Nay, lady. I would never play with another in such a manner. I may have committed many crimes in my life, but mockery has never been one of them."

She pulled the top letter off and removed the red ribbon. "Read this and tell me what you see."

A tic started in his jaw. "I can't read that."

"Why not?"

"Because I can't read. I never learned."

All the breath left her lungs at that. Stunned, she could do nothing but stare.

She'd wanted the truth and now she had it. Stryder was illiterate.

"Then who wrote this to me?"

"I did."

Chapter 3

Kenna turned to find Simon standing just behind her. His blue eyes were dark and stormy.

"*You* wrote to me as Stryder?" she asked.

He glanced to Stryder, then locked gazes with her. "Aye."

Pain and disbelief washed over her. Oh, she was such a fool! How could she have ever thought that a man as handsome, wealthy and well-famed as Stryder would ever settle for a plain woman such as she?

And yet Simon had made her believe. He had fed her mind full of fallacies and lies.

How could he?

"I see."

Her throat tight, she returned the ribbon to the letter, then handed the stack over to Simon.

"I hope the two of you have a good laugh over this. I'm sorry I disturbed you."

He captured her arm as she started past him. "Kenna, please. I . . ."

She waited for him to finish.

Instead, he just stared at her with his jaw flexed, his eyes snapping, as if he were debating with himself.

"You what?" she asked.

His gaze softened. "I never meant to hurt you."

"Then what did you mean by sending me those letters, knowing I thought they came from Stryder?"

Stryder promptly excused himself and headed for the stable's opening.

Alone now, Kenna stared up at Simon, whose eyes held a deep, inner torment. "I would never hurt you," he murmured.

She sensed his heartfelt sincerity, not that it mattered. What he had done had been wrong. Inexcusable.

And for what?

For sport?

For cruelty?

"But you did hurt me, Simon. You have embarrassed me and made me feel—"

He stopped her words with a hot, demanding kiss.

Kenna was shocked by his actions.

No man had ever dared such before. None. Her father would have had the heart of any man who dared handle her in such a fashion, and yet she found Simon's bold possession scintillating and wonderfully exciting.

Closing her eyes, she inhaled the warm, rich scent of him and moaned at his taste, at the sensation of his hot, firm lips on hers, of his tongue gently searching her mouth.

She'd lain awake for hours at night imagining what it would be like to kiss the author of her letters.

Only then she had imagined Stryder.

But it was Simon who had written them. Simon who had touched her heart and made her feel beautiful and needed.

She pulled back and looked up at him.

"I won't apologize for writing to you," he whispered. "I'm only sorry that you were embarrassed."

Her fury snapped at that. "Why didn't you tell me you weren't Stryder?"

"Would you have written to me if I had?"

"Of course," she said emphatically.

She saw the raw doubt in his eyes, and it made her ache in sympathy. How could he doubt her, especially after what he had done?

"Truly?" he asked. "Tell me, wasn't half the appeal of me the fact that you thought I was an earl and not some landless knight? I'm not a fool, Kenna. I learned long ago that whenever I'm with Stryder, Sin or Draven, women look past me to them. Because I hold no titles or land, I'm practically invisible. My only purpose has been to help women land titled husbands while I am seen as nothing more than a friend to them."

He stared at her, his gaze probing as if he could see the answer he needed in her eyes. "Had you known it was plain and simple Simon you were writing to, would you have continued to do so, or would you have written me a letter telling me what good friends we are and then set your gaze to another?"

Kenna opened her mouth, then paused.

She didn't want to think herself so shallow. She'd never been the kind of person to discount another because of their birth status.

Was there any truth to his claim?

Her gaze fell to the thin gold chain around his neck. She trailed her attention down to a small circle of gold that lay nestled between the laces of his tunic.

Before she could stop herself, she reached up and pulled it out. A simple, unadorned gold piece, it was warm from the heat of his body.

She opened it to find her lock of hair inside, just as he'd promised. "You kept it?"

"I told you I did. I know you don't believe me, but I swear that I never lied to you. I only omitted telling you what the *S* stood for because I didn't want to lose you. For once, I wanted something for myself."

Her hands shook as she closed the locket that held her hair. A thousand emotions flooded her. She was still angry over his falseness, but not even that could blot what she felt for him.

He had kept her close to his heart, just as he'd written. And as she thought of that, she remembered all the tender sentiments they had shared. All the secrets and disappointments of their pasts. Their hopes for the future.

The smiles and laughter his letters had brought to her . . .

"I'm not some great and noble champion, Kenna. I'm only a man who has nothing to offer a lady like you. For a time, your letters let me be more than what I am. Forgive me for the pain I've caused you."

He pulled back and turned away.

Tears welled in her eyes.

She knew this man. Knew him on a level that transcended friendship and lovers. It transcended understanding and reason.

It most certainly transcended a tiny omission of fact.

"I dwell in misery . . ."

He paused at her words and finished the sentence. ". . . my heart seeks the light that only your letters provide." He gave a half laugh. "Rather insipid, isn't it? Christopher of Blackmoor always said I should keep to my sword and not pick up his quill. He says I do far more damage with ink than I could ever do on a battlefield."

She smiled past the tears that choked her. "Nay, your words are beautiful. I treasured each one."

And she had. Every moment of every day she had watched for a messenger to come bearing another tie to her knight. She'd rushed from her duties to take the letters so that she could read them in solitude.

They had meant the world to her.

Just as he did.

Simon took a deep breath. "If you wish, I will help you to marry Stryder, my lady. I know ways to get past his defenses."

"You would do that for me?"

The sincerity on his handsome face made her shiver. "I would do *anything* you asked of me, Kenna."

A tear fell down her cheek at that. This was the man with whom she'd fallen in love.

Not Stryder and his reputation. Not some invincible champion.

She'd fallen in love with a man. One who had made her feel beautiful even though she didn't possess the great beauty of her cousin Caledonia. One who had made her laugh and filled her heart with warm, tender joy.

She took Simon's hand in hers and held it to her heart. "And if it's not Stryder I love?"

Simon couldn't breathe as her question rang in his ears.

Was she saying . . .

"Tell me what I can do, my lady, to make this right, and I will do it."

"I would make true my heart's fondest wish. A kiss from your tender lips and a pledge from my heart to yours."

He swallowed as she repeated the words he'd written in his last letter to her.

"Do you love me, Simon?"

"Aye."

Then she did the most unexpected thing of all. She released his hand, stepped into his embrace, and kissed him.

The feathery touch of her lips on his shook him profoundly. How could she want him?

It was unfathomable.

This woman whose warm humor had come to him like a gentle caress, giving him comfort on a level he'd never known existed. It still amazed him just how much he'd come to depend on her letters. How much he depended on her.

"I have nothing to offer you, Kenna."

"I only want your heart, Simon. I ask nothing else from you."

He smiled at her, unable to believe the reality of this moment. It was so much more than he'd ever dared to dream. "That I gladly give you, my lady." He lifted her hand to his lips and kissed it.

He wanted to keep her with him forever, but he knew the truth.

Her family would never allow him to marry her. Not even his friendship with Sin MacAllister or Stryder, or his blood relations to Draven would be enough to convince them.

She was an heiress of great wealth with ties to the Scottish throne. Her guardian would set his sights on a richer, more prestigious husband than a disinherited bastard.

It was only a matter of time before they were separated.

But even though fate decreed otherwise, he wanted to spend time with her. Wanted to pretend that there were no rules or expectations of others to govern their lives.

"Would you spend the day with me?" he asked.

"Where?"

He shrugged. "I'm not familiar with this area. Care to explore the countryside?"

Smiling, she nodded. "I would love to."

Simon left her only long enough to saddle his horse, then he led it over to her.

Kenna was puzzled as Simon approached her with only one mount.

Did he intend to leave her behind?

Before she could comment, he picked her up and set her on his horse. The feel of his arms and hands on her body made her heart pound. She'd never known anything better than the sensation of his touch against her flesh.

"Where are we to ride?"

"Wherever strikes our fancy." He gave her a

hot, searing look, then mounted his horse behind her.

The saddle tilted dangerously until he was settled behind her. His entire body was pressed against hers. It was intimate and intense. Electrifying.

Kenna trembled at his actions, especially when his arms came around her to take the reins. No man had ever done such with her. Men had always kept a respectful distance.

But not Simon.

He dared what no other would.

And she found herself wondering what other things he would dare with her before this day ended. She should be afraid to ride off with him alone, but she wasn't.

She wanted this man. Wanted to be his and his alone.

He was her champion.

Simon set his heels to the horse and whisked her out of the castle's bailey, through the barbican and out into the meadow that surrounded the castle.

They flew across the fields. The power of the horse was evocative, but not nearly as much as the strength of the man who held her. His heart pounded against her shoulder blade. Every step of the horse threw her back against him in a scintillating rhythm.

She could feel his hot breath on her neck, the steel of his arms coiled around her.

She'd never known anything like this.

Time seemed to stop as they rode far away from the world. Far away from any other living person.

Simon took her deep into the forest, where there was no one but the two of them.

He stopped by the shore of a shimmering lake that gently lapped at the mossy bank. He helped her down. Simon quickly rubbed his horse down before leaving the beast to graze and drink.

She waited patiently and admired the way his muscles flexed and bunched while he worked. It was the first time she'd ever noticed the way a man's body moved while he exerted himself. She was fascinated by the color that darkened his cheeks, by the look of his large hands being so gentle with his animal.

Simon was powerful. Strong, and yet tender in his caring. She smiled at the knowledge.

Once finished, he rejoined her. Taking her by the hand, he led her to where a small circle of rocks formed a strange table-and-chair design.

"What are we doing here?" she asked as she walked around the small outcropping of rocks.

"Nothing. I merely want to sit so that I can look at you and not have to worry about anyone else disturbing us."

Kenna frowned at his words. "Why would you wish to do that?"

"Because I have dreamed of your face every night for a year now. When next I leave, I want to make sure that I won't forget even the tiniest detail of you."

He sat down, then pulled her to sit beside him on the mossy grass.

Kenna didn't speak as she watched him. He leaned back against a rock, his gaze never wavering from hers.

The intensity of that icy blue stare unnerved her. She wasn't sure what she should say to him.

How strange. She'd always had plenty to say to him in letters. But then their letters had been safe.

There was nothing safe about the man beside her.

He *was* dangerous. She could sense it. This was a man who had stood single-handedly against his enemies. One who had put his life at risk for others, countless times.

"Edward used to tell me stories of how you would help—"

"Shh," he said, placing his fingertip over her lips. "I've no wish to remember my past. My time in Outremer was a nightmare best left forgotten."

She nodded. The horrors of their existence had haunted her brother until the day he'd died. Once Edward returned home, he'd refused ever to be in darkness. They had paid servants to stay awake all night long, keeping the fire and candles in his room burning until the dawn. Edward himself had purchased dozens of cats to make sure no rodents would ever be found in their hall.

For the first year of his return, Edward had been like a madman. Terrified and nervous. Screaming out for no apparent reason, sitting for hours curled up into a ball as he held on to himself and rocked endlessly.

All of them had feared for Edward's sanity until one night, when a stranger had shown up. To this day, she didn't know the man's name. He'd stayed with Edward for several months until her brother could again function as a man and not a scared animal waiting to be kicked.

When the man had left, he'd handed Edward

the badge she had returned to Stryder in Normandy—the mark of the Brotherhood of the Sword, a group of men whose ties to each other went far deeper than blood. Theirs was a brotherhood of sorrow and grief. One of unimaginable torment and pain.

Now there was Simon. He who had been in the thick of it and yet seemed to have somehow survived it whole and undamaged.

She marveled at his strength.

"What will you do after the tournament?" she asked.

"Stryder wishes to return to Normandy for a while."

Her stomach tightened at the thought of him so far away again. "You will go with him?"

"I haven't decided. What of you?"

She sighed as she thought it over. "I shall return home. The Angel sent word that there is another Scot who needs a resting place for a time before he returns to his family. I shall be there to make him welcome."

Simon nodded.

The Angel was the only woman who had been in their company during their days in Outremer. Only Simon and the other four members of the Quinfortis had known The Angel was a woman. The five of them had protected her carefully from their enemies.

He was grateful to Kenna for continuing to uphold her brother's oath to help save and protect those who had suffered the horrors of a Saracen prison.

Kenna was a good woman, one he would spend the rest of his life aching for.

How he wished things were different.

Simon sat quietly, watching the wind play in the tendrils of her brown hair, watching her long, graceful fingers toy with the trim of her dress.

He was captivated by those hands. Hands he wanted to feel on his skin. Fingers he wanted to taste and tease . . .

For the first time in his life, he felt awkward with a woman. He was so unsure of himself. So afraid of saying the wrong thing and making her demand that he leave her.

He watched as she picked up a blade of grass and used her hands to make a light whistle from it.

"What are you doing, my lady?"

She smiled, then blew against it again. "I'm calling the fey folk."

"Why?"

"So that they can give you back the silver tongue that wooed me so effectively. You are stiff with me now and I've no wish for you to be stiff."

He cleared his throat at her choice of words. She had no idea just how *stiff* he was.

She tossed the blade of grass aside. "Whatever can I do to make you relax?"

Lay with me and let me nibble every inch of you . . .

Simon cleared his throat at the lecherous thought.

"Well?" she prompted.

He started to lie to her, but couldn't. He'd never really lied to her before. They'd always had an open honesty between them where their feelings were concerned, and he had no desire to change that. "I dare not say it."

"Why not?"

His breathing ragged, he held her golden brown gaze with his. "Because what I want of you, my lady, is wholly indecent and improper, and should I speak these thoughts I fear you will run away from me."

A light frown puckered her brow. "And how are these thoughts indecent?"

Simon braced himself for her rejection as he

spoke the honest truth to her. "I want to taste you, Kenna, and not just your lips. I want to know every inch of your body. There has not been a single night over the last year that I haven't lain awake aching for your touch. Aching for your body."

Kenna shivered at his brazen words. Virgin she might be, but she well understood what it was he asked of her. Most importantly, she understood the consequences of desire met and unmet.

Her mother had once told her how precious a woman's maidenhead was.

Once gone, it could never be recovered.

Men the world over claimed it was a husband's right alone to take that from a woman, but her mother had been of a different mind.

Guard it well for the man you love with the whole of your heart. God willing, he shall be the one who marries you. But in the end, all women should know love the first time they take a man into their body. It is the most precious gift a woman can give to a man to let him know he is her first.

Kenna knew all too well the realities of her position. She was the king's cousin, which made her a direct link to the throne of Scotland. Love would have no place in her marriage. Politics and practicality were all that mattered. It was why Stryder would have been a good match.

But Simon . . .

Her cousin would never approve such a marriage. She knew that. And yet she wanted no other man.

She wanted her poetic knight. If she were forced to endure a marriage of alliance, then she wanted her one day of love. Her one moment spent with a man who made her feel like a woman.

For this one instant in her life, she didn't want to be the dutiful lady. She wanted something for herself.

That something was the man before her.

"Make love to me, Simon."

Simon's heart stopped at her whispered words. He couldn't quite believe his hearing, and yet there was no denying the sincerity on her face.

"Have you any idea what you're saying?"

She nodded.

Simon swallowed. He should get up and leave. He had no right to what she offered him and well he knew it. Women descended from kings didn't bother with knight-errants who had no prospects for anything better in life.

He was appalled at himself for not getting up immediately and returning her to the castle.

Yet he couldn't leave. His body refused to obey him, and his heart . . .

His heart needed her.

And when she leaned forward to kiss him, all of his sense left him. He couldn't think of leaving now. Not when all he wanted to do was stay.

He cupped her face in his hands, reveling at the softness of her skin.

Deepening his kiss, he laid her back on the warm grass and let the softness of her skin sweep him away from the realities of their situation.

He closed his eyes and allowed her to invade every sense he possessed. Her mouth was sweeter than honey, her touch sublime. He growled, needing more of her touch, desperate to lie with her, naked flesh to naked flesh.

Before this afternoon ended, they would both be well sated.

Kenna trembled at the foreign sensation of Simon on top of her. His weight felt so good to her, his lips even more so.

She felt his hand drop down to the laces of her kirtle while his hot, demanding kiss stole her breath.

Her senses reeled from the cascade of emotions and sensations that swept through her. The world around her careened. Her body seemed to be on fire, and it flamed even higher with every touch of his hand on her skin.

His fingers played with her laces until he spread her chemise open, baring her neck and the top swell of her breasts to his hot gaze.

Kenna watched in fascinated awe as he dipped his head down to tease her skin with his hot mouth. Desire coiled through her, pooling itself into a deep-seated throb at the center of her body.

Simon could barely draw his breath as he tasted her warm, sweet skin. Her lavender scent permeated his head, making him burn with aching need.

He couldn't remember ever being harder for a woman, ever wanting to taste one more.

She was his Aphrodite. Starving for more of her, he parted her kirtle even more until he could free her right breast.

A light flush covered her skin.

"Don't be embarrassed, my lady," he whispered, then he used his beard to lightly tease her taut nipple before he drew it deep into his mouth.

She moaned in response.

Arching her back, she laced her hands through his hair, pulling him close to her body, murmuring with pleasure while he licked and teased her taut areola.

He parted her gown even more until both her breasts were bare to his hungry gaze. Simon took his time sampling her, moving from one breast to the other while she ran her hands over him.

What he wouldn't give to make her his. To be able to claim her as her rightful husband.

He ached with the knowledge that one day she would lay like this with another man. Be forced to allow some other to touch her.

The thought wrung a bitter curse from him.

She stiffened. "Did I anger you?"

"Nay, love," he said, licking his way back to her lips. "You could never anger me."

"Then why—"

He kissed her to silence, unwilling to spoil the moment with what had ruined his mood.

But only for an instant. The taste of her warm, welcoming mouth was all he needed.

Kenna sighed in contentment as Simon gently teased her lips. Who knew kissing could be so pleasurable?

It whet her appetite for more, made her long to see him bare. With a courage that astounded her, she tugged at his surcoat and tunic.

He laughed at her eagerness before he pulled back long enough to divest himself of his garments.

Kenna swallowed at the sight of his bare, tawny skin gleaming in the sunlight. He was superb. Every part of him. Biting her lip, she reached out with her hand to trace the taut muscles of his shoulder down to his powerful biceps, then over to his pectorals.

He hissed at her touch and held himself still for her exploration. And explore him she did. She ran her questing hands down his chest to his hard, steely abdomen, where every muscle was well defined. Down to the small trail of hairs that ran from his navel to the waistband of his breeches.

Kenna hesitated to go any further. She desperately wished to see all of him, and yet she was a bit scared. She'd never seen a man naked before.

What would he look like?

"Don't stop there," he said, tugging at the laces at his waist.

Her throat dry, Kenna yielded to the curious part of herself and took courage in the hot, yearning look on his face as she gently sank her hand down into his breeches.

She found him instantly. He was swollen and wet and hard. Her hand trembling, she wrapped her fingers around his shaft. He groaned.

He held himself above her with one arm and used his other hand to cover hers. Kenna shivered as he showed her how to stroke him.

"You like this?" she asked, moving her hand down to the base of his shaft.

"Aye. I do."

Wanting to please him more, she cupped him in her palm while he teased the flesh of her neck with his mouth. Chills covered her from his hot breath.

She found it hard to believe that she was doing this with him, that they were about to share the most intimate of all experiences together—and yet why shouldn't they?

This was something she didn't want to share with anyone else. Only Simon had ever made her feel womanly. Desirable.

Oh, how she loved his hands on her. The feel of him in her own hands. He was so soft and hard as he rocked himself against her.

Simon pulled back and removed his boots and breeches.

Kenna licked her lips at the sight of his bare,

masculine form. He was all sinuous power. All golden skin and muscles. If she could, she'd spend the rest of her life staring at that lush, wonderful body.

Her desire for him tripled, leaving her breathless and weak.

He reached for her, then removed the rest of her clothes. Kenna shivered, feeling terribly vulnerable.

She knew she wasn't a beautiful woman. Knew she had never driven men wild with desire.

But she wanted to do that now with Simon.

"Am I disappointing to you?"

Simon was aghast at her question. "How could you ask that?" He'd never wanted any woman more than he wanted her.

She smiled at him. "I didn't want you to regret this."

"I could never regret you."

He gathered her into his arms and held her close. The feel of her body against his was enough to drive him to madness. He kissed his way slowly down her skin. From her neck to her breasts, then lower and lower.

There was no part of her he didn't want to sample. No part of her he didn't want to touch.

Kenna's eyes widened as she felt his hand

probe her between her legs. Her entire body burned as he slid his fingers in and around, teasing her with pleasure.

He pulled his hand away, then covered her fully with his body. Recapturing her lips with his, he parted her legs wide and slid himself deep inside her.

She hissed as pain spread through her.

"Shh," Simon breathed in her ear. "It'll pass in a moment, I promise."

She bit her lip and waited as he remained perfectly still. The fullness of him felt so strange. She'd tried to imagine what it would feel like to have a man inside her, but nothing had prepared her for the reality of it.

It was so intimate to have him there while he looked down at her.

He smiled tenderly. "You are beautiful, Kenna. A treasure truly."

She reached up and laid her hand against his cheek as she stared into those searing blue eyes. "I love you, Simon."

He dipped his head down and kissed her, then slowly started to move against her.

Kenna moaned at the sensation of his body thrusting against hers. She let her love for him wash over her. Her need.

He returned to her mouth, his breath stealing

hers as they kissed and stroked each other with their hands and bodies.

Simon could barely breathe as he lost himself to the softness of her. He had seldom known comfort in his life. Seldom known tenderness.

His life had been spent with those who'd had little to no regard for him. He'd always had to prove himself. But not with her. She loved him for what he was. Not for his sword arm, not for his ability to think quickly.

She loved him for his heart.

With her he didn't have to pretend to be anything he wasn't. He could be soft with her. Gentle.

It was so unfair that he couldn't keep her.

She ran her hands over his back, her touch searing him to his soul. She was all he'd ever wanted in a woman.

And everything he couldn't have.

But she was his for this moment.

Delighting in that fact, he lost himself to her.

Kenna moaned as all her pain faded away to the pleasure of Simon inside her. The hard strength of him filled her to overflowing. She'd never known anything more sublime than him sliding in and out of her, over and over, until she was breathless and weak.

"Oh Simon," she breathed in wonderment.

Her body clenched and unclenched with his movements. Her ecstasy mounted until she was sure she would die from it. And then, just as she was certain she could stand no more, her body burst around her.

Kenna held him close as she cried out from it.

Simon growled as he felt her climax. Unable to bear the pleasure of her body clutching his, he joined her in orgasm.

He nuzzled her neck with his lips as wave after wave of pleasure racked him. The scent of her filled his head, making him dizzy.

He didn't move for several minutes but stayed there in her arms, letting her softness soothe him.

Afraid he was hurting her with his weight, he pulled back. "Thank you, my lady."

Kenna smiled up at him. This was so strange. The feel of him still inside her while he spoke to her.

He was so handsome, his face flushed, his hair damp from exertion.

Reaching up, she brushed his damp bangs back from his forehead, then traced the line of his jaw.

How she wished they could stay like this. But it was impossible.

She saw the reluctance in his eyes before he

withdrew from her. He picked her up from the ground and carried her toward the water.

"What are you doing?"

"I plan to bathe you, my lady. Every part of you."

She bit her lip at his words as a rush of excitement went through her.

He carried her to the lake and set her down to stand waist deep in the water, then he made good on his promise. He ran his hands over her heated skin, bathing her with a tenderness that seemed at odds for a knight of his caliber.

He dipped his head under the water.

Kenna watched the water play over the muscles of his back as he broke the surface, then caught her up to him. It was a wicked sensation to have his wet body pressed up against hers.

"I am so glad you came with me today."

She smiled up at him as she touched the locket that held her hair. "As am I."

After they bathed, they lay naked on the grass, waiting for their bodies to dry in the sun.

Simon looked so good spread out under her. She particularly liked the way dark, auburn hair dusted his legs and chest. The way his shaft looked nestled in the dense hairs below his waist.

Truly, the man had no equal.

Kenna lay on her stomach, mostly for modesty's sake. She was draped over Simon's chest as he played with her hair and told her stories of his travels with Stryder.

"He does not snore," she said with a laugh at his latest declaration of Stryder's faults. If she didn't know better, she would swear he was only recounting the man's shortcomings out of jealousy.

"Like a bear. I swear it. There are times he's so loud that he wakes himself up with it. He'll grab his dagger and brandish it about, demanding to know who awakened him."

She laughed again. "He would kill you if he ever heard you repeat that."

Simon's smile made her heart light. "He's heard it oft enough. I make no pretense of niceties to him."

" 'Tis a wonder he tolerates you," she said as she ran her hand over Simon's chest. She'd been tracing circles over his skin the whole time they lay there.

For some reason, she couldn't get enough of touching his bare skin.

"Tolerates me? 'Tis a wonder I tolerate him. Truly the man is a beast."

"He can't be too bad if he sees the good in you."

Simon leaned up to capture her lips in a light kiss.

Kenna sighed in satisfaction. What a wonderful day this had turned out to be . . . and an emotional one.

This morning, she'd assumed she'd spend the day with Stryder. Never would she have guessed the day would end like this.

That the man of her dreams was Simon of Ravenswood.

Simon pulled back and sighed wistfully as her stomach rumbled. "I fear I should return you before you're missed and Sin sends a search party to find you."

"I wish we didn't have to. Can we not run away together?"

His fingers played across her cheek. "I wish we could. But I have my own oath to the Brotherhood to uphold. I am the only one Stryder trusts at his back. He has enemies who would do anything to see him dead."

"I know. But I wish . . ."

She couldn't finish the thought. Not that she needed to. Simon knew her wishes the same as she did.

Simon tucked a strand of her hair behind her ear. "And there is the matter of your cousin, who would never rest if he thought I had taken you away from your home. Malcolm would never leave us in peace."

Again he was right.

"Promise me that you won't just leave me, Simon. Swear to me that you'll always write to me."

"I promise."

Heartbroken, she moved away from him and got up. Neither of them spoke as they dressed and mounted the horse.

Kenna couldn't stand the thought of what was to come. It tore through her like a vicious blade, carving out her soul.

How she wished she had been born another. Some lesser-known lady whose position would have been equivalent to Simon's. Then perhaps there would have been a future for them.

All too soon they returned to the castle.

Simon rode them into the stable, and the first thing she saw there made her entire body run cold.

"Are you all right?" Simon asked as he slid down from his saddle.

Kenna couldn't answer. Her gaze was fastened onto the roan stallion in the nearest stall. It was a horse she knew well.

It belonged to her younger cousin Malcolm—the king of Scotland.

She shivered at the thought of why her cousin would be here.

But she didn't have to wonder for very long. No sooner had they entered the castle than she was besieged by the entire gathering of English and Scottish nobles.

A hush fell upon the crowd.

Swallowing, Kenna forced herself forward.

Malcolm was seated on the raised dias in the Great Hall, next to King Henry II of England.

Her spine straight, she forced herself to walk forward so that she stood before her cousin. Simon stayed by her side, his presence giving her comfort as she curtsied.

Malcolm looked uncomfortable. "Cousin Kenna, we have been searching for you all afternoon. Wherever have you been?"

She forced herself not to look at Simon lest she betray either one of them.

"Forgive me, Majesty," Simon's deep voice rumbled. "I fear I detained her."

Malcolm's look was harsh. "And you are?"

"Simon of Ravenswood," King Henry answered. "He is brother to the earl of Ravenswood."

"And a personal friend of mine."

Kenna passed a grateful look to Sin MacAllister, who spoke up from the small crowd that was gathered to her left. Sin was a friend and advisor to King Henry and had become a trusted ally to Malcolm as well. Both kings looked to the man favorably.

Malcolm relaxed. "Then he is trustworthy?"

"I would trust him with my life," Sin answered without hesitation.

"Good," Malcolm said. "I would hate for anything to come between my cousin and her marriage."

Dread consumed her.

"Marriage?" Kenna repeated.

It was then she saw Stryder of Blackmoor as he made his way through the dense crowd. The look on his face was one of hell wrath.

He passed a murderous glare to Simon, then offered her a forced smile.

"Dearest," Stryder said in a voice that was far from warm. "It appears that on the morrow we shall wed."

Chapter 4

"Pardon?" Kenna asked, unable to fathom what Stryder had just said.

With any luck, she'd gone deaf this afternoon and had misheard him.

Unfortunately, she wasn't so fortunate.

Malcolm smiled. "We are very proud of you, cousin. An English champion will make a fine alliance for our family. You have chosen very wisely for your husband."

Kenna struggled desperately to maintain composure. She dared a quick glance at Simon, who stood as still as a statue. There wasn't a single clue as to his mood, except for the angry tic in his jaw and the pain in his eyes.

"Majesty," she said, amazed at how level her voice sounded, given the fact that what she wanted to do was run screaming from the room. "Might I have a word with you in private?"

Malcolm hesitated.

"Now, please?" She pressed.

To her relief, he agreed. They were shown to a small antechamber just off the Great Hall, where they could speak without being overheard.

But to her further chagrin, King Henry came with them.

When Stryder tried to join their company, she put her foot down and banished him from the room.

If only she could do the same with Henry.

Not that it mattered. She refused to marry Stryder. Such a thing wouldn't be fair to either one of them now that she knew the truth.

"What is wrong?" Malcolm asked as soon as the three of them were sequestered.

Kenna took a deep breath and blurted out her desire. "I've no wish to marry Stryder of Blackmoor."

The two kings exchanged shocked looks.

"Caledonia assured us that you loved the earl," Malcolm said. "That you have spoken of nothing but him for months now."

She bristled uncomfortably. "I was wrong."

She cringed a bit more as the words came out sounding more like a question than a statement of fact.

"Wrong?" Henry repeated. "Lady, are you daft?"

Malcolm arched a regal brow at the harshness of the older king. "Our cousin is quite sound. Perhaps there is a flaw with *your* champion."

Henry scoffed. "Our champion is undefeated. Test his steel yourself and you shall see that none can touch him in prowess. We assure you, the flaw is not with Stryder."

"Please, Majesties," she said before they started a war over this. "I beg you not to fight. There is nothing wrong with Lord Stryder or myself, it's just—"

"You love someone else." It was Henry who spoke.

Kenna looked away.

"Is this true?" Malcolm demanded.

She nodded.

Her cousin sighed as he considered that. "And who is this man?"

She choked on the answer, too afraid that by speaking his name she might do him harm.

But then she didn't have to say it. Henry did. "Simon of Ravenswood. It is why the two of you were together."

Silence rang in the room for what seemed an eternity.

Kenna had no idea what to say. She was terrified of doing anything that might cause Simon to get into trouble for her actions.

"Kenna?" Malcolm's voice was deep and calm.

She met Malcolm's gaze levelly.

"What say you about this man?"

"I do love Simon, Majesty."

Malcolm's gaze turned steely. Speculative. "And again We ask you, who is this Simon of Ravenswood? Is he someone of rank or privilege?"

Henry shook his head. "He is a knight-errant who travels with our English champions. He has neither title nor any prospect for such."

Malcolm's gaze turned dull as he nodded in thanks for Henry's honesty.

When he looked back at Kenna, her heart shrank at the sadness and regret she saw on his face.

He would offer her no hope.

"Kenna, you know the wealth that comes with your hand. You are the last of your father's children. Would you have Us marry you to a landless knight?"

"If you're asking me for the answer in my

heart, Majesty, then the answer is aye. If you ask my head, then I know the truth. Please don't torture me with it. As always, I will do as you command."

Her cousin's gaze softened a degree. "We have come here to see you wed an English champion." He looked over to Henry. "You were to hold a show of arms tomorrow, were you not?"

"Aye."

"Then the winner shall take my cousin's hand."

Kenna was shocked by Malcolm's unexpected words. "What say you?"

The familiar determined fire returned to Malcolm's eyes. "Your Simon has but one chance to win you, Kenna. Pray tonight that he is as deft with his sword as he was with winning your heart."

Overjoyed by his words, Kenna threw herself into his arms and hugged him tightly. It was a breach of etiquette, but she knew her cousin wouldn't mind.

"Thank you!" She kissed his cheek.

Malcolm patted her on the back, then released her.

With a curtsy to both kings, Kenna took her leave and rushed to find Simon, who stood in a corner with Sin and Stryder.

None of them looked particularly happy.

Still overjoyed by her excitement, she had to force herself not to embrace Simon.

"All is not lost!" she announced to the dour group.

"How so?" Simon asked.

"Malcolm has granted us a reprieve," she replied. "If on the morrow you win the show of arms, he will allow us to marry."

Simon arched a disbelieving brow. "If *I* win?"

"Aye."

Her enthusiasm waned at the stunned look on Simon's face.

Stryder and Sin burst out laughing.

"What is so funny?" she demanded.

"You've never seen Stryder fight, have you?" Sin asked.

Kenna frowned at that. "Aye, I have."

"Then did you not notice the fact that no one bests me?" Stryder asked. "Least of all, Simon."

"Excuse me," Simon growled. "I happen to be second *only* to you, Sin and Draven."

"That would make you fourth then, wouldn't it?" Sin asked.

Simon cast him a feral glare. "I should have let the MacNeelys poison you."

"It doesn't matter who is best," Kenna said. "Simon will win tomorrow."

Stryder scoffed. "I doubt that most seriously."

Kenna lifted her chin as she eyed the handsome earl earnestly. "I do not. For if you win, my lord, and I am forced to wed you, then I can assure you, you will regret that victory for the rest of your life."

Stryder stiffened at her words. "Don't threaten me, my lady. I don't take kindly to it. And I will not lose to Simon or any other man. I have never in my life been defeated, and that is one title I will fight to the death to protect. No one will ever best me."

Before she could contradict him, Stryder spun about angrily and left them.

"How dare he!" Kenna started after him, but Simon stopped her.

"Pay him no mind, love. Stryder has good reason for his words."

"He might at that, but I will not let him win on the morrow." She met Sin's black gaze. "Can you not help Simon to train?"

Sin shook his head. "We have only one night."

"Aye, but surely—"

"It won't happen, Kenna," Simon said. "I will fight with every ounce of my strength for you, make no mistake about that. But I am not the fighter Stryder is. I have no delusions about that fact."

Perhaps, but she knew in her heart that it would work out. It had to.

"I think you will be surprised by what you can do."

Kenna and Simon spoke little for the rest of the night. After supper, Caledonia took Kenna upstairs to her room while Simon went to find Stryder, who hadn't shown himself to eat.

He found his old friend sitting up on the parapet with a flagon of ale nestled in his arms, much like a babe.

Simon let out a disgusted breath at the sight. "What is it with you and Sin that the two of you like to do this?"

Stryder didn't answer as he finished off his ale. "Why are you here, Simon?"

"I wanted to talk to you about tomorrow."

Stryder didn't turn to look at him. Instead, he continued to stare out at the inner bailey far below. "I'm not going to throw the match."

"I know." Simon would never ask such a thing from a man who had spent his entire life running from his past. Running from the little boy he had once been. It wasn't in Stryder to lose, and he would never ask his friend for such a sacrifice. "I don't want you to throw it."

"Then why are you here?"

"I wanted to make sure we are still friends."

"Friends . . ." Stryder laughed, and it was then Simon realized the man was drunk.

Extremely drunk, judging by the way Stryder wobbled as he tossed the flagon aside and reached for the second one that was set down by his foot.

Stryder righted himself and returned to staring out at the yard. "You get me betrothed to a woman I don't know and now I am told I have to fight to marry her on the morrow even though I want no wife, especially not one who is in love with someone else. If we weren't friends, you'd be dead now, Simon."

"I didn't mean for this to happen."

Stryder looked up at that, his eyes haunted. "Just as I never meant to get you and Edward captured."

Pain swept through Simon at the reminder. Stryder had barely earned his spurs when they had followed Simon's father down to Outremer. Still a squire, Simon had thought it a grand adventure, until they'd met up with the small band of Crusaders.

Simon's father had scoffed at the fools, but Stryder had been young and intent on proving himself.

Stryder had wanted to follow after the Crusaders so that he could win glory and fame.

Simon had chosen friendship and gone with Stryder, never knowing what would come of his decision. Three years of their lives had been sacrificed to that fateful day. Three years of living in filth and squalor. Of fighting rats and serpents for every scrap of food.

Simon's flesh still bore the scars of that time, but unlike Stryder, he had chosen to bury the internal scars. To try his best to forget every degradation and horror they had experienced.

"I never blamed you."

"And I've never understood why you didn't."

"We are brothers, Stryder." Just as he was brother to Sin and Draven. He'd had to align himself to all of them to survive. Their shared tragedies had bonded them.

Stryder took a deep breath. "Do you love her?"

"Aye."

"Then how can you stand here so casually when you know that on the morrow she will belong to me?"

"Because she never really belonged to me." The truth stung him deep, but both he and Stryder knew it. "I am truly the Wraith." He laughed bitterly at the irony of that. "She didn't see me until it was too late to do anything about it." His heart aching, he forced himself to add, "I know you will honor her."

"And if she dies because of the curse of my family?"

Simon rolled his eyes at the lunacy of that question. "You're not cursed, Stryder."

"Aye, but I am. Why else would I be forced to marry my best friend's love?" Stryder rubbed his hand over his head. "Why are you here with me anyway? You should be with her this night. God knows the two of you may never have another one."

Simon frowned at his words. "You're being remarkably understanding about all this."

"I'm being remarkably drunk, Simon. I plan to drink so much that this night will be nothing but an unremembered blur. Come the morrow, you and I shall have to fight." Stryder looked up at him. "I don't want to fight you, Simon. You are one of the few people I consider family, and family is something I have very little of. Now go. I want to be alone in my misery."

Simon nodded. He well understood that sentiment, though tonight, for the first time, he had no wish to be alone.

He wanted Kenna.

And yet he dare not seek her out.

If he did, he would spend this night with her, and he couldn't do that to Stryder.

He appreciated Kenna's confidence in his abilities, but he knew the limits of his prowess. He could never defeat Stryder.

Damn the Fates for it.

Clenching his teeth, he left Stryder to his ale and went to seek whatever comfort he could in his tent.

It was a calm, quiet night. Most of the knights were still in the hall, boasting of how well they intended to do on the morrow.

A sennight ago, Simon would have been headed back to his tent to write to Kenna, to tell her all about his day and to speculate on what the morrow might bring.

But he couldn't even take comfort in that anymore. Their days of writing letters to one another were over. It would be unseemly of him to continue to correspond with the countess of Blackmoor while he rode with her husband.

The pain of the thought was almost enough to send him to his knees.

Heartsick, Simon entered his tent and moved to disrobe. He had stripped down to his tunic and hose when he heard a light noise behind the curtain that separated his dressing area from the bed.

Suspicious of an intruder, he reached for his sword.

With it held at the ready, he pulled back the curtain, then froze.

There in his bed was the one woman he would sell his soul to possess.

Kenna.

Her thick, wavy hair was down around her face. She wore a gauzy white chemise that was so sheer he could easily see the bright pink tips of her breasts.

He'd never seen a more beautiful sight than her waiting for him.

"You shouldn't be here," he said, lowering his sword.

"This is the one place where I do belong. I don't want to be without you, Simon."

He was humbled by her words. By the fact that she would risk so much to be with him tonight when he needed her so desperately.

He should send her on her way. It would be the noble thing to do.

But having lived his life for others, he found himself selfish tonight.

For once, he wanted something for himself.

He wanted her.

He dropped his sword and made his way toward the bed where she lay waiting. How he wished he could have her with him like this always.

Kenna held her breath, half expecting Simon to send her away. He had a look about him that warned her he was divided in his intentions.

But there was no division in hers. She was concentrated on him and him alone.

She shivered as he drew near her and pulled back the covers.

"I know not what brought you here tonight, my lady. I am only glad that you came."

Kenna smiled at him. "I would always come for you, my knight. No matter where you go."

He pulled his tunic off and gathered her into his arms. Kenna sighed at the sensation of his skin under her hands. He was so steely and warm. She loved the way his muscles rippled beneath her hands. The way he stared at her as if she were some tasty morsel he longed to devour.

His locket fell down to nestle between her breasts. Fire tore through her as she welcomed him.

"Don't leave me, Simon," she whispered. "Please win for me tomorrow."

"I shall do all within my power to win you."

He separated her legs with his knee. Kenna moaned at the feel of his hard body lying against hers. She felt him from her lips to her toes.

He kissed her then, hot and passionately. She ran her hands over his back as he bulged against her. Her body throbbed, wanting him inside her again.

He opened her chemise and slid his hand down to her breast, which tightened and ached for him.

With a growl, he left her lips and dipped his head to take her swollen nipple into his mouth. She hissed at the feel of him there while she held his head to her.

She couldn't imagine anything more pleasurable than Simon touching her.

He took his time tasting her, teasing her, before he began a slow trail down her body.

Kenna had no idea what he intended. He lifted the hem of her chemise, baring her lower half to his hungry gaze.

She shivered at the sight of him staring at her most private place. He nudged her legs farther apart, then ran his finger down her wet cleft.

Just as she thought the pleasure couldn't get any better, he dipped his head down and took her into his mouth.

Kenna cried out in ecstatic surprise. She'd

never imagined a man doing this to her. He was relentless in his tasting of her.

And when she came for him, it tore her asunder.

She expected him to enter her then.

He didn't.

Instead, he pulled back and lowered the chemise to cover her. He moved to lay down by her side and pulled her so that he cradled her head against his bare chest.

"You didn't take your pleasure."

"Aye, love, I did. Your pleasure was mine tonight."

"I don't understand."

"I can't take you again, Kenna, knowing that on the morrow like as not you'll belong to someone else. I can't send you to Stryder carrying my child. It wouldn't be fair to any of us."

"And if I'm already carrying your child?"

"I can't undo that. I can only ensure that I don't cuckold him from this moment on."

Kenna swallowed the tears she longed to weep. This was so unfair. She was getting the very thing she'd wanted—marriage to Stryder. Only it wasn't what she needed.

She needed Simon.

She lay quietly, listening to Simon's heart beating beneath her cheek.

She sighed. "Do you remember what you wrote to me last Christmastide when you were in Flanders?"

"That I hate duck?"

She laughed. "Aye, you said that too. But I was thinking more of your telling me how you wished you could have a family celebration like the duke of Burgundy. You wrote of how his children had been around him as well as his brothers and sister. Do you remember it now?"

"Aye. Men ever seek to obtain what they know they can never have."

"The day might come—"

"Nay," he said, interrupting her. "Even if I were to become landed, there is no other I would have, Kenna. You are the only woman I would ever quest for."

"You would change your mind, Simon, if you were given lands."

"Nothing would change. I've known many women in my life, of all stations, and I know my heart. In all my journeys there has never been another woman who made me feel what you do. You are my friend and confidante. I have trusted you in ways I have never trusted anyone else. It's not in me to be so open with people, and yet I have told you every thought and dream I have ever possessed."

She was warmed by his words.

He balled her hair up in his hand and lifted it to his face. Closing his eyes, he inhaled the scent.

She was awed by the action. "I can't lose you, Simon."

His jaw flexed. "We do what we must."

"But—"

"Nay, Kenna. No matter what we want, the dawn will come and tomorrow will see us parted."

"But if we—"

"There are no buts. I will not see you running from the family that loves you and making them sick with worry. Stryder is a good man. He will see you cared for."

"Will he see me loved?"

His crystal blue eyes were dull, tortured. "Nay. He will never allow himself to love a woman."

"And I will never love him. Tell me where either Stryder or I will find happiness in that?"

"You will find it. Somehow."

Kenna growled at him. How she wanted to throttle the stubborn beast. What was it with men that they were ever blind?

He kissed her on the brow and held her face in his hand. "Sleep, Kenna. I need my rest if I am to fight."

She nodded, even though what she wanted was to argue more. She'd learned long ago that once a man set his mind to anything there was no changing it.

But as she lay nestled in his arms, she prayed for a miracle. One that would see her wed to the champion of her heart and not to the champion of England.

Chapter 5

The dawn found Simon waking up to feel Kenna pressed to his side. Her warm, silken body called out to his, while her precious, sweet scent clung to him, permeating his head.

He lay quietly just listening to her breathe, feeling her skin against his.

Odd how a few months ago he'd wanted nothing more than to spend the rest of his life helping the Brotherhood. He'd been content with his lot of second born, landless knight. Nothing had owned him and he had owned nothing.

His life had seemed good. Even desirable.

Kenna had changed that.

Now he wanted only to be with her. For the first time in his life, he desired to be a husband, a father.

He wanted to be everything to her. To see her grow round with his child and to hold his own son or daughter in his arms.

He wanted to grow old with her.

Ultimately, he wouldn't even be allowed to take part in her life at all. After this day, he would be forced to hand her over to Stryder and walk away.

It would be the hardest thing he'd ever had to do.

His heart heavy, he forced himself to leave her side and dress. There was much to be done in preparation for the day's events.

Once he was ready to leave, he returned to the bed and stole a quiet kiss from Kenna.

She didn't move.

Tracing her lips with his finger, he smiled sadly. "Sleep well, my love. I hope you have peace in your dreams." For he would never have any peace in his heart. Not so long as they were forced to live separate lives.

And with that, he left her and made his way to the list, where knights were already beginning to gather.

Stryder was in the list with his squire, Raven. The boy was adjusting Stryder's cuirass to allow Stryder a wider range of motion during the coming matches.

"How fare you?" Simon asked.

Stryder's eyes were rimmed and red. He snarled in greeting. "Don't speak so loudly."

Simon shook his head. "Given your current state, mayhap I stand a chance after all."

But even he knew better. He'd seen Stryder recover from far worse things than this and still fight like a lion amongst mice.

Stryder grunted in response.

Simon spent the morning training and resting for what would come that afternoon. But it was hard to focus on that while his thoughts continually drifted back to the woman he'd left in his tent.

"God," he whispered, looking up at the clear blue sky above his head, "grant me either the strength to win this or to be man enough to walk away and leave them in peace."

Kenna woke to the silence of an empty tent. There were no traces of Simon. Nothing other than the warm, manly scent of him on her skin.

Until her gaze fell to the pillow beside her, where he'd left a note.

Sitting up, she clutched the sheet to her while her hair trailed down her back. She broke the seal to find the flowing, masculine script that had come to mean the world to her.

Courage, my love. I need you to possess the same fire that led you from Scotland to Normandy that first day when we met. Whatever the day brings, know that I will always love you. You carry with you, my heart, my soul, my very being.

Be strong for me, Kenna.

Ever your knight,
S

Postscriptum
S doesn't stand for Stryder.

She laughed at that, even though her eyes were filled with tears.

Blinking them away, she quickly dressed and made her way to the castle before she was discovered missing.

But she didn't stay there long before she headed back toward the list, where the men were training.

As usual, none of them paid her any attention. It wasn't until a man knew her titles and status that their heads turned.

Except for Simon.

He cared for her person, not her birthright.

She found him by his horse, checking its shoes and rigging.

He straightened as soon as her shadow fell over him. His eyes widened in surprise.

"Kenna. I wasn't expecting to see you."

"I know." She handed him the small package in her hands. "But I wanted to bring you this."

He opened it to find the red ribbon she always wore in her hair. The one her father had given her as a present just days before he'd died.

Today was the first day in years she'd been completely without it.

"Since you lost the last one, I want you to wear my favor, my lord."

He smiled at her. "Always."

He kissed her lips lightly, then held his arm out so that she could tie her token around his mail-covered biceps. Her heart was weak and pain-filled at the thought of losing him today.

Silently, she wished him God's strength and mercy.

As soon as she was finished, she took a small step back. "Good luck, my lord."

He opened his mouth to speak, but the heralds called the knights forward to prepare for the march that would lead them to the show.

Simon kissed her hand, then turned and mounted his horse. He stared down at her from his saddle.

The gentle breeze tugged at his dark auburn

locks, and his eyes burned with fiery passion and promise.

Never had she seen a more breathtaking man.

"God's strength be with you," she said.

Simon nodded, then turned his horse away and joined the others.

Kenna couldn't move as she watched him head off. It was like something from a forgotten nightmare.

"Kenna?"

She turned to find Caledonia behind her.

"Don't fret, little cousin," Callie said, taking her arm. "Simon won't let another man win you."

"I pray you are right."

Callie pulled her off, toward the area that had been set up for spectators. Malcolm and Henry were already seated in the highest part, where a striped awning kept the sun from them.

Callie led her to a seat behind the two kings, where Sin, who was dressed all in black, was waiting.

"Are you not participating?" Kenna asked Sin.

He shook his head. "I never play at war and I've no desire to embarrass Stryder by taking this victory from him."

Kenna considered his boastful statement. "If you are sure you can win this, then I beg you to take the field."

"Why?"

"Should you win, I wouldn't have to marry Stryder."

Malcolm laughed at that. "We wouldn't let you out of this so easily, Kenna."

Aggravated by the fact her cousin was in earnest, Kenna sat quietly and waited for the event to start.

The day wore on slowly as knight after knight clashed and defeated each other.

Simon fought as if his life depended on the outcome; indeed it did.

Should he lose this day, she would kill him herself.

It was nearing dusk when it came down to the final match.

Stryder and Simon.

Kenna held her breath in expectation as the two knights faced each other.

Simon was exhausted. His entire body ached from the day's games. The last man he wanted to face was Stryder. Having sparred for years with the man in practice, he knew just how skilled a knight Stryder was.

He knew Stryder's weaknesses, just as Stryder knew his.

Not once in all these years had they faced each other in earnest.

That was about to change.

They were at war now, Stryder to protect his honor and reputation, Simon to win his lady.

Simon clenched the reins of his horse and eyed Stryder. He wouldn't lose this day. There was no way he was going to cede this victory to Stryder. Whatever it took, he would win this.

The earl of Blackmoor was about to taste his first defeat.

The herald lowered the flag.

Simon spurred his horse forward.

He came at Stryder full tilt, with his lance held at the ready. The thrumming of hooves droned in his ear alongside his rapid heartbeat. Sweat trickled down the back of his neck.

Stryder drew nearer.

Simon tensed, ready for the blows.

One . . .

Two . . .

He made contact with Stryder at the same time Stryder's lance slammed into the center of his chest. Simon growled fiercely at the pain of it.

The force of the blow knocked the wind from his body, but Simon held his saddle.

By all the angels in heaven, he would not be unhorsed. Not today and not by Stryder.

Struggling for breath, Simon tossed his broken lance to his squire and received a new one. He turned his horse about and walked it back toward the list.

Stryder inclined his head to him in a respectful salute. Simon returned the gesture as they waited for the signal to begin anew.

He glanced toward the stands where Kenna sat. He couldn't see anything more than the color of her gown, but he swore he could feel her eyes on him. Hear her voice urging him to victory.

He would not disappoint her.

The flag flew out.

For you, my love, for you. . . .

"Ya!" Simon urged his horse forward.

But no sooner had he started forward than Simon felt it. A slight loosening of his saddle. It was small at first, but with the pounding hoof beats, it became more pronounced.

Simon cursed as he realized he had no time to veer away from Stryder and the oncoming blow.

Grinding his teeth, he met Stryder's blow full force, but his weakened saddle wouldn't hold, and the force of Stryder's lance knocked him back.

The saddle girdle broke, sending him toward the ground.

In that moment, Simon felt the weight of his defeat.

Damn it all!

He slammed into the ground so hard that his teeth rattled, his bones jarred.

For a full minute, he couldn't breathe at all as the crowd roared with excitement over Stryder's victory.

Simon lay still, his broken heart hammering. His saddle lay off to the side, a testament of his ill luck.

Nay! How could he lose to a twisted piece of fate?

He wanted to scream out at the injustice of it.

"Simon?"

He barely recognized Stryder's voice from the ringing in his ears.

"Simon, are you all right?"

He snarled as he felt Stryder trying to help him up. "Leave me be." He jerked his helm from his head and glared at his friend.

Simon ached to decry what had happened,

but he wouldn't be so childish. Nor would he undignify himself. Such things happened.

He was defeated.

Stryder's eyes burned with guilt. "I'm sorry, Simon."

In his heart, he knew Stryder meant that. But it changed naught.

Kenna was lost to him now. Forever.

"Damn you, Stryder. Damn you to hell."

Stryder's eyes flared in anger. A muscle worked in his jaw.

Simon expected him to strike out.

He didn't.

Instead, Stryder turned about and headed back toward his horse.

Angry and hurt physically, mentally and spiritually, Simon released the laces of his coif and started to retrieve his helm from the ground where he'd tossed it. But as he reached for it, something caught his eye.

If he didn't know better, he'd swear it was the fading sun reflecting off a crossbow hidden on the parapets.

He'd fought enough wars and battles to well understand such tactics. And as he glanced to Stryder, he had a horrible realization.

The bow was aimed for Stryder.

If he dies, Kenna is yours.

The thought went through his mind before he could stop it. Not that it mattered.

He could never be happy with Kenna knowing he'd let his friend die.

Reacting on pure instinct, Simon raced for Stryder.

Stryder cursed as he caught sight of Simon charging him. "Simon, I swear—"

The words broke off as Simon fell forward into his arms. The man's weight made him stagger back.

At first he thought Simon was attacking him until he realized people around him were screaming.

Simon was bleeding.

Stryder gaped as he saw three crossbow bolts protruding from Simon's back.

"Nay!" he roared, placing Simon gently sideways on the ground. "Simon?"

Simon shook from the pain of his wounds. His brow was covered in sweat.

Suddenly Kenna was there, her face pale and her cheeks wet with tears.

"Simon?" she sobbed, cradling his head in her lap.

Simon swallowed, then coughed up blood. He held onto Kenna's hand, unwilling to let it go. He struggled to breathe against the pain that shredded him.

Stryder bellowed for a physician.

But it was too late. Simon knew that. He'd known there would be no saving him when he'd seen the assassin on the battlements.

"Don't you dare die, Simon," Kenna said, shaking him. "Don't you dare . . ."

He didn't bother to argue with her. Such things were never in the hands of men.

Instead, he kissed her hand and inhaled her warm, feminine scent.

"Damn it, Simon," Stryder snarled. "You weren't supposed to do this again. You swore to me you would never hazard yourself for my life."

Simon took Stryder's hand and placed it over Kenna's. "Take care of her for me, Stryder."

He swallowed back the pain and then let the darkness swallow him.

Chapter 6

Kenna paced outside the room where Simon was being tended. The hallway was gray and stark—a perfect mirror of her mood. Stryder, Sin and Caledonia, along with Malcolm and Henry, waited with her.

She had wanted to stay inside the room with Simon while Henry's royal physicians tended him, but Malcolm had refused to allow it.

"It was a remarkable thing he did," Malcolm said as if musing aloud.

"He's a rather remarkable man, Majesty," Sin said. "He never fails to protect those he loves, and he's loyal to a fault."

Kenna listened while both Sin and Stryder spoke of Simon's bravery to the kings. Sin told of how Simon, at great peril to himself, went to Scotland to make sure Sin didn't face his enemies alone.

Stryder told of Simon's bravery in the Holy Land and again of his loyalty to his brother Draven. How Simon had gotten Draven's wife, Emily, to safety while they'd been under attack by unknown assailants.

Not that Kenna needed to hear proof of his courage or deeds. She knew all too well just how noble and decent Simon was. It was why she loved him.

The door opened.

Kenna looked up hopefully and rushed forward.

The eldest of the three physicians came out, wiping his hands against a pale blue cloth.

"How does he?" Kenna asked.

"Not well, my lady. We have cauterized the wounds, but they are deep. We're not sure if they pierced a major organ or not. If he lives to morning, then he may yet rise and recover. Otherwise . . ."

Her stomach wrenched. "May I see him?"

He nodded.

Kenna didn't wait for the others. She rushed into the room, to see Simon unconscious on the bed while the other two physicians packed their instruments and supplies.

Simon lay on his stomach with a sheet pulled up over him. His face was pale and ghostly, and his body was covered with sweat.

Her heart aching, she sat down beside him and brushed his wet hair back from his forehead.

"Simon," she whispered. "Please come back to me."

For four days Kenna waited in fear and uncertainty for Simon to wake, but he never moved.

On the fifth day, Malcolm grew impatient. "Scotland needs a king on her throne, Kenna. We canna wait any longer for him to wake."

Kenna wanted to scream out her denial.

But she was honor bound to do as her cousin requested, because his requests weren't requests.

They were kingly demands.

Simon's brother, Draven, who had come to be with Simon, stood on the opposite side of the crimson bed. His handsome face was dour as he looked from the king to her. "I'll watch over him for you, Kenna. Believe me."

"Come, Kenna," Malcolm said. "Let us have this wedding done with so We can go home."

Her heart heavy, she nodded.

* * *

Simon came awake to a vicious pounding in his head. He heard whispering nearby, then the sound of a door closing.

He was hot all of a sudden. The covers over him seemed stifling, unbearable.

He tried to kick them away, only to find them too heavy and his limbs too weak. Why did he feel this way?

He was weaker than a newborn whelp, and his body ached as if he'd been slit open.

It wasn't until he focused on the sight of his brother that he remembered what had happened.

"Stryder?" Simon asked, hoping his friend hadn't been shot too.

Draven moved to his side and held him down against the bed. "Shh, lie back."

Simon did, even though he was anxious to learn what had happened after he'd passed out. He met his brother's gaze and noted that a few strands of gray were starting to mark Draven's ebony hair.

"Where's Stryder?" he asked.

"He left almost a sennight ago."

The words made Simon's head pound even more. "Gone?" he whispered.

Draven nodded.

Simon closed his eyes as despair washed over him. That would mean Kenna was gone, as well.

At least Stryder lives. . . .

Aye, his friend was alive, thanks to him, and married to the woman he loved. Again, thanks to him.

At that moment, he hated himself.

"Don't you wish to know how long you've been abed?"

Simon shook his head. He couldn't care less.

The only thing that mattered to him was the fact that Kenna wasn't here with him now.

"Would you like me to tell you about Kenna's wedding?"

Simon snarled at him. "Do so and I swear, brother or not, injuries or not, I shall run you through."

Draven arched both brows at Simon's rancor. "Fine then, sorry I tried."

Draven moved away from the bed, then returned with a cup.

Simon refused to take it.

"You need to drink something. You've been—"

"I don't need that."

What he needed was to see Stryder's wife.

Stryder's wife.

The words cut through him.

Simon rolled over to face the wall and let the pain of her loss seep through him.

Why couldn't he have just died? Surely no man could live with the pain in his heart that he felt.

Behind him, he heard Draven set the goblet down on the table beside the bed, then cross the floor.

The door opened, but Simon didn't bother to look. No doubt Draven was leaving him.

Good. He wanted to be alone.

"He's awake," he heard Draven say to someone in the hallway outside. "But a word of advice, my lady. Your husband is in a foul mood."

Simon frowned at the words.

He rolled over to see . . .

Nay, it couldn't be.

He blinked as he saw Kenna drawing near the bed.

Draven glared at him. "Be nice to her, brother."

Simon still couldn't breathe. He couldn't take his eyes off the vision that was Kenna.

Her pale face was bright and happy. Her brown eyes fair glowed. She wore a deep crimson gown that matched the hair ribbon she'd given him.

"You're awake," she breathed, her voice unsteady with her happiness.

She threw herself over him, holding his head in her hands as she squeezed him. "Thank the Lord and all his saints for their mercy!"

Simon was dumbfounded. He looked at Draven for an explanation, but his brother merely stood aside with his hands crossed over his chest, watching the two of them.

"What are you doing here?" he asked Kenna.

"Where else would I be?" she said, pulling back to stare at him.

"With your husband."

She laughed at that. "I *am* with my husband."

He was even more confused than before. "Draven said Stryder had left."

"Aye. He did."

"Then why are you still here?"

Draven was the one who laughed this time. "Take mercy on the poor man, Kenna, and tell him about your wedding. He didn't want to hear the details from me."

This was so odd. . . .

"What details?" Simon asked.

Kenna sat back and took his hand into hers.

"Malcolm had you and I married by proxy."

Simon blinked. Then blinked again.

Did she say what he heard?

"Beg pardon?"

Kenna's eyes turned warm, inviting. "After you were brought up here, we waited almost a week, but Malcolm had to go home. He had to be here to sign the papers in order for our marriage to be binding, and since you were nowhere near to waking, he allowed Stryder to stand in as proxy for you."

The king's reversal didn't make sense. "But why? I don't understand what made him change his mind. I lost the show of arms."

"Aye, but not fairly. Even Stryder pointed out that he won only because your saddle failed you. Not that it mattered in the end. Malcolm changed his mind because he thought a man so loyal to his friends, one who would sacrifice his own happiness to see Stryder safe, was worthy of marrying me. More so, in fact, since Malcolm figured you would never try to overthrow him."

"But I'm not titled."

Draven snorted. "You are now, Lord Simon of Anwyk. King Henry has a small barony for you to swear fealty over. Seems he rather likes the thought of having a baron who is married to a Scottish princess."

Simon looked back and forth between them, still not sure if he hadn't addled his brain in the fall. "Are you jesting?"

Draven shook his head.

"Nay, love," Kenna said with a bright smile. Then she turned serious. "Of course, you could always divorce me . . ."

"Nay," he said emphatically. "Never."

She smiled again. "I somehow didn't think you would mind."

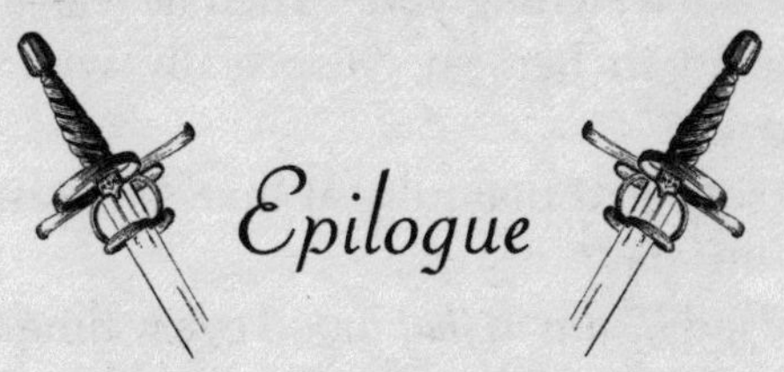

Epilogue

Simon paused outside the small donjon in Anwyk to watch his wife direct the servants who were helping her plant rosebushes in her private courtyard.

To his chagrin, a light blue veil covered her brown tresses. How he loved to brush his hands through those long, wavy locks at night. Bury his face deep in the fragrance of it every time they made love.

She grew more beautiful, more dear to him every day.

She looked up and saw him watching her.

The smile on her face made his heart pound.

"Greetings, my lord," she said. "Care to help us?"

"Nay," he said, closing the distance between them so that he could pull her into his arms. "I rather like watching you." Then he leaned and whispered in her ear, "Especially when you bend over."

She squealed playfully at that. "You are in a mood this day."

"My lady, I am in *that* mood every time I look at you."

She laughed at him, then gave him a smart, chaste kiss. "Be off with you, knave. I have work to be about."

Simon turned his head so that he could watch the youngest member of the work crew. The youth had been nothing more than a boy when he'd been imprisoned.

Stryder had sent him to them so that they could watch over and help him adjust to his newfound freedom. Under Kenna's care and kindness, the boy had come a long way in only a few weeks.

"You do great work, my lady," he said seriously. At least until the imp in him took over again.

He lifted Kenna up in his arms.

She shrieked in protest. "What are you doing?"

"It seems to me you still have a promise to fulfill."

"And what promise is that?"

"That you'd give me a child by next summer."

He kissed her then and carried her away from the others. Carried her to the castle that belonged to a man who had once had no prospects at all.

Well, he had them now, and he intended to make sure that he spent his life letting Kenna know just how grateful he was to her.

Simon sprinted to their upstairs room. He closed the door and frowned as he saw a letter on his bed.

Setting his wife down, he went to it.

Kenna came to stand behind him as he saw his own baronial seal. "What is this?" he asked. They hadn't written to each other since before their marriage.

She shrugged. "Read it and see."

He broke the seal and opened it.

My dearest champion,

Since all good news seems to come in written form, I thought I should tell you this.

I have kept my promise.

Ever your lady,
K

Postscriptum
The K is for Kenna just in case you might mistake me for another.

Simon's hand shook as he understood her meaning.

She carried his child.

He wanted to shout out in jubilation. He turned to face her. "Are you sure?"

She nodded.

Laughing aloud, he grabbed her up in his arms and whirled her around.

"Thank you," he said, then he lowered her down his body to capture her lips.

Every dream he'd ever possessed had come true, and he owed it all to one woman. . . .

His Kenna.

Multi-published, romance author, **SHERRILYN KENYON** knows men. She lives outside of Nashville, Tennessee, with her husband and three sons. Raised in the middle of eight boys, and currently outnumbered by the Y chromosome in her home, she realizes the most valuable asset a woman has for coping with men is a sense of humor—not to mention a large trash bag and a pair of tongs.

Writing as **KINLEY MACGREGOR** and Sherrilyn Kenyon, she is the best-selling author of several series including, *The Dark-Hunters, Brotherhood of the Sword* and *The MacAllisters.*

Julia Quinn
A Tale of Two Sisters

This one's for all those folks at all those Starbucks, who made me all those triple grande, nonfat, light vanilla Caramel Macchiatos, and then didn't say a word while I sat for hours, tapping away on my laptop.

And also for Paul, even though he says coffee is a "nasty, dirty, filthy habit," and that "no good ever came of it." (This apparently includes the time my mother almost missed her flight because we stopped for a latte on the way to the airport.)

I don't know how you ever made it through med school, babe.

Chapter 1

Ned Blydon let out a weary exhale and looked both ways before nudging his horse out of the stables. It was exhausting work, avoiding three women at once.

First, there was his sister. Arabella Blydon Blackwood had firm opinions about how her brother ought to live his life, opinions she wasn't shy about sharing.

Opinions that Ned had consistently ignored for the past eight or so years.

Belle was normally a perfectly lovely and reasonable person, but she seemed to feel that her status as a married woman gave her the right to dictate to him, even though he was, as he often reminded her, her elder by over a year.

Then there was his cousin Emma, who was, if possible, even more outspoken than Belle. The only reason she wasn't tied with his sister on his current list of women-to-be-avoided-at-all-costs was that she was seven months with child and couldn't move around very quickly.

If Ned was a bad person because he would run to escape a waddling pregnant woman, then so be it. His peace of mind was worth it.

Finally, he was ashamed to admit, there was Lydia.

He groaned. In three days' time, Lydia Thornton would be his wife. And while there was nothing particularly wrong with her, the time he spent in her company was all awkward pauses and looking at the clock.

It wasn't what he'd imagined for marriage, but it was, he had come to accept, all he could expect.

He'd spent the last eight seasons in London, a charming man about town, a bit of a rake, but not so much that nervous mamas steered their daughters away from him. He'd never consciously avoided marriage—well, not in the last few years, anyway—but at the same time, he'd never met any woman who inspired passion within him.

Desire, yes. Lust, most certainly. But true passion? Never.

And so as he approached the age of thirty the practical side of his mind had taken over, and he had decided that if he wasn't going to marry for love, he might as well marry for land.

Enter Lydia Thornton.

Twenty-two years of age, pretty blond hair, attractive gray eyes, reasonably intelligent and in good health. And her dowry consisted of twenty acres of very nice land that ran right along the eastern border of Middlewood, one of the Blydon family's smaller estates.

Twenty acres wasn't much for a man with family holdings scattered across the south of England, but Middlewood was the only property that Ned could truly call his own. The rest belonged to his father, the Earl of Worth, and would until he died and passed the title on to his son.

And while Ned understood that the earldom was his birthright and privilege, he was in no hurry to assume the rights and responsibilities that went with it. He was one of the few men in his circle of acquaintances who actually *liked* his parents; the last thing he wanted to do was bury them.

His father, in his infinite wisdom, had understood that a man such as Ned needed something of his own, and so on Ned's twenty-fourth birthday, he'd deeded over Middlewood, one of the earldom's unentailed properties.

Maybe it was the elegant house, maybe it was the superb trout pond. Maybe it was just because it was his, but Ned loved Middlewood, every last square inch of it.

And so when it had occurred to him that his neighbor's eldest daughter had actually grown old enough to marry—well, it had all seemed to make perfect sense.

Lydia Thornton was perfectly nice, perfectly dowered, perfectly attractive, perfectly everything.

Just not perfect for him.

But it wasn't fair to hold that against her. He'd known what he was doing when he'd proposed. He just hadn't expected his impending marriage to feel quite so much like a noose around his neck. Although in truth, it hadn't seemed so wretched until this past week, when he had come to Thornton Hall to celebrate the upcoming nuptials with his and Lydia's families. Not to mention fifty or so of their closest friends.

It was remarkable how many complete strangers could be found among such a group.

It was enough to drive a man mad, and Ned held little doubt that he'd be a candidate for

Bedlam by the time he left the village church that Saturday morning with his ancestral family ring firmly ensconced on Lydia's finger.

"Ned! Ned!"

It was a shrill female voice. One he knew all too well.

"Don't try to avoid me! I see you!"

Bloody hell. It was his sister, and if all went as it usually did, that meant that Emma would be waddling along behind her, ready to offer her own lecture as soon as Belle paused for breath.

And—good God—come tomorrow his mother would be in residence to complete the terrifying triumvirate.

Ned shuddered—an actual physical shudder—at the thought.

He spurred his horse into a trot—the fastest he could manage so close to the house—planning to move into a full-fledged gallop once he could do so without endangering anyone.

"Ned!" Belle yelled, clearly unconcerned with decorum, dignity, or even danger as she came running down the lane, heedless of the tree root that snaked out into her path.

Thud!

Ned closed his eyes in agony as he drew his horse to a halt. He was never going to escape now. When he opened them, Belle was sitting in the dust, looking rather disgruntled but no less determined.

"Belle! Belle!"

Ned looked past Belle to see his cousin Emma waddling forward as fast as her rather ducklike body would allow.

"Are you all right?" Emma asked Belle before turning immediately to Ned and asking, "Is she all right?"

He leveled a gaze at his sister. "Are you all right?"

"Are *you* all right?" she countered.

"What kind of question is *that*?"

"A rather pertinent one," Belle retorted, grabbing onto Emma's outstretched hand and hauling herself to her feet, nearly toppling the pregnant woman in the process. "You've been avoiding me all week—"

"We've only been here two days, Belle."

"Well, it *feels* like a week."

Ned could not disagree.

Belle scowled at him when he did not reply. "Are you going to sit there on your horse, or are you going to dismount and speak with me like a reasonable human being?"

Ned pondered that.

"It's rather rude," Emma put in, "to remain

on horseback while two ladies are on their feet."

"You're not ladies," he muttered, "you're relations."

"Ned!"

He turned to Belle. "Are you certain you're not injured in any manner?"

"Yes, of course, I—" Belle's bright blue eyes widened once she discerned his intentions. "Well, actually, my ankle feels a little tender, and—" She coughed a few times for good measure, as if that might help to prove her claim of a turned ankle.

"Good," Ned said succinctly. "Then you won't require my help." And with that he spurred his horse forward and left them behind. Rude maybe, but Belle was his sister and she had to love him no matter what. Besides, she was only going to try to talk with Ned about his upcoming marriage, and that was the last thing he wanted to discuss.

He took off heading west, firstly because that was the direction of the road offering the easiest escape, but also because he could soon expect to find himself among Lydia's dowered lands. A reminder of why he was getting married might be just the thing he needed to keep his mind on an even keel. They were lovely lands, green and fertile, with a picturesque pond and a small apple orchard.

"You like apples," Ned muttered under his breath. "You've always liked apples."

Apples were good. It would be nice to have an orchard.

Almost worth marrying for.

"Pies," he continued. "Tarts. Endless pies and tarts. And applesauce."

Applesauce was a good thing. A very good thing. If he could just keep equating his marriage with applesauce, he ought to retain his sanity until the following week, at the very least.

He squinted into the distance, trying to judge how much farther it was until he reached Lydia's lands. Not much more than five minutes' ride, he should think, and—

"Hello! Hello! Hell-oooooo!"

Oh, wonderful. Another female.

Ned slowed his mount, looking around as he tried to figure out just where the voice was coming from.

"Over here! Please help!"

He turned to his right and then behind him, and immediately ascertained why he hadn't noticed the girl before. She was sitting on the ground, her green riding habit a rather effective camouflage against the grass and low shrubs around her. Her hair, long and medium brown, was pulled back in a manner that would never have passed muster in a London drawing room, but on her the queue was rather fetching.

"Good day!" she called out, sounding a bit uncertain now.

He drew to a reluctant halt and dismounted. He wanted nothing more than a bit of privacy, preferably on horseback as he rode hell-for-leather over rolling fields, but he was a gentleman (despite his admittedly shabby treatment of his sister), and he couldn't ignore a lady in distress.

"Is something amiss?" he inquired mildly as he approached.

"I've turned my ankle, I'm afraid," she said, wincing as she tried to tug off her boot. "I was walking, and—"

She looked up, blinked her large gray eyes several times, then said, "Oh."

"Oh?" he echoed.

"You're Lord Burwick."

"Indeed."

Her smile was oddly lacking in warmth. "I'm Lydia's sister."

* * *

Charlotte Thornton felt like a fool, and she hated feeling like a fool.

Not, she supposed, that anyone was particularly fond of the sensation, but she found it especially irritating, as she had always judged common sense to be the most laudable of traits.

She'd gone for a walk, eager to escape the throngs of rather annoying houseguests who'd invaded her home for the week preceding her older sister's wedding.

Why Lydia needed her nuptials witnessed by fifty people she didn't know, Charlotte would never understand. And that didn't even count everyone who was planning to arrive on the day of the ceremony.

But Lydia had wanted it, or rather, their mother had wanted it, and so now their house was filled to the rafters, as were the neighbors' homes and all the local inns. Charlotte was going straight out of her mind. And so, before anyone could flag her down and beg her assistance in some *terribly* important endeavor, like making sure that the best chocolate was delivered to the Duchess of Ashbourne, she'd donned her riding habit and made her escape.

Except that when she'd reached the stables, she'd discovered that the grooms had given her mare to one of the guests. They had insisted that her mother had given them permission to do so, but that had done little to brighten Charlotte's foul mood.

So she'd taken off on foot, stomping down the lane, looking for nothing but a bit of blessed peace and quiet, and then she'd gone and stepped in a mole hole. She hadn't even hit the ground before she'd realized that she'd turned her ankle. It was already swelling in her boot, and this day progressing as it was, of course, she was wearing her boots that pulled on, not the ones with the flimsy black laces that would have made removal so quick and easy.

The only bright spot in her morning was that it wasn't raining, although with her luck lately, not to mention the gray sky above, Charlotte wasn't even counting on that.

Now her savior was none other than Edward Blydon, Viscount Burwick, the man who was supposed to marry her older sister in three days' time. According to Lydia, he was a complete rake and not at all sensitive to a woman's tender emotions.

Charlotte wasn't precisely certain what constituted a tender emotion, and in fact she rather doubted that she herself had ever possessed such a feeling, but still, it didn't speak well of the young viscount. Lydia's description had made him sound like a bit of a boor, and an overbearing one at that. Not at all the sort of gentleman best suited to rescue a damsel in distress.

And he certainly looked like a rake. Charlotte might not be the romantic dreamer that Lydia was, but that didn't mean she was oblivious to a man's aspect and appearance. Edward Blydon—or Ned, rather, as she'd heard Lydia mention him—possessed the most startlingly bright blue eyes she had ever seen grace a human face. On anyone else, they might have seemed effeminate (especially with those sinfully long dark lashes), but Ned Blydon was tall and broad, and anyone would have realized that he was rather lean and athletic under his coat and breeches, even someone who wasn't really looking, which she most assuredly was *not*.

Oh, very well, she was. But how could she help it? He was looming over her like some dangerous god, his powerful frame blocking out what was left of the sun.

"Ah, yes," he said, somewhat condescendingly, in her opinion. "Caroline."

Caroline? They'd only been introduced *three* times. "Charlotte," she bit off.

"Charlotte," he repeated, with grace enough to offer her a sheepish smile.

"There *is* a Caroline," fairness compelled her to say. "She's fifteen."

"And thus too young to be off on her own, I imagine."

Implying that *she* was too young as well. Her eyes narrowed at the vague sarcasm in his voice. "Are you scolding me?"

"I wouldn't dream of it."

"Because I'm *not* fifteen," she said pertly, "and I go for walks by myself all the time."

"I'm sure you do."

"Well, not walks very often," she admitted, somewhat mollified by his bland expression, "but I do ride."

"Why aren't you riding, then?" he asked, kneeling down beside her.

She could feel her lips twist into an extremely unpleasant expression. "Someone took my mare."

His brows rose. "Someone?"

"A guest," she ground out.

"Ah," he said sympathetically. "There seem to be quite a lot of those milling about."

"Like a plague of locusts," she muttered, before realizing that she had just been unforgivably rude to a man who thus far was not proving to be the unpleasant boor her sister had painted him to be. One man's locusts were another man's wedding guests, after all. "I'm sorry," she said quickly, glancing up at him with hesitant eyes.

"Don't be," he replied. "Why do you suppose *I'm* out for a ride?"

She blinked. "But it's your wedding."

"Yes," he said wryly, "it is, isn't it?"

"Well, yes," she replied, taking his query literally, even though she knew he hadn't intended it thus, "it is."

"I'll let you in on a little secret," he said, lightly touching his hands to her boot. "May I?"

She nodded, then tried not to whimper as he tugged the boot off her foot.

"Weddings," he announced, "are for women."

"One would think they require at least *one* man," she returned.

"True," he acceded, at last easing the boot all the way off. "But truly, does the groom have much to do besides stand there and say, 'I will'?"

"He has to *propose*."

"Pfft." He gave a dismissive snort. "That

takes but a moment and besides, it's done months in advance. By the time one gets around to the actual wedding, one can hardly remember it."

Charlotte knew his words to be true. Not that anyone had ever bothered to propose to her, but when she'd asked Lydia what the viscount had said when he'd asked her to marry him, Lydia had just sighed and said, "I don't recall. Something terribly ordinary, I'm sure."

Charlotte offered a commiserating smile to her future brother-in-law. Lydia had never spoken highly of him, but he really didn't seem like a bad sort at all. In fact, she rather felt a kinship with him in that they'd both fled Thornton Hall looking for peace and quiet.

"I don't think you've broken it," he said, lightly pressing his fingers to her ankle.

"No, I'm quite sure I haven't. It'll be better by tomorrow, I'm certain."

"Are you?" Ned asked, quirking one corner of his mouth into a dubious expression. "I'm certain it won't. It'll be at least a week before you're able to walk without discomfort."

"Not a week!"

"Well, perhaps not. I'm certainly no surgeon. But you'll be limping for a while yet."

She sighed, a long-suffering sort of sound. "I shall look splendid as Lydia's maid of honor, don't you think?"

Ned hadn't realized that she'd been offered the position; in truth, he'd paid only scant attention to the wedding details. But he was rather good at feigning interest, so he nodded politely and murmured something that wasn't meant to make much sense, then tried not to look quite so surprised when she exclaimed, "Maybe I won't have to do it now!" She looked at him with palpable excitement, her wide, gray eyes gleaming. "I can pass it off to Caroline and hide in the back."

"In the back?"

"Of the church," she explained. "Or the front. I don't care where. But maybe now I won't have to take part in this wretched ceremony. I—oh!" Her hand flew to her mouth as her cheeks turned instantly red. "I'm sorry. It's *your* wretched ceremony, isn't it?"

"As wretched as it is to admit it," he said, unable to keep a sparkle of amusement from his face, "yes."

"It's a yellow dress," she grumbled, as if that would explain everything.

He glanced down at her green riding habit, quite certain that he would never understand the workings of the female brain. "I beg your pardon?"

"I'm supposed to wear a yellow dress," she told him. "As if having to sit through the ceremony isn't bad enough, Lydia picked out a yellow dress for me."

"Er, why will the ceremony be so dreadful?" Ned asked, suddenly feeling rather afraid.

"Lydia ought to know I look wretched in yellow," Charlotte said, completely ignoring his query. "Like a plague victim. The congregation is likely to run screaming from the church."

Ned should have felt alarmed by the thought of his wedding erupting into mass hysteria; instead, he was alarmed by the fact that he found the image rather comforting. "What's wrong with the ceremony?" he asked again, giving his head a little shake as he reminded himself that she hadn't answered his previous question.

She pursed her lips as she poked her fingers against her ankle, paying him little mind. "Have you *seen* the program?"

"Er, no." Which he was beginning to think might have been a mistake.

She looked up, her large, gray eyes clearly pitying him. "You should have done," was all she said.

"Miss Thornton," he said, using his sternest voice.

"It's very long," she said. "And there will be birds."

"Birds?" he echoed, choking on the word until his entire body collapsed into a spasm of coughing.

Charlotte waited for his fit to subside before her face assumed a suspiciously innocent expression, and she asked, "You didn't know?"

He found himself unable to do anything but scowl.

She laughed, a decidedly mellow and musical sound, then blurted out, "You're not at all how Lydia described you."

Now *that* was interesting. "Am I not?" he asked, keeping his voice carefully mild.

She swallowed, and he could tell that she regretted her loose tongue. Still, she had to say something, so he waited patiently until she tried to cover for herself with, "Well, in truth, she hasn't said much of anything. Which I suppose led me to believe you were a bit aloof."

He sat down on the grass beside her. It was rather comfortable to be in her presence after having to be at constant attention among all the crowds back at Thornton Hall. "And why would you reach that conclusion?" he asked.

"I don't know. I suppose I just imagined that if you weren't aloof, your conversations with her would have been a bit more . . ." She frowned. "How do I say it?"

"Conversational?"

"Exactly!" She turned to him with an exceptionally sunny smile, and Ned found himself sucking in his breath. Lydia had never smiled at him like that.

Worse, he'd never wanted her to.

But Charlotte Thornton . . . now there was a woman who knew how to smile. It was on her lips, in her eyes, radiating from her very skin.

Hell, by now that smile was traveling down his midsection to areas that should never be touched by one's sister-in-law.

He should have stood immediately, should have made up some sort of excuse about getting her back home—anything to end their little interview, because there was nothing more unacceptable than desiring one's sister-in-law, which was exactly what she would be in three days' time.

But his excuses would have made rather transparent falsehoods, as he'd just told her that he wanted nothing more than to escape the pre-wedding festivities.

Not to mention the fact that those unmentionable areas of his anatomy were behaving in a manner that might be termed a bit too obvious when one was in a standing position.

And so he decided simply to enjoy her company, since he hadn't enjoyed anyone's company since he'd arrived two days earlier. Hell, she was the first person he'd come across who wasn't trying to congratulate him or, in the case of his sister and cousin, attempting to tell him how to conduct his life.

The truth was, he found Charlotte Thornton rather charming, and since he was quite certain his reaction to her smile was a freakish, one-time sort of occurrence—not to mention that it wasn't terribly urgent, just potentially embarrassing—well, there was really no harm in prolonging their encounter.

"Right," she was saying, clearly oblivious to his physical distress. "And if your conversations with her had been more conversational, I imagine she'd have had more about which to tell me."

Ned rather thought it was a good thing that his future wife wasn't one for indiscreet talk. Score one for Lydia. "Perhaps," he said, a little more sharply than he ought, "she doesn't tell tales."

"Lydia?" Charlotte said with a snort. "Hardly. She always tells me everything about—"

"About what?"

"Nothing," she said quickly, but she didn't meet his eyes.

Ned knew better than to push. Whatever it was that she'd been about to say, it wasn't complimentary toward Lydia, and if there was one thing he could already tell about Charlotte Thornton, it was that she was loyal when it counted. And she wasn't going to reveal any of her sister's secrets.

Funny. It hadn't even occurred to him that a woman like Lydia might have secrets. She'd always seemed so . . . bland. In fact, it had been that blandness that had convinced him their marriage was not an ill-advised endeavor. If one wasn't going to love one's wife, one might as well not be bothered by her.

"Do you suppose it's safe to return?" Ned queried, motioning with his head in the direction of Thornton Hall. He'd much rather stay here with Charlotte, but he supposed it would be rather unseemly to remain alone in her company for very much longer. Besides, he was feeling a bit more . . . settled now, and he thought he ought to be able to stand up without embarrassing himself.

Not that an innocent like Charlotte Thornton would probably even know what it meant for a man to have a bulge in his breeches.

"Safe?" she echoed.

He smiled. "From the plague of locusts."

"Oh." Her face fell. "I doubt it. I think Mother has arranged for some sort of ladies' luncheon."

He smiled broadly. "Excellent."

"For you, perhaps," she retorted. "I'm probably expected."

"The maid of honor?" he asked with a wicked smile. "For certain you're expected. In fact, they probably can't begin without you."

"Bite your tongue. If they get hungry enough, they won't even notice I'm gone."

"Hungry, eh? And here I thought women ate like birds."

"That's only for the benefit of men. When you're gone, we go mad for ham and chocolate."

"Together?"

She laughed, a rich, musical sound. "You're quite funny," she said with a smile.

He leaned forward with his most dangerous expression. "Don't you know you're never supposed to tell a rake that he's funny?"

"Oh, you can't possibly be a rake," she said dismissively.

"And why is that?"

"You're marrying my sister."

He shrugged. "Rakes have to get married eventually."

"Not to Lydia," she said with a snort. "She'd be the worst sort of wife for a rake." She looked up at him with another one of those wide, sunny smiles. "But you have nothing about which to worry, because you are obviously a very sensible man."

"I don't know that I've ever been called sensible by a woman," he mused.

"I can assure you I mean it as the highest of compliments."

"I can see that you do," he murmured.

"Common sense seems like such an easy thing," she said, punctuating her words with a wave of her hand. "I can't understand why more people don't possess it."

Ned chuckled despite himself. It was a sentiment he shared, although he had never thought to phrase it in quite those terms.

And then she sighed, a soft, weary sound that went straight to his heart. "I'd best be getting back," she said, not sounding at all excited by the prospect.

"You haven't been gone long," he pointed out, absurdly eager to prolong their conversation.

"*You* haven't been gone long," she corrected. "I left an hour ago. And you're right. I can't avoid the luncheon. Mother will be terribly cross, which I suppose I could bear, since Mother is often terribly cross, but it wouldn't be fair to Lydia. I am her maid of honor, after all."

He rose to his feet and held out his hand. "You're a very good sister, aren't you?"

She looked at him intently as she placed her fingers against his palm. Almost as if she were trying to gauge his very soul. "I try to be," she said quietly.

Ned winced as he thought of his sister, yelling up at him as she sat in the dust. He probably ought to go and apologize. She was his only sibling, after all.

But as he rode back to Thornton Hall, Charlotte Thornton tucked neatly behind him in the saddle, her arms around his waist, he didn't think of Belle at all.

Or Lydia.

Chapter 2

The luncheon was just as Charlotte had imagined it would be.

Dull.

Not quite unbearable. The food was rather good, after all. But definitely dull.

She filled her plate with ham and chocolate (she could hardly believe her mother had served both at the same time, and she simply had to take servings of each in the viscount's honor) and found a chair in the corner, where she hoped no one would bother her.

And no one did, at least not until the very end, when Lydia slid into the seat next to her.

"I need to speak with you," Lydia said in a harsh whisper.

Charlotte looked to the right, then to the left,

trying to discern why Lydia felt the need to announce it. "Then speak," she said.

"Not here. Privately."

Charlotte chewed her last bite of chocolate cake and swallowed. "You'd be hard-pressed to find any place less private," she commented.

Lydia shot her an extremely annoyed look. "Meet me in your bedchamber in five minutes?"

Charlotte glanced toward the festivities with a doubtful expression. "Do you really think you're going to be able to escape in five minutes? Mother looks as if she's enjoying herself exceedingly well, and I doubt she'll want—"

"I'll be there," Lydia assured her. "Trust me. You go now, so no one sees us leave together."

That was more than Charlotte could let pass without comment. "Really, Lydia," she said, "we're sisters. I hardly think anyone will take notice if we leave a room together."

"All the same," Lydia said.

Charlotte decided not to ask what, precisely, was all the same. Lydia tended to assume the air of a Drury Lane actress when she had it in her head that she was talking about something important, and Charlotte had long since realized that it was often best not to inquire about her convoluted thoughts. "Very well," she said, setting her plate down on the empty chair beside her. "I'll be there."

"Good," Lydia said, looking furtively around her. "And not a word to anyone."

"For heaven's sake," Charlotte said, even though Lydia had already walked away. "Who would I tell?"

"Oh, my lord!" Charlotte did not so much say as chirp. "Fancy meeting you here."

Ned glanced slowly around the hall. Hadn't he just dropped her off right here, barely an hour ago? "It's not so very strange a coincidence," he felt compelled to point out.

"Er, yes," she said, "but seeing as how our paths have never crossed before, twice in one day seems quite remarkable."

"Indeed," he said, although he didn't think it remarkable at all. Then he motioned to the woman at his side. "May I introduce you to my sister? Miss Thornton, my sister, Lady Blackwood. Belle, Miss Charlotte Thornton. She is Lydia's younger sister," he explained to Belle.

"We have been introduced," Belle said with a gentle smile, "although we have never been given the opportunity to exchange anything other than the most basic of pleasantries."

"I'm pleased to further our acquaintance, Lady Blackwood," Charlotte said.

"Please, do call me Belle. We will be sisters of a sort in just a few days' time."

She nodded. "And I am Charlotte."

"I met Charlotte earlier this morning," Ned said, not at all certain why he was offering that information.

"You had never met Lydia's sister?" Belle asked, surprised.

"No, of course I had," he said. "I just meant that I stumbled across her outside."

"I turned my ankle," Charlotte said. "He was prodigiously helpful."

"How *is* your ankle?" Ned asked. "You really shouldn't be walking on it."

"I'm not. I'm—"

"Limping?"

She gave him a guilty smile. "Yes."

"I saw her out on the fields," Ned said, directing his explanation to his sister, but not really looking at her. "I'd gone to escape the crowds."

"As had I," Charlotte put in. "But I had to walk."

"One of the grooms gave her horse to a guest," Ned said. "Can you believe it?"

"My mother did give him permission to do so," Charlotte said with a roll of her eyes.

"Still."

She nodded her agreement. "Still."

Belle gaped at the two of them. "Do you realize you're finishing each other's sentences?"

"No, we weren't," Charlotte said, just as Ned offered a considerably more disdainful, "Don't be absurd."

"We were talking rather quickly," Charlotte said.

"And ignoring you," Ned put in.

"But we weren't finishing each other's sentences," Charlotte added.

"Well, you did just then," Belle said.

Charlotte's response was nothing more than a blank stare. "I'm sure you're mistaken," she murmured.

"I'm sure I'm not," Belle replied, "but it hardly signifies."

An awkward silence descended upon the group, until Charlotte cleared her throat and said, "I must leave, I'm afraid. I'm meant to meet Lydia in my room."

"Do give her my regards," Ned said smoothly, wondering why she winced right after she told him she was meeting Lydia.

"I will," she said, and now her cheeks were turning slightly pink.

Ned felt his brow furrow in thought. Was

Charlotte lying about meeting Lydia upstairs? And if so, why would she think he'd care? What secret could she possibly possess that would affect him?

"Have a care with that ankle," he said. "You might want to prop it up on a pillow once you get to your room."

"An excellent idea," she said with a nod. "Thank you."

And with that, she limped around the corner and disappeared from view.

"Well, that was interesting," Belle said, once Charlotte was obviously out of earshot.

"What was interesting?" Ned asked.

"That. Her. Charlotte."

He stared at her uncomprehendingly. "I speak only English, Belle."

She jerked her head in the direction in which Charlotte had departed. "That's the one you ought to be marrying."

"Oh, God, Belle, *don't* start."

"I know I've said—"

"I don't know what you *haven't* said," he snapped.

She glared at him, then glanced furtively about. "We can't talk here," she said.

"We're not talking anywhere."

"Yes, we are," she returned, yanking him into a nearby salon. Once she'd shut the door, she turned on him with the full force of sisterly concern. "Ned, you must listen to me. You cannot marry Lydia Thornton. She is all wrong for you."

"Lydia is perfectly acceptable," he said, his tone clipped.

"Do you hear what you're saying?" she burst out. "Perfectly acceptable? You don't want to marry someone acceptable, Ned. You want to marry someone who makes your heart sing, someone who makes you smile every time she enters the room. Trust me. I know."

He did know. Belle and her husband loved each other with a fierce devotion that should have been nauseating to behold, but somehow Ned had always just found it rather warm and comforting.

Until now, when it was starting to make him feel—good God—jealous.

Which of course only served to put him in a ripping bad mood.

"Ned," Belle persisted, "are you even listening to me?"

"Very well, then," he snapped, unable to prevent himself from taking his foul temper out on his sister, "you tell me how I'm meant to get out of it. Am I supposed to jilt her three days before the ceremony?"

Belle did nothing but blink, but Ned wasn't fooled. His sister's brain was working so fast he was surprised he didn't see steam coming out of her ears. If there was a way to break an engagement three days before a wedding, he could be sure that Belle would think of it.

She was silent for just long enough that Ned thought their conversation might actually be over. "If that's all, then," he said, stepping toward the door.

"Wait!"

He let out a weary groan. It had really been too much to hope for.

"Do you realize what you said?" she asked, placing her hand on his sleeve.

"No," he said baldly, hoping that might be the end of it.

"You asked me to tell you how you could get out of your marriage. Do you know what that means? It means you *want* to get out of it," she finished, rather smugly, in his opinion.

"It means nothing of the sort," Ned snapped. "We can't all be lucky enough to marry for love, Belle. I'm almost thirty. If it hasn't happened yet, it's not going to. And I'm not getting any younger."

"You've hardly one foot in the grave," she scoffed.

"I'm getting married in three days' time," he said in a hard voice. "You ought to accustom yourself to the notion."

"Is the land really worth it?" Belle asked, her soft voice more arresting than any shout could ever be. "Twenty acres, Ned. Twenty acres for your life."

"I'm going to pretend you didn't say that," he said stiffly.

"Don't try to fool yourself into thinking this is anything but the most mercenary of endeavors," Belle said.

"And if it is," Ned returned, "am I so very different from most of our class?"

"No," she acceded, "but it's very different from *you*. This isn't right, Ned. Not for you."

He gave her an insolent stare. "May I go now? Does that conclude our interview?"

"You're better than this, Ned," she whispered. "You may not think so, but I know so."

He swallowed, his throat suddenly tight and dry. He knew she was right, and he hated it. "I'm marrying Lydia Thornton," he said, barely able to recognize his voice. "I made my decision months ago, and I will stand by it."

She closed her eyes for a moment. When she

reopened them, they were sad and shiny with tears. "You're ruining your life."

"No," he said shortly, unable to tolerate the discussion any further. "What I'm doing is leaving the room."

But when he reached the hall, he didn't know where to go.

It was a sensation he seemed to feel quite a bit lately.

"What took you so long?"

Charlotte started in surprise as she entered her room. Lydia was already there, pacing like a caged cat.

"Well," Charlotte said, "I turned my ankle earlier today and I can't walk very quickly. And—" She stopped herself. Better not to mention to Lydia that she'd stopped to talk with the viscount and his sister. Because she'd accidentally mentioned that she was planning to rendezvous with Lydia, and Lydia had told her quite explicitly not to tell anyone.

Not that Charlotte could see what the harm was. But still, Lydia didn't seem to be in the most even of moods. Charlotte saw no reason to disturb her further.

"How bad is it?" Lydia demanded.

"How bad is what?"

"Your ankle."

Charlotte looked down as if she'd forgotten it was even there. "Not too terrible, I suppose. I don't think I'll be winning any footraces anytime soon, but I don't need a cane."

"Good." Lydia stepped forward, her gray eyes—so very like Charlotte's own—glittering with excitement. "Because I need your help, and I can't have you lame."

"What are you talking about?"

Lydia's voice dropped to a whisper. "I'm eloping."

"With the viscount?"

"No, not with the viscount, you dolt. With Rupert."

"Rupert?" Charlotte nearly shouted.

"Will you keep your voice down?" Lydia hissed.

"Lydia, are you mad?"

"Madly in love."

"With Rupert?" Charlotte returned, unable to keep the disbelief from her voice.

Lydia gave her an affronted glare. "He's certainly more worthy of it than the viscount."

Charlotte thought about Rupert Marchbanks, the golden-haired self-described scholar who'd lived near the Thornton family for years. There was nothing wrong with Rupert, Charlotte supposed, if one preferred the dreamy type.

The dreamy type who talked too much, if such a thing could exist.

Charlotte grimaced. Such a thing most certainly did exist, and his name was Rupert. The last time he'd been over, Charlotte had feigned a head cold just to escape his never-ending drone about his new volume of poetry.

Charlotte had tried to read his work. It seemed only polite, after all, given that they were neighbors. But after a while, she'd simply had to give up. "Love" always rhymed with "dove," (Where, she wondered, did one locate that many doves in Derbyshire?) and "you" rhymed so often with "dew," that Charlotte had wanted to grab Rupert by the shoulders and yell, "Few, hue, new, woo, Waterloo!" Good gracious, even "moo" would have been preferable. Rupert's poetry could surely have been improved by a cow or two.

Saying moo on cue at Waterloo.

But Lydia had always seemed to like him a great deal, and in fact, Charlotte had heard her dub him "Brilliance personified," on more than one occasion. In retrospect, Charlotte probably should have realized what was going on, but in truth, she found Rupert so ridiculous that it was difficult to imagine anyone might see fit to fall in love with him.

"Lydia," she said, trying to keep her voice reasonable, "how can you possibly prefer Rupert to the viscount?"

"What do you know of it?" Lydia retorted. "You don't even know the viscount. And you *certainly*," she said with a haughty sniff, "don't know Rupert."

"I know he writes bloody awful poetry," Charlotte muttered.

"What did you just say?" Lydia demanded.

"Nothing," Charlotte said quickly, eager to avoid *that* conversation. "Just that I finally had a chance to speak with the viscount today, and he seems like a most reasonable man."

"He's awful," Lydia said, flinging herself onto Charlotte's bed.

Charlotte rolled her eyes. Please, no hysterics. "Lydia, he's not at all awful."

"He has never once recited poetry to me."

Which seemed to Charlotte like a point in his favor. "And this is a problem?"

"Charlotte, you would never understand. You're much too young."

"I'm eleven months younger than you!"

"In years, perhaps," Lydia said with a dramatic sigh. "But decades in experience."

"In *months*!" Charlotte nearly yelled.

Lydia placed a hand over her heart. "Charlotte, I don't want to have a row with you."

"Then stop talking like a madwoman. You're engaged to be married. In three days. Three days!" Charlotte threw up her hands in desperation. "You can't elope with Rupert Marchbanks!"

Lydia sat up so suddenly that Charlotte felt dizzy. "I can," she said. "And I will. With your help or without it."

"Lydia—"

"If you don't help me, I'll ask Caroline," Lydia warned.

"Oh, don't do that," Charlotte groaned. "For heaven's sake, Lydia, Caroline is barely fifteen. It wouldn't be fair to drag her into something like this."

"If you won't do it, I'll have no choice."

"Lydia, why did you accept the viscount if you dislike him so?"

Lydia opened her mouth to reply but then fell silent, and an uncharacteristically thoughtful expression crossed her face. For once she wasn't being dramatic for the sake of drama.

For once she wasn't going on about love and romance and poetry and tender emotions. And when Charlotte looked at her, for once all she saw was her beloved sister with whom she'd shared almost everything. Her very childhood, even.

"I don't know," Lydia finally said, her voice soft and tinged with regret. "I suppose I thought it was what was expected. No one ever thought I'd receive a proposal from an aristocrat. Mother and Father were so thrilled by the offer. He's quite eligible, you know."

"I'd gathered," Charlotte said, since she'd had no firsthand experience on the marriage mart herself. Unlike Lydia, she'd never had a London season. The money simply hadn't been there. But she hadn't minded. She'd spent her entire life in the southeast corner of Derbyshire, and she fully expected to spend the remainder there as well. The Thorntons weren't on their way to the poorhouse, but they were forever robbing Peter to pay Paul—it was *expensive,* Mrs. Thornton was always saying, to keep up appearances. Charlotte thought it a wonder that they'd never had to sell off the parcel of land that was serving as Lydia's dowry.

But Charlotte hadn't minded the lack of the season. The only way they would have been able to pay for one would have been to sell off every last horse in the stables, which her father was not willing to do. (And the truth was, neither was Charlotte; she was much too fond of her mare to trade her in for a couple of fancy dresses.) Besides, twenty-one wasn't considered too old to marry in these parts, and she certainly didn't feel like an old maid. Once Lydia was married and out of the house, Charlotte was sure that her parents would turn their attention to her.

Although she wasn't quite certain that was a *good* thing.

"And I suppose he's handsome," Lydia conceded.

Far more so than Rupert, Charlotte thought, but she kept that to herself.

"And he's wealthy," Lydia said with a sigh. "I'm not mercenary—"

Obviously not, if she was planning to wed penniless Rupert.

"—but it's difficult to refuse someone who is going to provide dowries and seasons for one's younger sisters."

Charlotte's eyes widened. "He is?"

Lydia nodded. "He hasn't said as much, but the money would be a pittance to him, and he did tell Father that he would make sure the Thorntons would be provided for. Which would have to include the lot of you, wouldn't it? You're Thorntons, just as much as I am."

Charlotte sank down into her desk chair. She had no idea that Lydia had been making such a sacrifice on her behalf. And on Caroline's and Georgina's, of course. Four daughters were a stunning burden on the Thornton family budget.

Then an awful thought occurred to Charlotte. Who was paying for the wedding festivities? The viscount, she supposed, but one could hardly expect him to do so if Lydia was going to jilt him. Had he already forwarded funds to the Thorntons, or had her mother made all of the (very expensive) arrangements with the understanding that Lord Burwick would reimburse her?

Which he most certainly would not do after he was left dangling at the altar.

Dear God, what a coil.

"Lydia," Charlotte said with renewed urgency, "you must marry the viscount. You must." And she told herself that she wasn't saying it simply to save her own skin or to save her family from ruin. She honestly believed that of Lydia's two suitors, Ned Blydon was the better man. Rupert wasn't *bad;* he wasn't going to do anything to hurt Lydia. But he spent money he didn't have and was forever talking about things like metaphysics and higher emotions.

Truly, it was often difficult to listen to him without laughing.

Ned, on the other hand, seemed solid and dependable. Handsome and intelligent, with a rapier wit, and when he spoke, it was about topics that were actually interesting. He was everything a woman could want in a husband, at least in Charlotte's opinion. Why Lydia couldn't see that, Charlotte would never understand.

"I can't do it," Lydia said. "I just can't. If I didn't love Rupert, it would be different. I could accept marriage to someone I didn't love if that were my only choice. But it's not. Don't you see? I have another choice. And I choose love."

"Are you certain you love Rupert?" Charlotte asked, knowing she was wincing as she asked the question. But what if this was just a silly infatuation? Lydia wouldn't be the first woman to ruin her life over a schoolgirl crush, but Charlotte didn't care about all those other unhappy women—they weren't her sister.

"I do," Lydia whispered. "With all of my heart."

Heart, Charlotte thought dispassionately. She thought she remembered Rupert rhyming it with *dart*. And once with *cart*, although that had seemed rather odd.

"And besides," Lydia added, "it's too late."

Charlotte glanced at the clock. "Too late for what?"

"For me to marry the viscount."

"I don't understand. The wedding isn't for another three days."

"I can't marry him."

Charlotte fought the urge to growl. "Yes, you've said as much."

"No, I mean I *can't*."

The word hung ominously in the air, and then Charlotte felt something explode inside of her. "Oh, no, Lydia, you didn't!"

Lydia nodded, and not with a single ounce of shame or remorse. "I did."

"How could you?" Charlotte demanded.

Lydia sighed dreamily. "How could I not?"

"Well," Charlotte retorted, "you could have said no."

"You can't say no to Rupert," Lydia murmured.

"Well, *you* can't, that's for certain."

"No one could," Lydia said, now smiling beatifically. "I'm so lucky he's chosen me."

"Oh, for the love of God," Charlotte muttered. She got up to pace the floor, then nearly howled in pain when she remembered her poor, abused ankle. "What are you going to do?"

"I'm going to marry Rupert," Lydia said, the dreamy look in her eyes rather startlingly replaced by clearheaded determination.

"You're not being fair to the viscount," Charlotte pointed out.

"I know," Lydia said, her face colored by enough remorse that Charlotte rather thought she meant it. "But I don't know what else to do. If I tell Mother and Father, they will lock me in my room for certain."

"Well, then, for heaven's sake, if you're going to elope, you must do so tonight. The sooner the better. It's not fair to leave the poor man hanging."

"I can't do it until Friday night."

"Why the devil not?"

"Rupert won't be ready."

"Well, then, make him be ready," Charlotte ground out. "If you don't elope until Friday night, no one will know until Saturday morning, and that means that everyone will be gathered in the church when *you* don't show up."

"We can't go without money," Lydia explained, "and Rupert can't get the bank to release his funds until Friday afternoon."

"I didn't know Rupert *had* funds," Charlotte muttered, unable to be polite at such a moment.

"He doesn't," Lydia said, apparently not taking any offense. "But he does receive a quarterly allowance from his uncle. And he won't get that until Friday. The bank is most insistent."

Charlotte groaned. It made sense. If she were in charge of doling out Rupert's quarterly allowance, she wouldn't give it to him a day earlier than the first of April, either.

Her head sank into her hands as her elbows rested on her knees. This was awful. She'd always been exceedingly good at finding the bright side of a situation. Even when things looked utterly bleak, she could usually find some interesting angle, some positive avenue to pursue that could lead out of trouble.

But not today.

Only one thing was certain. She was going to have to help Lydia elope, as distasteful as it seemed. It wouldn't be fair for Lydia to marry the viscount after she had already given herself to Rupert.

But it wasn't just about the viscount. Lydia

was her sister. Charlotte wanted her to be happy. Even if that meant Rupert Marchbanks for a brother-in-law.

But she couldn't shake the awful feeling in the pit of her stomach as she finally lifted her head to face Lydia and said, "Tell me what I need to do."

Chapter 3

"Ah-Ah-Ah-"

"Is she ill?" came a kindly female voice, belonging to whom, Charlotte would never know, as her eyes were closed in intense concentration.

Not to mention that they had to be closed for a convincing sneeze.

"Ah-CHOO!"

"I say!" Rupert Marchbanks said loudly, flicking his head so that his moppy blond locks flew out of his eyes. "I think I'm making her sneeze."

"Ah-CHOO!"

"Good gracious," Lydia said, all concern, "you don't look right at all."

Charlotte wanted—more than anything—to spear her sister with a sarcastic glare, but she could hardly do that in front of such a large audience, so instead—

"Ah-CHOO!"

"I *know* I'm making her sneeze," Rupert announced. "It has to be me. She started right when I came up next to her."

"Ah-CHOO!"

"Do you see," Rupert added, to no one in particular, "she's sneezing."

"That much," drawled a low male voice that could only belong to Ned Blydon, "is hardly disputable."

"Well, she can't be my partner in the scavenger hunt," Rupert said. "I'd probably kill the chit."

"Ah-CHOO!" Charlotte made that one a little softer, just for variation.

"Did you use a strange scent?" Lydia asked Rupert. "Or maybe a new soap?"

"A new scent!" Rupert exclaimed, his eyes flashing as if he'd just discovered, oh, say, gravity. "I *am* wearing a new scent! Had it sent specially from Paris, of course."

"Paris?" Lydia asked delightedly. "You don't say?"

Charlotte wondered if she could smack her sister in the ribs without anyone noticing.

"Yes," Rupert continued, always pleased to

have an audience for a discussion of fashion or hygiene. "It's a delightful combination of sandalwood and persimmon."

"Not perthimmon," Charlotte wailed, attempting to get back to the matter at hand. "Perthimmon makes me thneeze." She tried to make it sound like there were tears pouring forth from her eyes. Which of course there weren't, since until the day before she hadn't even been certain what a persimmon was.

Lydia looked over at Ned and batted her eyes. "Oh, my lord," she pleaded, "you must trade places with Rupert for the scavenger hunt. We can't expect Charlotte to spend the afternoon in his company."

Ned looked over at Charlotte with one raised brow. She looked back up at him and sneezed.

"No," he said, delicately drawing a handkerchief from his pocket and wiping his face, "clearly we can't."

Charlotte sneezed again, mentally sending up a short plea for forgiveness that she was certain she was going to have to expand upon in church on Sunday. What Lydia knew, and what in fact all of her sisters knew, was that no one could fake a sneeze like Charlotte. The Thornton girls had always had great fun with Charlotte's false sneezes. Luckily, their mother had never caught on, or she surely would have been looking upon the scene with great suspicion.

But as it was, Mrs. Thornton was busy with some guest or another, and so she'd just patted Charlotte on the back and instructed her to drink some water.

"Then you'll agree?" Lydia asked Ned. "We shall meet up again after the hunt, of course."

"Of course," he murmured. "I should be happy to pair with your sister. I could hardly refuse a damsel in such, ah—"

"Ah-CHOO!"

"—distress."

Charlotte flashed him a grateful smile. It seemed like the right thing to do.

"Oh, thank you, my lord," Lydia gushed. "We'll be off right away, then. I must remove Rupert from Charlotte's presence immediately."

"Oh yes," he said mildly, "you must."

Lydia and Rupert scurried off, leaving Charlotte alone with Ned. She looked up at him hesitantly. He was leaning against the wall as he stared down at her, his arms crossed.

Charlotte sneezed again, this time for real. Maybe she *was* allergic to Rupert. Heaven knew, whatever scent he'd doused himself in still hung rather noxiously in the air.

Ned raised his brows. "Perhaps," he suggested, "you'd do well with a bit of fresh air."

"Oh, yes," Charlotte said eagerly. If she were outside, there would be all sorts of logical things for her to look at. Trees, clouds, small furry animals—anything would do as long as she didn't have to look the viscount in the eye.

Because she had a sneaking suspicion that he knew she was faking it.

She'd told Lydia this wasn't going to work. Ned Blydon was clearly no milksop. He was not going to be taken in by batted eyelashes and a few false sneezes. But Lydia had insisted that she desperately needed the time alone with Rupert to plan their elopement, and thus they had to be partnered together for the scavenger hunt.

Their mother, unfortunately, had already drawn up the list of teams, and of course she'd put Lydia with her betrothed. Since Charlotte had been paired with Rupert, Lydia had come up with the mad scheme of having Charlotte sneeze her way into a switch. But Charlotte had never thought it was going to fool Ned, and in fact, just as soon as they were outside and had taken a few deep breaths of the crisp spring air, he smiled (but only ever-so-slightly) and said, "That was quite a performance."

"I beg your pardon?" she said, stalling for

time because really, what other choice did she have?

He glanced at his fingernails. "My sister has always faked a rather impressive sneeze."

"Oh, my lord, I assure you—"

"Don't," he said, his blue eyes catching hers rather directly. "Don't lie and make me lose respect for you, Miss Thornton. It was an excellent show, and it would have convinced anyone who wasn't related to my sister. Or you, I suppose."

"Fooled my mother," Charlotte muttered.

"It did, didn't it?" he said, looking a little . . . well, heavens, could he be *proud* of her?

"I would have fooled my father, too," she added, "if he'd been there."

"Do you want to tell me what it was about?"

"Not especially," she said brightly, taking advantage of the yes-or-no phrasing of his question.

"How is your ankle?" he asked, the sudden change of subject making her blink.

"Much improved," she said warily, not certain why he'd given her a reprieve. "It barely hurts now. It must have been less of a sprain than I'd thought."

He motioned toward the lane leading away

from the house. "Shall we walk?" he murmured.

She nodded hesitantly, because she couldn't quite believe that he would actually let the subject drop.

And of course, he didn't.

"I should tell you something about myself," he said, glancing up at the treetops in a deceptively casual manner.

"Er, what is that?"

"I generally get what I want."

"Generally?"

"Almost always."

She gulped. "I see."

He smiled mildly. "Do you?"

"I just said I did," she muttered.

"Therefore," he continued, neatly brushing her comment aside, "it's probably safe to assume that before we finish this scavenger hunt that your mother has so kindly devised as entertainment, you will tell me why you were working so hard to ensure that we were partners today."

"Er, I see," she said, thinking she sounded an absolute fool. But the alternative was silence, and given the tenor of the conversation, that didn't seem much better.

"Do you?" he asked, his voice terrifyingly silky. "Do you really?"

She *did* stay quiet for that; she couldn't imagine any right answer to that query.

"We could make things easy," he said, still carrying on as if he were talking about nothing less mundane than the weather, "and come clean right now. Or," he added meaningfully, "we could make things very, very difficult indeed."

"We?"

"I."

"I rather thought that," she mumbled.

"So," he said, "are you prepared to tell all?"

She looked him straight in the eye. "Are you always so calm and controlled?"

"No," he replied. "Not at all. In fact, I've been told that my temper is about as vicious as they come." He turned to her and smiled. "But I generally manage to lose it only once or twice a decade."

She swallowed nervously. "That's rather well done of you."

He continued to speak in that horribly controlled manner. "I don't see any reason to lose my temper now, do you? You seem a reasonable young lady."

"Very well," Charlotte said, since the bloody

man would probably tie her to a tree (with a calm smile on his face) if she didn't offer some sort of explanation. "As it happens, it had nothing to do with you."

"Really?"

"Is that so difficult to believe?"

He ignored her sarcasm. "Continue."

She thought quickly. "It's Rupert."

"Marchbanks?" he queried.

"Yes. I cannot abide him." Which wasn't so far from the truth, really. Charlotte had, on more than one occasion, thought she might go mad in his company. "The thought of spending the entire afternoon in his company set me into a positive panic. Although I must say, I didn't expect Lydia to offer to trade."

He seemed more interested in her previous sentence. "A panic, you say?"

She planted a level look squarely on his face. "You try spending three hours listening to him recite his poetry, and then we'll see who's panicking."

Ned winced. "He writes poetry?"

"And *talks* about writing poetry."

He looked pained.

"And when he's not doing that," Charlotte said, now getting into the spirit of the conversation, "he's talking about the analysis of poetry and explaining why most people lack the proper intellectual capabilities to understand poetry."

"But he does?"

"Of course."

He nodded slowly. "I should make a confession at this point. I'm not much for poetry myself."

Charlotte couldn't help herself; she beamed. "You're not?"

"It's not as if we speak in rhyme in our ordinary conversations," he said with a dismissive wave of his hand.

"I feel precisely the same way!" she exclaimed. "When, I ask you, have you ever said, 'My love is like a dove'?"

"Good God, I hope never."

Charlotte burst out laughing.

"I say!" he suddenly exclaimed, pointing up toward the canopy of leaves above them. "That tree! It's like my knee!"

"Oh, please," she said, trying to sound disdainful but laughing all the while. "Even I could do better."

He shot her a devilish grin, and Charlotte suddenly knew why he was reputed to have broken so many hearts in London. By God, it ought to be illegal to be so handsome. One smile and she felt it down to her toes.

"Oh, really?" he scoffed. "Better than—I saw my sister, and I . . ."

"And you what?" she prompted, as he floundered for words. "Poorly done of you to pick such a difficult word to rhyme, my lord."

"And I wished her!" he finished triumphantly. "Wished her to . . . well, I don't know where, but not to perdition." His face took on a very cheeky expression. "That would be impolite, don't you think?"

Charlotte would have replied, but she was laughing too hard.

"Right," he said, looking very satisfied with himself. "Well, now that we've established that I'm the better poet, what is the first item on our list?"

Charlotte looked down at the scrap of paper she'd forgotten she was clutching. "Oh, yes," she said. "The scavenger hunt. Um, let's see, it's a feather, although I don't think we have to find everything in order."

He tilted his head to the side as he tried to read her mother's neat handwriting. "What else do we need?"

"A red brick; a hyacinth bloom—that will be

easy, I know exactly where they are in the garden; two sheets of writing paper, not from the same set; a yellow ribbon; and a piece of glass. A piece of glass?" she echoed, looking up. "Where on earth are we supposed to find that? I don't think Mother intended us to be breaking windows."

"I'll steal my sister's spectacles," he said offhandedly.

"Oh. That's quite clever." She gave him an admiring glance. "And devious, too."

"Well, she *is* my sister," he said modestly. "Even if I don't wish her to perdition. But she's quite blind without them, and one must be devious in all dealings with siblings, don't you agree?"

"Certainly dealings of this nature," Charlotte said. She and her sisters generally got along well, but they were forever teasing and pulling pranks on one another. Stealing spectacles to win a scavenger hunt—now that was something she could respect.

She watched his face as he gazed off in the distance, his mind apparently somewhere else. And she couldn't help but reflect upon what a good sort he'd turned out to be.

Ever since she'd agreed to help Lydia jilt him

she'd felt rather guilty about it, but not until now had she felt truly horrible.

She had a feeling that the viscount didn't love her sister; in fact, she was quite certain he did not. But he *had* proposed to her, so he must have wanted Lydia as a bride for some reason or another. And like all men, he had his pride. And she, Charlotte Eleanor Thornton, who liked to think of herself as an upstanding and principled human being, was actually helping to orchestrate his downfall.

Charlotte suspected that there were more embarrassing things in life than being left at the altar, but at that moment, she couldn't think of a one.

He was going to be mortified.

And hurt.

Not to mention furious.

And he'd probably kill her.

The worst part was, Charlotte had no idea how to stop it. Lydia was her sister. She had to help her, didn't she? Didn't she owe her first loyalties to her flesh and blood? And besides, if there was one thing this afternoon had shown her, it was that Lydia and the viscount really wouldn't suit. Good God, Lydia *expected* her suitors to speak to her in poetry. Charlotte couldn't imagine they'd make it through more than a month of marriage before trying to murder one another.

But still . . . this wasn't right. Ned—when had she begun to think of him by his Christian name?—didn't deserve the shabby treatment he was about to receive. He might be a bit high-handed, and he certainly was arrogant, but underneath all that, he seemed to be a good man—sensible and funny and at heart a true gentleman.

And that was when Charlotte made a solemn vow. There was no way she would allow him to wait in the church on Saturday morning. She might not be able to stop Lydia and Rupert from eloping—she might even be *helping* them—but she would do all in her power to save Ned from the worst sort of embarrassment.

She gulped nervously. It meant seeking him out in the dead of night, just as soon as Lydia was safely away, but she had no other choice. Not if she wanted to live comfortably with her conscience.

"You look rather serious of a sudden," he remarked.

She started in surprise at the sound of his voice. "Just woolgathering," she said quickly, glad that about this, at least, she wasn't lying.

"Your sister and the poet seem to be in rather deep conversation," he said quietly, nodding his head to the left.

Charlotte jerked her head around. Sure enough, Lydia and Rupert were about thirty yards away, talking earnestly and quickly.

Thank *God* they were too far away to be overheard.

"They're rather good friends," Charlotte said, hoping that the warmth she was feeling in her cheeks did not mean that she was blushing. "We've known Rupert for years."

"Does that mean my future wife is a great fan of poetry?"

Charlotte smiled sheepishly. "I'm afraid so, my lord."

When he looked at her, his eyes were twinkling. "Does that mean she will expect me to recite poetry to her?"

"Probably," Charlotte replied, giving him a sympathetic look that she was not faking at all.

He sighed. "Well, I suppose no marriage can be perfect." Then he straightened. "Come along then. We've feathers to pluck and spectacles to steal. If we must participate in this foolish scavenger hunt, we might as well win."

Charlotte set her shoulders back and stepped forward. "Indeed, my lord. My sentiments exactly."

And they were. It was odd, actually, how often he said something that was her sentiments exactly.

Chapter 4

Friday night was the occasion of a pre-wedding soirée that Ned supposed differed in some critical manner from Wednesday's and Thursday's pre-wedding soirées, but as he stood at the back of the room, idly holding a glass of champagne and a plate with three strawberries on it, he couldn't for the life of him discern how.

Same people, different food. That was really all there was to it.

If he'd been in charge of the details, he would have done away with all this prenuptial nonsense and merely shown up before the vicar at the appointed time and place, but no one had seen fit to ask his opinion, although to be fair, he'd never given any indication that he cared one way or another.

And in truth, it hadn't even occurred to him until this week—this astoundingly, no, hellishly, long week—that he did care.

But everyone else looked to be having a jolly time, which he supposed was a good thing, since as far as he knew, he was paying for all of this. He sighed, vaguely recalling some conversation during which he'd said some nonsense along the lines of, "Of course Lydia must have the wedding of her dreams."

He looked down at the three strawberries on his plate. There had been five when he'd begun, and the two presently in his stomach constituted his entire supper for the evening.

Most expensive damned strawberries he'd ever consumed.

It wasn't that he could ill afford the festivities; he had funds to spare and wouldn't want to begrudge any girl the wedding of her dreams. The problem, of course, was that the girl getting the wedding of her dreams had turned out not to be the girl of *his* dreams, and it was only now—when it was far too late to do anything about it—that he was coming to realize that made a difference.

And the saddest part was he hadn't even realized that he'd *had* dreams. It hadn't occurred to him that he might really enjoy a grand love affair and romantic marriage until right now, which was, if one had no reason to doubt the clock in the corner, approximately twelve hours before he hauled himself into a church and ensured that he would have neither.

He leaned against the wall, feeling far more tired than a man of his age ever ought. How soon, he wondered, could he leave the festivities without being rude?

Although, truth be told, no one seemed to be noticing him. The partygoers appeared to be enjoying themselves quite handily without sparing any attention for the groom. Or, for that matter, Ned realized as he scanned the room in surprise, the bride.

Where was Lydia?

He frowned, then shrugged, deciding it didn't signify. He'd spoken with her earlier, when they'd performed their obligatory waltz, and she'd been pleasant enough, if a trifle distracted. Since then, he'd spotted her across the crowd from time to time, chatting with the guests. She was probably off in the ladies' retiring room, mending her hem or pinching her cheeks or doing whatever it was ladies did when they thought no one was looking.

And they always seemed to leave the party in pairs. Charlotte had gone quite missing as well, and he'd have bet three strawberries (which, in the context of the evening, was no small sum indeed) that she'd been dragged off by Lydia.

Why this irritated him so much, he didn't know.

"Ned!"

He stood up straight and pasted a smile on his face, then decided he didn't need to bother. It was his sister, squirming her way through the crowds, pulling their cousin Emma behind her.

"What are you doing over here alone?" Belle asked once she'd reached his side.

"Enjoying my own company."

He hadn't meant it as an insult, but Belle must have taken it as such, because she pulled a face. "Where is Lydia?" she asked.

"I have no idea," he said quite honestly. "Probably with Charlotte."

"Charlotte?"

"Her sister."

"I know who Charlotte is," she said peevishly. "I was simply surprised that you—" She shook her head. "Never mind."

Just then Emma poked her way into the conversation, belly-first. "Are you going to eat those strawberries?" she asked.

Ned held out the plate. "Help yourself."

She thanked him and plucked one off the

dish. "Hungry all the time these days," she commented. "Except, of course, when I'm not."

Ned just stared at her as if she were speaking ancient Greek, but Belle was nodding as if she understood perfectly.

"I fill up quickly," Emma said, taking pity on his ignorance. "It's because—" She patted his arm. "You'll understand soon enough."

Ned thought of Lydia heavy with his child, and it just seemed *wrong*.

Then her face changed. Not very much, since it didn't have to change much. The eyes were the same, after all, and probably the nose as well, although definitely not the mouth. . . .

Ned sagged back against the wall, feeling suddenly quite ill. The face hovering over the pregnant body in his mind was Charlotte's, and *she* didn't seem wrong at all.

"I have to go," he blurted out.

"So soon?" Belle queried. "It's barely nine."

"I have a big day tomorrow," he grunted, which was true enough.

"Well, I suppose you might as well," his sister said. "Lydia's gone off, and what's good for the goose and all that."

He nodded. "If anyone asks . . ."

"Don't worry about a thing," Belle assured him. "I'll make excellent excuses."

Emma nodded her agreement.

"Oh, and Ned," Belle said, her voice just soft enough to catch his full attention.

He looked over at her.

"I'm sorry," she said quietly.

It was the sweetest—and the most awful—thing she could have said. But he nodded anyway, because she was his sister and he loved her. Then he slipped out the French doors to the patio, intending to make his way around the house and back in the side door, from which he was hoping he could make it back up to his room without running into anyone desiring a conversation.

And then, of course—he looked down and realized he was still holding his plate—he could eat another few thousand pounds' worth of strawberries.

"You have to go back, Lydia!"

Lydia gave her head a frantic shake as she thrust another pair of shoes into her valise, not even bothering to look at Charlotte as she said, "I can't. I don't have time."

"You're not meant to meet Rupert until two," Charlotte said. "That's five hours from now."

Lydia looked up, horrified. "That's all?"

Charlotte looked at Lydia's two bags. They

weren't small, but they couldn't possibly require five hours to fill. She decided to try another tack. "Lydia," she said, doing her best to sound exceptionally reasonable, "it is your party downstairs. You will be missed." And then, when Lydia did nothing but hold up two sets of unmentionables, clearly weighing one against the other, she repeated herself. "Lydia," Charlotte said, probably more loudly than she ought, "are you listening to me? *You will be missed.*"

Lydia shrugged. "You go back, then."

"I am not the bride," Charlotte pointed out, jumping in front of her sister.

Lydia looked at her, then back at her unmentionables. "The lavender or the pink?"

"Lydia . . ."

"Which one?"

Charlotte wasn't sure why—maybe it was the sheer farce of the moment—but she actually looked. "Where did you get those?" she asked, thinking of her own all-white repertoire of underthings.

"From my trousseau."

"For your marriage with the viscount?" Charlotte asked in horror.

"Of course," Lydia said, deciding on the lavender and tossing it in her valise.

"Lydia, that's sick!"

"No, it's not," Lydia said, giving Charlotte her full attention for the first time since they'd stolen into her room. "It's practical. And if I'm going to marry Rupert, I can't afford not to be."

Charlotte's lips parted with surprise. Until that moment, she hadn't really thought that Lydia understood just what she was getting herself into by marrying a spendthrift like Rupert.

"I'm not as flighty as you think I am," Lydia said, embarrassing Charlotte by reading her thoughts exactly.

Charlotte was silent for several moments, then, her soft words holding an unspoken apology, she said, "I like the pink."

"Do you?" Lydia said with a smile. "I do, too. I think I'll bring both."

Charlotte swallowed uncomfortably as she watched her sister pack. "You should try to slip back to the party for a few minutes, at least," she said.

Lydia nodded. "You're probably right. I'll return once I finish here."

Charlotte walked to the door. "I'm going back now. If someone asks about you, I'll . . ." She moved her hands helplessly through the air as she tried to figure out what she was supposed to say. "Well, I'll make something up."

"Thank you," Lydia said.

Charlotte did nothing but nod, feeling too off balance from the encounter to say anything more. She slipped quietly from the room, shutting the door behind her before scurrying down the hall to the stairs. She was *not* looking forward to this; she supposed she was a good enough liar when she had to be, but she hated doing it, and most of all, she hated doing it to the viscount.

It all would have been so much easier if he hadn't been so *nice.*

Nice. Somehow that made her smile. He would hate being called that. Dashing, maybe. Dangerous, definitely. And devilish also seemed rather appropriate.

But whether the viscount liked it or not, he *was* a nice man, and he was good and true, and he certainly didn't deserve the fate Lydia had in store for him.

Lydia and . . .

Charlotte stopped on the landing and closed her eyes, pausing while she waited for a wave of guilt-induced nausea to pass. She didn't want to think about her own part in this upcoming fiasco. Not yet, at least. She needed to focus, to concentrate on getting her sister safely on her way.

And then she could do right by the viscount—find him and warn him so that he would not . . .

Charlotte shuddered, imagining the scene in the church. She couldn't let that happen. She *wouldn't*. She—

"Charlotte?"

Her eyes flew open. "My lord!" she croaked, unable to believe that he was standing before her. She hadn't wanted to see him until it was done, hadn't wanted to speak with him. She wasn't certain her conscience could take it.

"Are you all right?" he asked, breaking her heart with the concern in his voice.

"I'm fine," she said, swallowing until she was able to manage a wobbly smile. "Just a little . . . overwhelmed."

His lips twisted dryly. "You should try being one of the prospective spouses."

"Yes," she said, "I'm sure. It must be very difficult. I mean, of course it shouldn't be difficult, but . . . well . . ." She wondered if she had ever uttered a less meaningful sentence. "I'm sure it's difficult nonetheless."

He stared at her oddly, intensely enough to make her squirm, then murmured, "You have no idea." He held up the small plate in his hand. "Strawberry?"

She shook her head; her stomach was far too unsettled to even consider filling it. "Where are you going?" she asked, mostly because the ensuing silence seemed to ask for it.

"Upstairs. Lydia left, and—"

"She's nervous, too," Charlotte blurted out. Surely he didn't mean to visit Lydia in her room. It would be beyond improper, but even worse, he'd catch her packing. "She went to lie down," she said quickly, "but she promised me she would go back to the party soon."

He shrugged. "She should do as she likes. We've a long day ahead of us tomorrow, and if she wants rest, she should get it."

Charlotte nodded, slowly exhaling as she realized that he'd never intended to seek out Lydia.

And then she made the biggest mistake of her life.

She looked up.

It was strange, because it was dark, with just one flickering sconce behind her, and she oughtn't to have been able to see the color of his eyes. But as she looked at him, her gaze caught by his, they glowed so hot, so blue, and if the entire house had started to fall down around them . . .

She didn't think she could have looked away.

* * *

Ned had been sneaking up the side staircase with the express purpose of avoiding all human contact, but when he'd seen Charlotte Thornton on the landing, something had clicked into place inside of him, and he'd realized that *all human contact* simply didn't include her.

It hadn't been as he'd feared it might be, that he'd wanted her, although every time he allowed his gaze to slip down to her lips he felt something clench in his gut that should never, ever clench in the company of one's sister-in-law.

It was more that when he'd seen her, just standing there with her eyes closed, she'd seemed a lifeline, a stable anchor in a world tipping drunkenly around him. If he'd somehow been able to touch her, just take her hand, everything would be all right.

"Do you want to dance?" he asked, the words surprising him even as they left his lips.

He saw the surprise in her eyes, heard it in the soft rush of her breath before she echoed the question, "Dance?"

"Have you?" he asked, quite certain he was leading himself down a very dangerous road but quite unable to do anything about it. "Danced, I mean. There wasn't much of it this evening, and I didn't see you on the floor."

She shook her head. "Mother has had me busy," she explained, but she sounded distracted, as if her words had absolutely nothing to do with what was going on in her brain. "Party details and all that."

He nodded. "You should dance," he said, really meaning, *You should dance with me.*

He set his plate down on a nearby stair, murmuring, "What's the point of turning your ankle if you don't have fun with it once it's healed?"

She said nothing, just stood there staring at him, not as if he were a madman, although he was quite certain he was that, at least for this evening. She just stared at him, as if she couldn't quite believe her eyes, or maybe her ears, or maybe just the moment.

Music was drifting up from below; the staircase was twisted in such a way that no one could have seen them on the small landing from either below or above.

"You should dance," he said again, and then, proving that one of them still had a sane thought in their brain, Charlotte shook her head.

"No," she said, "I should go."

His hand fell to his side, and it was only then that he realized he'd lifted it with every intention of placing it at the small of her back for a waltz.

"Mother will be looking for me," she said. "And then I should check on Lydia."

He nodded.

"And then I should—" She looked up at him . . . just for a moment. Just one single fraction of a second, but it was long enough for their eyes to meet before she pulled away.

"But I shouldn't dance," she said.

And they both knew she meant, *I shouldn't dance with you.*

Chapter 5

Later that night, as Ned was finding solace in a glass of brandy and the quiet of Hugh Thornton's sparsely filled library, he couldn't shake the feeling that he was about to step off a bridge.

He'd known, of course, that he was entering into a loveless marriage. But he'd thought himself reconciled to the notion. It was only recently—only this week, in fact—that he'd come to realize that he was about to be miserable, or, at the very least, mildly discontent, for the rest of his life.

And there was nothing he could do about it.

Maybe in another time, another place, a man could back out of a marriage mere hours before the ceremony, but not in 1824 and not in England.

What had he been thinking? He didn't love the woman he was about to marry, she didn't love him, and quite frankly, he wasn't even certain they *knew* each other.

He hadn't been aware, for example, that Lydia considered herself such an aficionado of poetry until Charlotte had told him so during the scavenger hunt (which they had, of course, won. What was the point of playing silly games, otherwise?).

But wasn't that the sort of thing a man ought to know about his wife? Especially if the man in question had made it a point not to include any volumes of poetry in his own library?

And it made him wonder what else might be lurking behind Lydia Thornton's pretty gray eyes. Did she like animals? Was she a reformer, given to charitable pursuits? Could she speak French? Play the pianoforte? Carry a tune?

He didn't know why these questions hadn't plagued him before this night; it certainly seemed like they should have. Surely any sensible man would want to know more about his prospective bride than the color of her hair and eyes.

As he sat in the darkness, pondering his life ahead, he couldn't help but think that this was what Belle had been trying to tell him all these months.

He sighed. Belle might be his sister, but, much as it pained him to admit it, that didn't mean that she wasn't occasionally right.

He didn't *know* Lydia Thornton.

He didn't know her, and he was going to marry her anyway.

But, he thought with a sigh, as his eyes settled aimlessly on a stack of leather-bound books in the corner, that didn't necessarily mean that his marriage would be a failure. Plenty of couples found love after marriage, didn't they? Or if not love, contentment and friendship. Which was all, he had to allow, that he'd been aiming for in the first place.

And it was, he realized, what he would have to learn to live with. Because he *had* gotten to know Lydia Thornton a little bit better this past week. Just enough to know that he would never love her, not the way a man ought to love his wife.

And then there was Charlotte.

Charlotte, at whom he probably would never have glanced twice in London. Charlotte, who made him laugh, with whom he could tell stupid jokes and not feel embarrassed.

And, he reminded himself fiercely, who would be his sister in about seven or so hours.

He looked down at the empty glass in his hand, wondering when he'd finished his drink. He was seriously considering pouring another when he heard a sound through the door.

Funny, he'd thought everyone had gone to bed. It was—he glanced over at the clock on the mantel—nearly two in the morning. Before he'd left the party, he'd heard the Thorntons express their intentions to end the festivities at the unfashionable hour of eleven, stating their desire for all of the wedding guests to be well rested and refreshed for the Saturday morning ceremony.

Ned had not bothered to close the door all the way, so he crept up to the open crack and peered out. There were no clicks of locks or squeaks of doorknobs to alert anyone to his presence, and he was able to satisfy his curiosity as to who was up and about.

"Shhhh!"

Definitely a female doing the shushing.

"Did you have to pack so much?"

He frowned. That sounded a bit like Charlotte. He'd spent so much time with her in the past few days that he probably knew her voice better than Lydia's.

What the devil was Charlotte doing up and about in the middle of the night?

Ned suddenly felt as if he'd been punched in the stomach. Did she have a lover? Surely Charlotte wouldn't be so foolish.

"I can't go with only one morning dress!" came a second female voice. "Would you have me appear a pauper?"

Hmmm. He supposed he did know Lydia's voice better than he thought, because that sounded remarkably like her.

His ears pricked. Forget Charlotte—what was *Lydia* up to? Where the hell did she think she was going the night before their wedding?

He moved his face closer to the crack, glad that the moon was out that night. There had been so much light flowing through the windows that he'd decided not to light a candle when he'd sat down with his drink. With no light streaming from the library, there was no indication that the room was inhabited. Unless Charlotte and Lydia made a point of peering into the library, they would not see him when they passed.

Keeping his eyes trained on the staircase, he watched as they descended, each carrying a large valise. The only light came from the candle Charlotte held in her free hand. Lydia was quite obviously dressed in traveling clothes, and Charlotte was wearing a serviceable day dress in some sort of drab color that he couldn't quite discern in the semidarkness.

Neither was wearing anything one might expect on a female in the middle of the night.

"Are you certain Rupert will be waiting for you at the end of the drive?" Charlotte whispered.

Ned didn't hear Lydia's reply, didn't even know if she did reply or if she only nodded. The roaring in his ears blocked out all sound, eliminated all thought except for the one that was painfully pertinent.

Lydia was jilting him. Sneaking out in the middle of the night mere hours before he was planning to meet her in the village church.

She was *eloping*.

With that idiot fop Marchbanks.

He'd been sitting here resigning himself to a marriage he didn't even want, and his blushing bride had been planning to toss him over all along.

He wanted to scream. He wanted to put his fist through a wall. He wanted to—

Charlotte. Charlotte was helping her.

His rage trebled. How could she do this to

him? Damn it all, they were friends. Friends. He'd known her a scant few days, but in that time he'd come to *know* her, truly know her. Or so he'd thought. He supposed Charlotte wasn't as loyal and true as he'd imagined her to be.

Charlotte. His body tensed even more, every muscle straining with fury. He'd thought she was better than this.

She had to know what she was doing to him as she ushered Lydia out of the house. Or had she even given a thought to what he would go through the next morning, standing at the altar in front of hundreds of onlookers, waiting for a bride who would never arrive?

The two young women were moving slowly, hampered by the large cases. Lydia was dragging hers now, obviously not as strong as Charlotte, who at least managed to clear the floor by two inches. Ned waited as they approached, his jaw clenching tighter by the second, and then, just as they reached the hinged end of his doorway—

He stepped out.

"Going somewhere?" he asked, amazed at the disdainful drawl of his voice. He'd been quite certain the words would come out as a roar.

Lydia jumped back a foot, and Charlotte let out a little scream, which changed tenor when she dropped her valise on her foot.

He leaned one shoulder against the doorframe as he crossed his arms, aware that he needed to keep a very tight leash on his emotions. One little spark and he was going to explode. "It's a bit late to be up and about, don't you think?" he asked, keeping his voice purposefully mild.

The two Thorntons just stared at him, shaking.

"Past two, I would guess," he murmured. "One would think you'd be in your night rails by now."

"This isn't what it looks like," Charlotte blurted out.

He looked to Lydia to see if she'd found her tongue, but she seemed terrified beyond speech.

Good.

He turned back to Charlotte, since she was obviously a more worthy opponent. "That's interesting," he said, "because I'm not certain *what* it looks like. Perhaps you could edify me?"

Charlotte gulped and wrung her hands together. "Well," she said, obviously stalling for time. "Well . . ."

"If I were a less intelligent man," he mused,

"I might think it looked as if my beloved bride was eloping the night before our marriage, but then I thought to myself, *'Surely that cannot be.'* The Thornton girls would never be so foolish as to attempt such a stunt."

He'd done it. He'd silenced them. Charlotte was blinking furiously, and he could almost see her mind behind her eyes, working frantically for something to say, but coming up with nothing. Lydia just looked as if she'd stared into the sun a bit too long.

"So," he continued, enjoying this in a rather sick and pathetic way, "since you are obviously not eloping, and you"—he turned to Charlotte and speared her with a hostile glance—"are obviously not helping her, perhaps you could tell me what you *are* doing."

Lydia looked to Charlotte, her eyes imploring. Charlotte swallowed several times before she said, "Well, actually, I . . ."

He watched her.

She raised her eyes to his.

His gaze never wavered.

"I . . . I . . ."

And still their eyes were locked.

"She's eloping," Charlotte whispered, her gaze finally sliding to the floor.

"Charlotte!" Lydia exclaimed, her voice piercing the silent night. She turned to her sister with an expression of irritation and disbelief. "How could you?"

"Oh, for heaven's sake, Lydia," Charlotte shot back, "he obviously already knew."

"Maybe he—"

"How stupid do you think I am?" Ned asked her. "Good God, you'd marry a man who wasn't bright enough to figure *this*"—he jerked his hand through the air—"out?"

"I told you this wouldn't work," Charlotte said to her sister, her voice urgent and pained. "I told you it wasn't right. I told you you'd never get away with it."

Lydia turned to Ned. "Are you going to beat me?"

He stared at her in shock. Well, bloody hell. Now she'd managed to silence *him*.

"Are you?" she repeated.

"Of course not," he spat out. "Although you can be assured that if I were ever to strike a woman, you'd be the first I'd consider."

Charlotte grabbed Lydia's arm and attempted to pull her back toward the stairs. "We'll return," she said hurriedly, her eyes meeting his for what seemed like an eternally long second. "She's sorry. I'm sorry. We're both sorry."

"And you think that's good enough?" he demanded.

She swallowed convulsively, and her skin looked quite pale, even amid the flickering candlelight. "We'll prepare for the wedding," she said, yanking up both valises. "I'll make sure that she is in the church on time. You can trust me."

And that did it. *You can trust me.* How dare she even think those words?

"Not so fast," he bit off, halting their admittedly slow progress.

Charlotte whirled around, her eyes flashing with desperation. "What do you want?" she cried out. "I told you I would have her ready. I told you I would make sure she was at the church on time. I'll see to it that no one knows what transpired this eve, and that you will know no embarrassment due to Lydia's foibles."

"Very generous of you," he said. "But in light of recent events, marriage to Lydia no longer seems quite so appetizing."

Lydia's mouth fell open at the insult, and he had to look away, so disgusted was he by her reaction. What the hell did she expect?

And so his gaze fell on Charlotte, who all of a sudden looked startlingly lovely in the candlelight, her hair catching the reddish hue of the flames. "What do you want?" she whispered, her lips trembling on the words.

She looked as she had on the landing, her lips parted, her eyes turning silver in the candleglow. He'd wanted to dance with her then.

And now— Now that everything had changed, now that Lydia was halfway out the door, he could finally admit that he'd wanted more.

His mind filled with thoughts, carnal and seductive, and something more he couldn't quite name.

He looked straight at Charlotte, directly into those magical gray eyes, and he said, "I want *you.*"

For a moment, nobody spoke.

No one even breathed.

And then finally Charlotte managed, "You're mad."

But the viscount simply grabbed Lydia's two valises and lifted them into the air as if they were filled with feathers.

"Where are you going with those?" Lydia

shrieked (quietly, if such a thing was possible, which apparently it was, because no one came running down the stairs inquiring after the commotion).

He strode to the front door and tossed them out. "Go," he said harshly. "Get the hell out of here."

Lydia's eyes bugged out. "You're letting me leave?"

His answer was an impatient snort as he strode back, roughly grasped her arm, and started hauling her toward the door. "Do you really think I'd want to marry you after this?" he hissed, his voice rising slightly in volume. "Now, get out."

"But I have another quarter mile before I reach Rupert," Lydia protested, her head turning rapidly between her sister and Ned. "Charlotte was supposed to help me carry my bags."

Charlotte watched in horror as Ned turned to Lydia with quite the most malevolent expression imaginable. "You're a big girl," he said. "You'll figure something out."

"But I can't—"

"For the love of God, woman," he exploded, "get Marchbanks to come back for them! If he wants you badly enough, he'll carry your damned bags."

And then, while Charlotte stared at the scene with gaping mouth, he pushed Lydia through the door and slammed it shut.

"Lydia," she just managed to squeak before he turned on her.

"You" he said.

It was just one word, but all she could think was, *Thank God it wasn't more.*

But—

"Wait!" she cried out. "I have to say good-bye to my sister."

"You'll do what I say you can—"

She brushed past him and ran to the door. "I have to say good-bye," she said again, her voice cracking on the words. "I have no idea when I'm going to see her again."

"I pray it's not anytime soon," he muttered.

"Please," Charlotte pleaded. "I have to—"

He'd caught her around the waist, but then his arms went slack. "Oh, for the—fine," he muttered. "Go. You have thirty seconds."

Charlotte didn't dare argue. He was the wronged party in this awful scene, and much as she hated his anger, she rather thought he had a right to it.

But what the *devil* had he been thinking when he'd said he wanted *her*?

Enough. She couldn't think about that now. Not when her sister was running off into the night.

Not when the mere memory of his face made her tremble. Eyes so blue, so intense as he'd said it.

I want you.

"Lydia!" she called out, her voice desperate. She pushed the door open and ran outside as if the fires of hell were on her heels.

And the truth was—she wasn't so sure they weren't.

"Lydia!" she called again. "Lydia!"

Lydia was sitting under a tree, sobbing.

"Lydia!" Charlotte cried in horror as she rushed to her side. "What's wrong?"

"It wasn't supposed to be like this," Lydia said, looking up at her through watery eyes.

"Well, no," Charlotte agreed, shooting a nervous glance toward the door. Ned had said thirty seconds, and she rather thought he meant it. "But this is how it is."

But that didn't seem good enough for Lydia. "He wasn't supposed to find me," she protested. "He was supposed to be upset."

"He certainly was *that,*" Charlotte replied, wondering what was *wrong* with her sister. Didn't she want to marry Rupert? Wasn't she getting exactly what she wanted?

Why on earth was she complaining?

"No," Lydia gasped, wiping her cheeks with the back of her hand. "But it was all supposed to happen after I left. I wasn't supposed to have to *think* about it."

Charlotte gritted her teeth. "Well, that's too bad, Lydia."

"And I didn't think he'd be quite so glad to have me g-g-*gone*!" At that Lydia began to wail anew.

"Get up," Charlotte ground out, yanking Lydia to her feet. This was really too much. She had a furious viscount inside waiting to tear her to pieces, and Lydia was *complaining*? "I have had enough of this!" she seethed. "If you didn't want to marry the viscount, you shouldn't have said yes."

"I told you why I accepted! I did it for you and Caroline and Georgina. He promised dowries for you."

She had a point, but as much as Charlotte appreciated the sacrifice Lydia had almost made, she wasn't terribly inclined to offer any compliments just then. "Well, if you were going to elope," she said, "you should have done so weeks ago."

"But the bank said—"

"I don't care one whit about Rupert's abysmal finances," Charlotte snapped. "You have been behaving like a child."

"Don't talk to me like that!" Lydia shot back, finally straightening her shoulders. "I am older than you!"

"Then act like it!"

"I will!" And with that, Lydia actually lifted both of her valises into the air and started to walk away. She made it about eight steps before muttering, "Oh, bloody hell," and letting them thunk to the ground. "What the devil did I pack?" she asked, planting her hands on her hips as she stared at the offending baggage.

And suddenly Charlotte was smiling. "I don't know," she said helplessly, shaking her head.

Lydia looked over with a soft expression. "I probably do need more than one day dress."

"Probably," Charlotte agreed.

Lydia looked down at the bags and sighed.

"Rupert will get them for you," Charlotte said softly.

Lydia turned around and caught her sister's gaze. "Yes," she said, "he will." Then she smiled. "He'd better."

Charlotte lifted her hand in farewell. "Be happy."

To which Lydia replied, with a fearful glance toward Ned, who had come through the front door and was now striding rather purposefully in their direction, "Be careful."

And then she ran into the night.

Charlotte watched her sister disappear down the lane and took a deep, fortifying breath as she attempted to gird herself for the battle that was sure to come. She could hear Ned approaching; his footfalls were low and heavy in the noiseless night. By the time she turned around, he was right beside her, so close that she couldn't help but catch her breath.

"Inside," he bit off, jerking his head toward the house.

"Can't this wait until morning?" she asked. He'd given her considerably longer than thirty seconds to say good-bye to Lydia; maybe he was feeling generous.

"Oh, I don't think so," he said in an ominous tone of voice.

"But—"

"Now!" he ground out, taking her by the elbow.

But even as he half-dragged her to the house, his touch was surprisingly gentle, and Charlotte found herself tripping along behind him, her gait forced into a half-run in order to keep up with his long strides. Before she knew it, she was in her father's library, with the door shut tightly behind them.

"Sit," he ordered, stabbing his finger toward a chair.

She gripped her hands together. "I'd rather stand, if you don't mind."

"Sit."

She sat. It seemed a foolish battle to pick, when the larger war was clearly looming in the near future.

For a moment he did nothing but stare at her, and she actually wished he would just open his mouth and yell. Anything would be better than this silent, disdainful stare. The moonlight was just strong enough to illuminate the blue in his eyes, and she felt pierced to the quick by his gaze.

"My lord?" she finally said, dying to break the silence.

That seemed to spark him. "Do you have any

idea what you've done?" he demanded. But his voice was soft, and in a strange way worse than any shout would have been.

Charlotte made no immediate reply. She didn't think he really wanted an answer, and she was proven correct not three seconds later when he continued with, "Were you still planning on donning your maid of honor costume? Going to sit in the front pew while I waited for Lydia to arrive at the church?"

She recoiled at the expression on his face. He looked furious, but also . . . stricken. And he was clearly trying so hard to hide it.

"I was going to tell you," she whispered. "I swear, on the grave of—"

"Oh, do spare me the melodrama," he snapped, pacing the room now with such restless energy that Charlotte half expected the walls to push back in deference.

"I was going to tell you," she insisted. "Right after I saw Lydia safely off, I was going to find you and tell you."

His eyes glittered. "You were going to come to my room?" he asked.

"Well . . ." she hedged. "You were actually here in the library."

"But you didn't know that."

"No," she admitted, "but—" She swallowed

the remainder of her words. He'd closed the space between them in under a second, and both of his hands were now planted on the arms of her chair.

His face was very close.

"You were going to come to my room," he repeated. "How interesting that would have been."

Charlotte said nothing.

"Would you have roused me from my sleep?" he whispered. "Gently touched my brow?"

She looked down at her hands. They were shaking.

"Or maybe," he said, moving in even closer, until she could feel his breath on her lips, "you would have woken me with a kiss."

"Stop," she said in a low voice. "This is beneath you."

He jerked back at that. "You're hardly in a position to cast aspersions on someone else's character, Miss Thornton."

"I did what I thought was right," she said, holding herself ramrod straight in her chair.

"You thought this was *right*?" Ned asked, disgust evident in every syllable.

"Well, maybe not right," she admitted. "But it was best."

"Best?" he echoed, nearly spitting the word.

"It's best to humiliate a man in front of hundreds of people? It's best to steal out in the middle of the night, rather than face—"

"What would you have had me do?" she demanded.

Ned was silent for a long while, and then, trying to regain control of his emotions, he walked to the window and leaned heavily on the ledge. "There is nothing in this world," he said in a gravely serious voice, "that I prize more than loyalty."

"Nor I," she said.

His fingers gripped the wood so tightly that his knuckles turned white. "Oh, really?" he asked, not trusting himself even to turn around to look at her. "Then how do you explain *this*?"

"I don't understand your meaning," came her voice from behind him.

"You betrayed me."

Silence. And then, "I beg your pardon?"

He whirled around so quickly that she flattened against the back of her chair. "You betrayed me. How could you do such a thing?"

"I was helping my sister!"

Her words reverberated through the room, and for a moment he couldn't even move. She was helping her sister. Of course, he thought, almost dispassionately. Why would he have expected her to do otherwise? He had once ridden hell-for-leather all the way from Oxford to London, just to prevent his sister from making a hasty marriage. He, of all people, ought to understand loyalty to siblings.

"I am so sorry about what we were doing to you," Charlotte continued, her voice soft and almost dignified in the near-darkness. "But Lydia is my sister. I wanted her to be happy."

Why would he have thought that Charlotte would owe her first loyalties to him? Why would he have even dreamed that she might consider their friendship more important than her blood bond with her sister?

"I was going to tell you," she continued, and he heard her rise to her feet. "I would never have allowed you to wait in vain at the church. But . . . but . . ."

"But what?" he asked, his voice raw and ragged. He turned around. He didn't know why it was suddenly so important to see her face; it was almost like a magnet was drawing him in, and he had to see her eyes, to know what was in her heart, in her soul.

"You wouldn't have been very well suited," she said. "Not that that excuses Lydia's behavior, or even mine, I suppose, but she wouldn't have made a very good wife to you."

He nodded, and then everything began to fall into place. Something began to bubble within him, something light and delicious, something almost giddy. "I know," he said, leaning closer, just so he could breathe her in. "And that is why I'll take *you* instead."

Chapter 6

Charlotte was quite sure that she now knew what it felt like to strangle. "What," she gasped, trying to speak over the squeezing sensation that seemed to have wrapped around her throat, "do you mean, er, precisely?"

His brows arched. "Wasn't I clear?"

"My lord!"

"Tomorrow morning," he stated in the sort of tone that brooked no dissent, "I will see you at the wedding. You look as if you will fit into Lydia's gown." He gave her a wicked, one-sided grin as he walked to the door. "Don't be late."

She stared helplessly at his back before blurting out, "I can't marry you!"

He turned slowly around. "And why not? Don't tell me you've some idiot poet waiting for you at the end of the lane as well."

"Well, I—" She fought for words. She fought for reasons. She fought for anything that would give her the strength to make it through what had to be the most illogical and surreal night of her life. "To start with," she blurted out, "your banns were read with Lydia's name!"

He shook his head dismissively. "That's not a problem."

"It is to me! We haven't a license." Her eyes bugged out. "If we marry it couldn't possibly be legal."

He appeared unconcerned. "I'll have a special license by morning."

"Where do you think you're going to get a special license in the next ten hours?"

He took a step in her direction, his eyes glittering with satisfaction. "Luckily for me, and for you as well, as I'm quite certain you'll soon come to realize, the Archbishop of Canterbury is planning to attend."

Charlotte felt her jaw drop. "He won't grant you a special license. Not for such an irregular situation."

"Funny," he mused, "I thought special licenses were *for* irregular situations."

"This is madness. There is no way he'll allow us to be married. Not when you came so close to marrying my sister."

Ned only shrugged. "He owes me a favor."

She sagged against the edge of her father's reading table. What kind of man was he that the Archbishop of Canterbury owed him a favor? She'd known that the Blydons were considered an important family in England, but this was beyond comprehension.

"My lord," she said, twisting her fingers together as she tried to formulate a cogent and well-reasoned argument against his mad plan. Surely he appreciated a cogent and well-reasoned argument. He'd certainly seemed to when she'd spent time with him this past week. It was why she'd liked him so well, actually.

"Yes?" he asked, his lips turning up ever-so-slightly at the corners.

"My lord," she said again, clearing her throat. "You seem the sort to listen to a cogent and well-reasoned argument."

"Indeed." He crossed his arms and leaned against the reading table right next to her. They were hip to hip—most distracting.

"My lord," she said again.

"Under the circumstances," he said, his eyes now sparkling with amusement, "don't you think you ought to familiarize yourself with my given name?"

"Right," she said. "Yes, of course. If we were to be married, I would of course—"

"We *are* to be married."

Good heavens, he was positively a brick wall. "Perhaps," she said placatingly. "But be that as it may . . ."

He touched her chin, nudging her until their eyes locked. "Call me Ned," he said softly.

"I'm not certain—"

"*I'm* certain."

"My lord—"

"Ned."

"Ned," she finally acquiesced.

His lips curved. "Good."

He let go of her and leaned back, and Charlotte finally remembered how to breathe again. "Ned," she said, although his name felt odd and thick on her tongue, "I think you ought to take a deep breath and consider what it is you're saying. I'm not sure you've given this adequate thought."

"Really?" he drawled.

"We barely exchanged a word before this week," she said, her eyes imploring him to listen to her words. "You don't know me."

He shrugged. "I know you a damn sight better than I do your sister, and I was prepared to marry her."

"But did you want to?" she whispered.

He stepped forward and caught her hand. "Not half as much as I want you," he murmured.

Her lips parted, but no words came forth, only a soft rush of air as she gasped. He was pulling her closer . . . closer . . . and then his arm snaked around her waist, and she could feel him against her, the entire thrilling length of him.

"Ned," she somehow managed to whisper, but he placed his index finger against her lips with a, "Shhh," followed by, "I have been wanting to do this for days."

His lips found hers, and if he still felt any anger toward her, it was not there in his kiss. He was soft and sweetly gentle, his mouth brushing against hers with the barest of friction.

And yet she felt it all the way to her toes.

"Have you ever been kissed before?" he whispered.

She shook her head.

His smile was very satisfied and very, *very* male. "Good," he said, before dropping his lips back down to hers.

Except this kiss was one of possession, of desire and need. His mouth claimed hers hungrily, even as his hands splayed against her back, pulling her tightly against him. Charlotte found herself sinking into it all, letting herself melt into his body, reaching until her hands found the powerful muscles of his upper back through the fine, thin linen of his shirt.

This, she realized, somewhere in the foggy hazes of her mind, was desire. This was desire, and Lydia was a damn fool.

Lydia!

Good God, what was she doing? Charlotte wrenched herself from his arms. "We can't do this!" she gasped.

Ned's eyes were glazed and his breathing was shallow, but still he managed to sound rather in control as he said, "Why not?"

"You're engaged to marry my sister!"

He quirked a brow at that.

"Very well," she replied, frowning. "I suppose you're not engaged to her any longer."

"It's difficult to remain engaged to a married woman."

"Right." She swallowed. "Of course she's not married yet. . . ."

He stared at her with one arched brow. It was, Charlotte thought miserably, far more effective than words.

"Right," she muttered. "Of course. She might as well be married now."

"Charlotte."

"And it's really too much to expect—"

"Charlotte," he said again, with a touch more volume.

"—you to retain any loyalties to her at such a time—"

"Charlotte!"

She shut her mouth.

His eyes were so intent on hers that she couldn't have looked away if five handsome men were dancing naked out the window.

"There are three things you ought to know this evening," he said. "First, I am alone with you, and it is the middle of the night. Second, I am going to marry you in the morning."

"I'm not sure—"

"*I'm* sure."

"I'm not," she mumbled in a pathetic attempt to get the last word.

He leaned down with a wolfish smile. "And third, I have spent the last few days wracked with guilt because when I went to bed at night, I never, ever—not even once—thought about Lydia."

"No?" she whispered.

He shook his head slowly. "Not Lydia."

Her lips parted of their own accord, and she couldn't take her eyes off him as he leaned in closer, his breath whispering across her skin.

"Only you," he said.

Her heart was clearly a traitor, because it positively sang.

"All my dreams. Only you."

"Really?" she breathed.

His hands cupped her derrière, and she found herself pressed rather intimately against him. "Oh yes," he said, pulling her in even more tightly.

"And you see," he continued, his mouth nipping gently at her lips, "it all falls together rather nicely, because"—his tongue traced the outline of her mouth—"there is no reason I can think of why I shouldn't kiss the woman I plan to marry in less than ten hours, especially if I am fortunate enough to find myself alone with her"—he sighed contentedly against her lips—"in the middle of the night."

He kissed her again, his tongue sliding between her lips in a deliberate attempt to seduce her senseless. "Especially," he murmured, his words caressing her skin, "when I've been dreaming of it for days."

Ned touched her cheeks with his hands, holding her face with near reverence as he pulled back to gaze into her eyes. "I think," he said softly, "that you must be mine."

Her lips parted, and her tongue darted out to wet them, a movement that was so achingly seductive, and yet completely unpracticed. She was so pretty in the moonlight, beautiful in a way that Lydia could never hope to achieve. Charlotte's eyes flashed with intelligence, with fire, with an animation that most women lacked. Her smile was infectious, and her laugh pure music.

She would make a fine wife. At his side, in his heart, in his bed. He didn't know why he hadn't thought of it sooner.

Hell, he thought with a shaky laugh, he probably ought to send a case of the finest smuggled French brandy to Rupert Marchbanks. Heaven knew, he owed the bloody fool his eternal thanks. If he hadn't eloped with Lydia, Ned would have married the wrong sister.

And spent his life pining after Charlotte.

But now she was here in his arms, and she would be his—no, she *was* his. She might not realize it quite yet, but she was.

Suddenly he couldn't help it—he was smiling. Grinning really, rather like an idiot, he supposed.

"What is it?" she asked, rather cautiously if truth be told, almost as if she were afraid he'd gone quite mad.

"I find I'm rather pleased by the recent turn of events," he told her, reaching down and entwining his fingers in hers. "You were quite right earlier this evening. Lydia would not have suited me at all. But you, on the other hand . . ." He lifted her hand to his lips and kissed her knuckles. It was the sort of gesture he'd done a thousand times before, usually just to cater to a woman's desire for romance.

But this time was different. This time it was *his* sense of romance that had been tickled. When he kissed her hand he wanted to linger there, not because he was bent on seduction (although he certainly was *that*), but because he adored the feel of her hand in his, her skin under his lips.

Slowly, he turned her hand over and placed another, more intimate kiss against her palm.

He wanted her—oh, how he wanted her. It was like nothing he'd ever experienced—lust from the inside out. It started at his heart and spread to his body, not the other way around.

And there was no way he was going to allow her to flee.

He grasped her other hand and then held both up. Their arms were bent, their wrists at a level with their shoulders. "I want you to make me a vow," he said, his voice low and serious.

"Wh-what?" she whispered.

"I want you to promise me that you will marry me in the morning."

"Ned, I've already said—"

"If you give me your vow," he said, brushing aside her protest, "then I will allow you to return to your room to sleep."

She let out a slightly panicked giggle. "You think I could sleep?"

He smiled. This was going better than he'd hoped. "I know you, Charlotte."

"You do?" she asked doubtfully.

"Better than you think, and I know that your word is your bond. If you give me your word that you won't do anything silly like run away, I will let you go to your room."

"And if I don't?"

His skin grew hot. "Then you will remain here with me in the library. All night."

She swallowed. "I give you my word that I won't run off," she said solemnly. "But I cannot promise to marry you."

Ned considered his options. He was fairly certain that he could convince her to marry him in the morning if it came to that. She already felt guilty enough over her role in Lydia's elopement. That was certainly something he could twist to his advantage.

"And you'd have to talk to my father in any case," she added.

He allowed their fingers to untangle, then

slowly slid his down her arms until they dropped to his sides. The battle was won. If she was suggesting that he talk to her father, she was all but his.

"I will see you in the morning," he said, nodding his head in a gesture of respect.

"You're letting me go?" she whispered.

"You gave me your word you would not run off. I need no other assurances."

Her lips parted, and her eyes grew wide with some emotion he couldn't quite identify.

But it was good. It was definitely good.

"I will meet you here," he said, "at eight in the morning. Will you see to it that your father is in attendance?"

She nodded.

He stepped back and executed a smart bow. "Until tomorrow then, my lady."

When she opened her mouth to correct his use of such an honorific, he held up a hand and said, "Tomorrow you will be a viscountess. You'll soon grow accustomed to people referring to you as one."

She gestured toward the door. "I should leave on my own."

"Of course," he said, irony tugging at his lips. "We wouldn't want to be caught together in the middle of the night. There would be talk."

She smiled in a rather fetchingly self-deprecating manner. As if there wasn't going to be talk already. Their marriage was sure to be the height of gossip for months.

"Go," he said softly. "Get some sleep."

She shot him a look that said she couldn't even hope to sleep, and then slipped out the door.

He stared at the open doorway for several seconds after she'd disappeared, then whispered, "Dream of me."

Luckily for Charlotte, her father was a notoriously early riser, and so when she entered the small breakfast room at fifteen minutes before eight the following morning, he was there as usual, his plate laden with gammon steak and eggs.

"Good morning, Charlotte," he boomed. "Excellent day for a wedding, isn't it?"

"Er, yes," she said, trying to smile but failing miserably.

"Smart of you to come here to break your fast. Your mother's got everyone else in the formal dining room, not that many of that lot is willing to rise from bed at this hour."

"Actually, I heard a few people milling about as I passed," Charlotte said, not certain why she was even bothering to tell him this.

"Hmmph," he snorted dismissively. "As if a body could digest a proper plate of eggs amidst all that commotion."

"Father," she said haltingly, "I need to tell you something."

He looked at her with raised brows.

"Er, perhaps I should just show you this." She held out the note Lydia had left for their parents, explaining what she had done.

Then Charlotte took a healthy step back. Once her father read the contents of Lydia's message, his roar would be deadly indeed.

But when his eyes finished scanning the lines, all he did was whisper. "Did you know about this?"

More than anything, Charlotte wanted to lie. But she couldn't, and so she nodded.

Mr. Thornton did not move for several seconds, the only proof of his anger his whitening knuckles as his fingers gripped the edge of the table.

"The viscount is in the library," she said, swallowing convulsively. Her father's silence was far more fearsome than his bellows. "I think he would like to speak with you."

Mr. Thornton looked up. "He knows what she's done?"

Charlotte nodded.

And then her father uttered several words that she had never imagined crossing his lips, including one or two that she had never even heard of. "We're ruined now," he hissed, once he was through cursing. "Ruined. And we have your sister—and you—to thank."

"Perhaps if you just see the viscount," Charlotte said miserably. She had never been close to her father, but oh, how she had always craved his approval.

Mr. Thornton rose abruptly and threw down his napkin. Charlotte scooted out of his way and then followed him down the hall, remaining a respectful three paces behind the entire way.

But when her father reached his library, he turned to her and said, anger evident in his every word, "What do you think you're doing here? You've done quite enough already. Go to your room immediately, and do not come out until I have given you my leave to do so."

"I think," came a deep voice from down the hall, "that she should stay."

Charlotte looked up. Ned was descending the last few steps on the staircase, looking splendidly handsome in his wedding suit.

Her father jabbed her in the ribs and hissed, "I thought you said he knew."

"He does."

"Then what the devil is he doing dressed like that?"

Charlotte was saved from replying by Ned's arrival. "Hugh," he said, nodding at Mr. Thornton.

"My lord," her father replied, surprising her. She'd thought he used Ned's given name. But maybe his nerves forced him to show more respect this morning.

Ned motioned with his head toward the library. "Shall we?"

Mr. Thornton stepped forward, but Ned cut him off smoothly. "Charlotte first."

Charlotte could tell that her father was dying of curiosity, but he held his counsel and instead stepped back and allowed her to pass. As she walked into the room, however, Ned leaned forward and murmured, "Interesting choice of dress."

Charlotte felt her skin redden. She had donned one of her ordinary morning dresses, not Lydia's wedding gown, as he'd instructed.

A moment later they were all in the library, with the door closed firmly behind them.

"My lord," Mr. Thornton began, "I must assure you, I had no idea—"

"Enough," Ned said, standing at the center of the room with remarkable self-possession. "I have no wish to discuss Lydia or her elopement with Marchbanks."

Mr. Thornton swallowed forcefully, his Adam's apple bobbing up and down in his fleshy neck. "You don't?"

"Naturally, I was angered by your daughter's betrayal—"

Which daughter? Charlotte wondered. He'd seemed far more angry with her last night than he'd been with Lydia.

"—but it will not be difficult to set matters aright."

"Anything, my lord," Mr. Thornton assured him. "Anything at all. If it is within my power—"

"Good," Ned said mildly. "Then, I'll take her"—he motioned to Charlotte—"instead."

Mr. Thornton did nothing but blink. "Charlotte?" he finally asked.

"Indeed. I have no doubt she will make a finer wife than Lydia would have done."

Mr. Thornton's head snapped back and forth between his daughter and his other daughter's fiancé several times before saying again, "Charlotte?"

"Yes."

And that was enough to convince him. "She's yours," Mr. Thornton said emphatically. "Whenever you want her."

"Father!" Charlotte cried out. He was speaking of her as if she were nothing more than a sack of flour.

"This morning will do," Ned said. "I've arranged for a special license, and the church is already set up for a wedding."

"Wonderful, wonderful," Mr. Thornton said, relief evident in his every nervous motion. "I have no objections, and the . . . er . . . settlements will remain the same?"

Ned's expression turned wry at Mr. Thornton's eager glance, but all he said was, "Of course."

This time Mr. Thornton didn't even bother to hide his relief. "Good, good. I—" He cut himself off as he turned to Charlotte. "What are you waiting for, girl? You need to get ready!"

"Father, I—"

"Not another word about it!" he boomed. "Begone with you!"

"You might consider speaking to my future wife in more polite tones," Ned said, his voice deadly quiet.

Mr. Thornton turned to him and blinked in shock. "Of course," he said. "She's yours now, anyway. Whatever you want."

"I think," Ned said, "that what I want is a few moments alone."

"Absolutely," Mr. Thornton agreed, grabbing Charlotte's wrist. "Come along. The viscount wants his privacy."

"Alone with Charlotte," Ned edified.

Mr. Thornton looked first to Ned, then to Charlotte, then back again. "I'm not certain that's a wise idea."

Ned merely quirked a brow. "Many unwise ideas have been carried out recently, don't you think? This, I should think, is the least unwise of the lot."

"Of course, of course," Mr. Thornton mumbled, and he left the room.

Ned watched his chosen bride as she watched her father's departure. She felt helpless; he could see that on her face. And probably manipulated as well. But he refused to feel any guilt over that. He knew, in his heart, in his very bones, that marrying Charlotte Thornton was the absolute right thing to do. He regretted that he'd had to be so high-handed to achieve his goal, but Charlotte wasn't exactly innocent in the recent turn of events, was she?

He stepped forward and touched her cheek. "I'm sorry if you feel that this is all happening too fast," he said softly.

She said nothing.

"I can assure you—"

"He didn't even ask me," she said, her voice breaking.

Ned slid his fingers to her chin and tipped her face up to his. He asked his question with his eyes.

"My father," she said, blinking against tears. "He didn't even once ask me what I wanted. It was like I wasn't even here."

Ned watched her face, watched as she tried so hard to remain strong and expressionless. He saw her courage and her strength of character, and he was suddenly overcome by the urge to make this right for her.

Charlotte Thornton might be getting a rushed wedding that had been planned for her sister, but by God, she would receive a proposal that was hers alone.

He sank down to one knee.

"My lord?" she squeaked.

"Charlotte," he said, his voice rich with emotion and need, "I am humbly asking for your hand in marriage."

"Humbly?" she echoed, eyeing him doubtfully.

He took her hand and brushed it softly against his lips. "If you do not say yes," he said, "I shall spend my every last hour pining for you, dreaming of a better life, a perfect wife—"

"You rhymed," she said, laughing nervously.

"Not on purpose, I assure you."

And then she smiled. Really smiled. Not that wide, radiant grin that had marked the beginning of his downfall, but something softer, shyer.

But no less real.

And as he watched her, his eyes never leaving her face, it all became clear.

He loved her.

He loved this woman, and God help him, he didn't think he could live without her.

"Marry me," he said, and he didn't try to hide his urgency or need.

Her eyes, which had been focused on some spot on the wall behind him, returned to his.

"Marry me," he said again.

"Yes," she whispered. "Yes."

Chapter 7

Two hours later Charlotte was a viscountess. Six hours after that, she stepped into a carriage and said good-bye to everything that was familiar in her life.

Ned was taking her to Middlewood, his small estate that was located only fifteen miles from her own home. He didn't want to spend his wedding night at Thornton Hall, he'd said. His intentions required more privacy.

The wedding was a blur. Charlotte was still in such a state of shock, still so completely stunned by Ned's romantic proposal, that she hadn't been able to concentrate on anything other than making sure she said, "I will," at the appropriate time. Someday, she was sure, she'd hear about all the gossip that was flying back and forth between the guests, who had been expecting a different bride to walk down the aisle, but for today at least, she didn't hear a whisper.

She and Ned didn't say much during the ride, but it was an oddly comfortable silence. Charlotte was nervous, and she should have felt awkward, but she didn't. There was something about Ned's presence that was comforting, reassuring.

She liked to have him near. Even if they weren't speaking, it was nice to know he was close. Funny how such a deeply seated emotion could take root in so short a time.

When they arrived at what she supposed was her new home—one of them, at least—Ned took her hand.

"Are you nervous?" he asked.

"Of course," she replied without thinking.

He laughed, the warm, rich sound spilling from the carriage as a footman opened the door. Ned jumped down, then reached up to aid in Charlotte's dismount. "What bliss to have married an honest wife," he murmured, letting his lips trail past her ear.

Charlotte swallowed, trying not to concentrate on the shiver of warmth that seemed to ripple through her.

"Are you hungry?" Ned inquired as he led her inside.

She shook her head. It was impossible to think of food.

"Good," he said approvingly. "Neither am I."

Charlotte looked around as they entered the house. It was not an exceedingly large dwelling, but it was elegant and comfortable.

"Do you come here often?" she asked.

"To Middlewood?"

She nodded.

"I'm more often in London," he admitted. "But we may choose to spend more time here if you would like to be near your family."

"I would," she said, her lower lip catching between her teeth for an instant before she added, "if you would."

He nudged her toward the stairs. "What happened to the firebrand I married? The Charlotte Thornton I know would hardly ask my permission for anything."

"It's Charlotte Blydon now," she said, "and I told you, I'm nervous."

They reached the top of the stairs and he took her hand, leading her down the hall. "There's nothing to be nervous about," he said.

"Nothing?"

"Well, very little," he admitted.

"Only a little?" she asked dubiously.

He offered her a wicked smile. "Very well.

There's a great deal about which to be nervous. I am going to show you some things"—he led her through an open doorway and shut the door firmly behind them—"that will be very, very new."

Charlotte gulped. In the chaos of the day, her mother had forgotten to have a mother-daughter talk with her. She was a country girl, and thus knew a bit about what happened between women and men, but somehow that seemed little reassurance as her husband stood before her, positively feasting on her with his eyes.

"How many times have you been kissed?" he asked, shrugging off his coat.

She blinked in surprise at the unexpected question. "Once," she replied.

"By me, I presume?" he asked mildly.

She nodded.

"Good," he said, and it was only then that she realized he'd undone his cuffs.

She watched as his fingers went to the buttons on his shirt, her mouth going dry as she asked, "How many times have you been kissed?"

His lips curved. "Once."

Her eyes flew to his face.

"Once I kissed you," he said huskily, "I realized that all the others weren't worthy of the name."

It was as if lightning had struck right there in the room. The air went quite electric, and Charlotte no longer held any confidence in her ability to remain standing.

"But I trust," Ned murmured, closing the distance between them and bringing both of her hands to his lips, "that I won't end my days with only one kiss."

Charlotte managed to give her head a little shake. "How did this happen?" she whispered.

He cocked his head curiously. "How did what happen?"

"This," she said, as if the simple pronoun could explain everything. "You. Me. You're my husband."

He smiled. "I know."

"I want you to know something," she said, the words rushing from her mouth.

He looked slightly amused by her earnestness. "Anything," he said quietly.

"I fought you on this," she said, aware that the moment was very important. Her marriage had been rushed, but it would be based on honesty, and she had to tell him what was in her heart. "When you asked me to take Lydia's place—"

"*Don't* say it that way," he interrupted, his voice low but intense.

"What do you mean?"

His blue eyes focused on hers with stunning fire. "I don't ever want you to feel you've taken someone else's place. You are my wife. You. Charlotte. You are my first choice, my only choice." His hands closed tightly around hers, and his voice grew even more intense. "I thank God for the day your sister decided she needed a little more poetry in her life."

Charlotte felt her lips part in surprise. His words made her feel more than loved; she felt cherished. "I want you to know—" she said again, afraid that if she focused too much on his words, and not on her own, that she would melt into his arms before she said what she needed to say. "I want you to know that I know, with every inch of my heart, that I made the right decision when I married you this morning. I don't know how I know, and I don't think it makes any sense, and heaven knows, there's nothing I value above sense, but . . . but . . ."

He gathered her into his arms. "I know," he said, the words floating into her hair. "I know."

"I think I might love you," she whispered against his shirt, only able to find the courage to say the words now that she wasn't actually looking at him.

He froze. "What did you say?"

"I'm sorry," she said, feeling her shoulders slump at his reaction. "I shouldn't have said anything. Not yet."

His hands went to her cheeks, and he tipped her face up until she had no choice but to gaze straight into his eyes.

"What did you say?" he repeated.

"I think I love you," she whispered. "I'm not sure. I've never loved someone before, so I'm not familiar with the emotion, but—"

"*I'm* sure," he said, his voice rough and unsteady. "I'm sure. I love you, Charlotte. I love you, and I don't know what I would have done if you hadn't agreed to marry me."

Her lips trembled with an unexpected laugh. "You would have found a way to convince me," she said.

"I would have made love to you right there in your father's library if that's what it would have taken," he replied, his lips curving devilishly.

"I believe you would have done," she said slowly, her own mouth slipping into a smile.

"And I promise you," he said, softly kissing her ear as he spoke, "that I would have been very, very convincing."

"I have no doubt," she said, but her voice was growing breathless.

"In fact," he murmured, his fingers working the buttons at the back of her gown, "I might need to convince you now."

Charlotte sucked in her breath as she felt a cold rush of air against the skin on her back. Any moment now her bodice would fall away, and she would be standing before him as only a wife stood before a husband.

He was so close she could feel the heat rising from his skin, hear the very tenor of his breath. "Don't be nervous," he whispered, his words touching her ear like a caress. "I promise I will make this good for you."

"I know," she said, her voice trembling. And then somehow she smiled. "But I can still be nervous."

He hugged her to him, gruff laughter shaking both of their bodies. "You can be anything you want to be," he said, "as long as you're mine."

"Always," she vowed. "Always."

He stepped away to shrug off his shirt, leaving Charlotte standing there, clutching at her bodice, marveling at the cool air on her back.

"Would you like me to leave?" he asked quietly.

Her eyes widened. She hadn't expected that.

"So that you might have privacy while you climb into bed," he explained.

"Oh." She blinked. "Is that how it's done?"

"It's how it is often done," he said, "although it's not how it has to be done."

"How do you want it to be done?" she whispered.

His eyes grew hot. "I want to remove every last scrap of your clothing myself."

She shivered.

"And then I want to lay you down on the bed so I can see you."

Her heart began to pound.

"And then," he said, his shirt falling to the floor as he took a step toward her, "I think I might kiss every inch of you."

She stopped breathing.

"If you don't mind," he added with a wicked, one-sided smile.

"I don't mind," she blurted out, then turned beet red as she realized what she'd said.

But Ned only chuckled as his hands covered hers and gently eased her bodice down. Charlotte held her breath as she was bared to him, unable to tear her eyes off his face—or to contain the rush of pride she felt when she saw his expression.

"You're so beautiful," he breathed, and his

voice held a touch of reverence in it, a tinge of awe. His hands cupped her, testing the weight and feel of her, and for a moment he almost looked as if he were in pain. His eyes closed, and his body shook, and when he looked at her again, there was something in his face Charlotte had never seen before.

It went beyond desire, past need.

He nudged her gown from her body, then picked her up and laid her on the bed, stopping briefly to remove her stockings and slippers. Then, in less time than ought to have been possible, he'd stripped himself of the rest of his clothing and had covered her body with his.

"Do you know how much I need you?" Ned whispered, groaning as he pressed his hips intimately against hers. "Could you possibly understand?"

Charlotte's lips parted, but the only word she managed was his name.

He let out a ragged breath as he ran his hands along her sides to her hips, and then underneath until he could squeeze her bottom. "I have been dreaming of this since the moment I met you, wanting it so desperately even when I knew it was wrong. And now you're mine," he growled, moving his face so that he could nuzzle her neck. "Forever mine."

He trailed his lips down the elegant line of her throat to her collarbone, then to the gentle swell of her breast. With one hand he cupped her, nudging her flesh until her nipple rose in the air. It was soft and pink, and thoroughly irresistible. He forced himself to stop, just to look at her and savor the moment, but then he could hold back no longer. He captured her in his mouth, stopping only to smile when she let out a squeal of surprise.

She was soon whimpering with pleasure, and squirming beneath him, obviously eager for something she didn't even understand. Her hips were pushing up against his, and every time he moved his hands, squeezed, touched, caressed, she moaned.

She was everything he'd ever dreamed a woman could be.

"Tell me what you like," he whispered against her skin. He grazed her nipple with the palm of his hand. "This?"

She nodded.

"This?" This time he took her entire breast in his hand and squeezed.

She nodded again, her breath coming fast and urgent over her lips.

And then he slid his hand between them and touched her intimately. "This?" he asked, turning his face so she wouldn't see his wicked smile.

All she did was let out a little, "Oh!"

But it was a perfect, "Oh!"

Just as she was perfect in his arms.

He touched her more deeply, easing one finger inside of her to prepare for his entry. He wanted her so badly; he didn't think he'd ever felt this particular intensity of need. It was more than lust, deeper than desire. He wanted to possess her, to consume her, to hold her so close and tight that their souls melded to one.

This, he thought, burying his face against the side of her neck, was love.

And it was like nothing he'd ever experienced. It was more than he'd hoped, bigger than he'd dreamed.

It was perfection.

Beyond perfection. It was bliss.

It was hard to hold back, but he held his desire in check until he was certain she was ready for him. And even then, even though his fingers were moist with her passion, he still had to be sure, had to ask her, "Are you ready?"

She looked at him with questioning eyes. "I think so," she whispered. "I need . . . something. I think I need you."

He hadn't thought he could want her more,

but her words, simple and true, were like a jolt to his blood, and it was all he could do not to plunge recklessly into her then and there. Gritting his teeth against this all-consuming need, he positioned himself at her entrance, trying to ignore the way her heat was beckoning him.

With carefully controlled motions, he pushed forward, a back and forth slide, until he reached the proof of her innocence. He had no idea if he was going to hurt her; he suspected he might, but if so, there was no way to avoid it. And since it seemed foolish to warn her of pain—surely that would just make her anxious and tense?—he simply plunged forward, finally allowing himself to feel her fully around him.

He knew he should stop to make sure she was all right, but by the heavens above, he couldn't have stopped moving if his very life depended on it. "Oh, Charlotte," he moaned. "Oh, my God."

Her answer was equal in desire—a thrust of her hips, a gasp on her lips—and Ned knew that she was with him, awash in pleasure, any pain all but forgotten.

His motions gained rhythm, and soon his every muscle was focused on not allowing himself release until he could be sure that she too reached a climax. It wasn't common for a virgin, he'd been told, but this was his wife—this was *Charlotte*—and he didn't know if he could live with himself if he didn't ensure her pleasure.

"Ned," she gasped, her breath coming faster and faster. She looked so beautiful it brought tears to his eyes. Her cheeks were flushed, her eyes unfocused, and he couldn't seem to stop thinking, *I love her*.

She was nearly there; he could see it. He didn't know how much longer he could possibly hold out against his own body's raging need, and so he slipped a hand between them, his fingers finding her most sensitive nub of flesh.

She screamed.

He lost all control.

And then, as if in a perfectly choreographed dance, they both tensed and arched at the same precise moment, motion stopped, breathing stopped until they simply collapsed, weary and spent. . . .

And blissfully content.

"I love you," he whispered, needing to say the words even if they were lost into the pillow.

And then he felt, more than heard, her reply. "I love you, too," she whispered against his neck.

He propped himself up on his elbows. His exhausted muscles protested, but he had to see her face. "I will make you happy," he vowed.

She offered him a serene smile. "You already do."

He thought to say something more, but there were no words to express what was in his heart, so he lay back down on the mattress, gathering her against him until they were two nestled spoons.

"I love you," he said again, almost embarrassed by his desire to say this once every minute or so.

"Good," she said, and he could feel her giggling against him.

Then she flipped over quite suddenly, so that they were face-to-face. She looked rather breathless, as if she'd just thought of something quite astonishing.

He quirked a brow in question.

"What," she asked, "do you suppose Rupert and Lydia are doing right now?"

"Do I care?"

She smacked his shoulder with the heel of her hand.

"Oh, very well," he sighed, "I suppose I do care, given that she *is* your sister, and that he *did* save me from marrying her."

"What do you think they are doing?" she persisted.

"Much the same as us," he said, "if they're lucky."

"Their lives will not be easy," Charlotte said soberly. "Rupert hasn't two pennies to rub together."

"Oh, I don't know," Ned said with a yawn. "I think they shall make out just fine."

"You do?" Charlotte asked, closing her eyes as she settled deeply into the pillows.

"Mmmm."

"Why?"

"You're a persistent wench, has anyone told you that?"

She smiled, even though he couldn't see it. "Why?" she asked again.

He closed his eyes. "Don't ask so many questions. You'll never be surprised."

"I don't want to be surprised. I want to know everything."

He chuckled at that. "Then know this, my dear Charlotte: You have married an exceedingly clever man."

"Have I?" she murmured.

It was a challenge that could not be ignored. "Oh, yes," he said, rolling until he was once again looming over her. "Oh, yes."

"Very clever, or just a little bit clever?"

"Very—*very*—clever," he said wickedly. His body might be too spent for a rematch, but that didn't mean he couldn't torture *her*.

"I might need proof of this cleverness," she said. "I—oh!"

"Proof enough?"

"Oh!"

"Oh."

"Ohhhh."

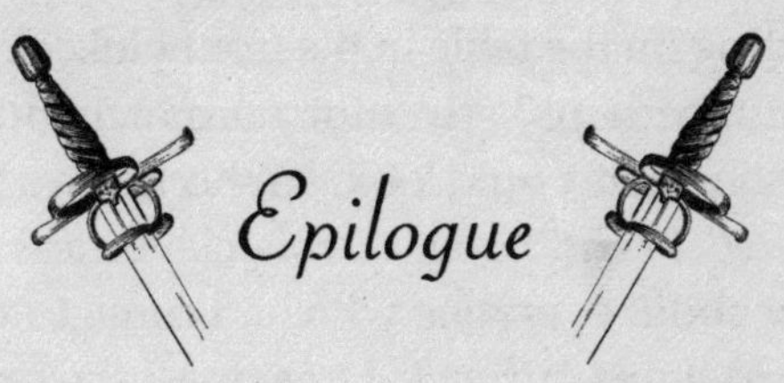

Epilogue

One week later

"Here you are, Mrs. Marchbanks!"

Lydia smiled dreamily as Rupert carried her over the threshold of Portmeadow House. It wasn't as grand as Thornton Hall, which actually wasn't very grand itself, and it wasn't even theirs, at least not until Rupert's elderly uncle finally passed on.

But none of that seemed to signify. They were married, and they were in love, and as long as they were together, it didn't matter if they were in a borrowed home.

Besides, Rupert's uncle wasn't due back from London for another week.

"I say," Rupert said, narrowing his eyes as he set her down. "What's this?"

Lydia followed his gaze to a brightly wrapped box sitting on the table in the front hall. "A wedding gift, perhaps?" she murmured hopefully.

He shot her a wry look. "Who knows we're married?"

"Just about everyone who had come to watch me marry Lord Burwick, I imagine," she replied. They had already heard the news of his marriage to Charlotte in her stead. Lydia couldn't even imagine what the gossip must be like.

Rupert's attention, however, was already on the box. With careful motions, he tugged an envelope free of the ribbons and slid a finger under the sealing wax. "It's expensive," he commented. "A real envelope. Not just a folded piece of paper."

"Open it," Lydia urged.

He stopped just long enough to shoot her a peevish expression. "What do you think I'm doing?"

She snatched it from his hands. "You're too slow." With eager fingers, she tore the envelope open and removed the paper inside, unfolding it so that they could read the contents together.

'Tis with this note that I give thee thanks
And promise that you may avoid all banks.

When you stole my bride, you did me a favor
And gave me a wife that I may savor.
In this box you'll find French brandy
And a selection of the finest candy.
But my true gift to you lies in this verse
So you may avoid money's worst curse.
The deed to a home, not five miles away
That you may call your own, both night and day.
And a modest income, yours for life
Because when you eloped, you gave me my wife.
I wish you happiness, health and love
(My wife assures me this rhymes with dove.)

—Edward Blydon, Viscount Burwick

A full minute passed before Rupert or Lydia could speak.

"How very generous of him," Lydia murmured.

Rupert blinked several times before saying, "Why do you suppose he wrote it in verse?"

"I couldn't begin to imagine," Lydia said. "I had no idea he was so addled in the brain." She swallowed, and tears pricked her eyes. "Poor Charlotte."

Rupert placed an arm around her shoulder. "Your sister is made of stern stuff. She shall overcome."

Lydia nodded and allowed him to lead her to the bedroom, where she promptly forgot she had any siblings at all.

Meanwhile, at Middlewood . . .

"Oh, Ned, you didn't!" Charlotte clapped a horrified hand to her mouth when he showed her a copy of the note he'd sent to Rupert and Lydia.

He shrugged. "I couldn't help myself."

"It's very generous of you," she said, trying to appear solemn.

"Yes, it is, isn't it?" he murmured. "You shall have to demonstrate your gratitude, don't you think?"

She pursed her lips to keep from laughing. "I had no idea," she said, desperately trying to maintain an even expression, "that you were such a talented poet."

He waved a hand through the air. "Rhyming isn't so difficult once you put your mind to it."

"Oh, really?"

"Indeed."

"How long did it take you to compose that, er, poem?" She looked down at the sheet of paper and frowned. "Although it does seem terribly unfair to Shakespeare and Marlowe to call it such."

"Shakespeare and Marlowe have nothing to fear from me—"

"Yes," she murmured, "that much is clear."

"—I have no plans to write more verse," Ned finished.

"And for that," Charlotte said, "we all thank you. But you never did answer my question."

He looked at her quizzically. "You asked me a question?"

"How long did it take you to write this?" she repeated.

"Oh, it was nothing," he said dismissively. "Only four hours."

"Four hours?" she repeated, choking on laughter.

His eyes twinkled. "I wanted it to be *good,* of course."

"Of course."

"There's little point in doing anything if you're not going to be good at it."

"Of course," she said again. It was all she could say, since he had wrapped his arms around her and was now kissing her neck.

"Do you think we could stop talking about poetry?" he murmured.

"Of course."

He nudged her toward the sofa. "And maybe I could ravish you here and now?"

She smiled. "Of course."

He pulled back, his face serious and tender all at once. "And you'll let me love you forever?"

She kissed him. "Of course."

JULIA QUINN is the *New York Times* bestselling author of twelve historical romance novels, including the wildly popular Bridgerton series. A graduate of Harvard and Radcliffe Colleges, she lives in the Pacific Northwest with her family, where they occasionally while away the rainy days by watching the tape of her recent appearance on the game show "The Weakest Link." To find out if she won, visit her website at *www.juliaquinn.com.*